No Girl Needs a Husband Seven Days a Week

By Nina Foxx

No Girl Needs a Husband Seven Days a Week
Just Short of Crazy
Marrying Up
Going Buck Wild
Get Some Love

No Girl Needs a Husband Seven Days a Week

Nina Foxx

AVON

An Imprint of HarperCollins*Publishers*

NO GIRL NEEDS A HUSBAND SEVEN DAYS A WEEK. Copyright © 2007 by Nina Foxx Holder. All rights reserved. Printed in the United States of America. No part of this book may be used or reproduced in any manner whatsoever without written permission except in the case of brief quotations embodied in critical articles and reviews. For information address HarperCollins Publishers, 10 East 53rd Street, New York, NY 10022.

HarperCollins books may be purchased for educational, business, or sales promotional use. For information please write: Special Markets Department, HarperCollins Publishers, 10 East 53rd Street, New York, NY 10022.

FIRST EDITION

Designed by Rhea Braunstein

Library of Congress Cataloging-in-Publication Data
Foxx, Nina.
   No girl needs a husband seven days a week / Nina Foxx. — 1st ed.
      p. cm.
   ISBN 978-0-06-133527-3
   1. African American women—Fiction.   2. Female friendship—Fiction.   I. Title.

   PS3556.O98N6   2007
   813'.54—dc22   2007014803

ISBN: 978-0-06-133527-3
ISBN-10: 0-06-133527-4

07 08 09 10 11   WBC/RRD   10 9 8 7 6 5 4 3 2 1

The Dating Cycle

T his was the most perfect date Kennedy had been on in at least six months. She and Troy met by chance at a Starbucks, and as far as she could see, there was nothing wrong with him. He had a good job, straight teeth, and an excellent command of the English language. If shoe size was an indication, he would do the job she had in mind just fine.

"Don't you think so, Kennedy?" he asked.

What had he just said? Kennedy had been so busy staring at him like a piece of meat, she'd missed an entire conversation. She raised her eyebrows and tried to look amused, then nodded. The man was fine as hell and trying hard to find something for them to talk about, but the way he looked, it was hard to focus. Muscular arms, a yoga body, and a designer-jean ass. He had the total package.

Kennedy sat back in her chair with her legs crossed at the ankles in her favorite "come hither" body position. They were eating at Fonda San Miguel's, known for its great Mexican food and trademark automatic white curtain at the door. It slid open with a metal *shushing* sound as new patrons entered, and, being that she was facing the door, Kennedy couldn't help but be distracted. Lack of sex made it hard for her to concentrate. Troy, or at least she thought that was his name, had been talking endlessly about himself since they'd sat down. He'd chosen to sit with his back to the door and didn't even flinch at the noise the curtain made as it slid along its track and didn't notice the group of three women that entered, but Kennedy did. Like Kennedy, they were dressed to the nines. She squinted and tried to focus. Her breath caught in her throat as she recognized one of the dresses as one she and her friend Marie had shopped for together. *What are the chances?* She thought. *They'd certainly made more than one.*

She hoped that Marie wasn't the one in the dress. The two of them had been best friends since college, where they'd pledged their sorority together. They'd added Mai later when they all ended up living near one another. She was a few years older, and she was also their sorority sister. Over the years, she was often the glue that kept the three of them together.

There was no need for Troy to meet any friends or family or anyone like that. He probably wouldn't be around too long. Or at least that was the plan.

As a general rule, Kennedy tried not to get into anything that might be construed as a relationship. It made things too complicated. *Strictly short term* had become her mantra. She was successful because she'd thought like a man and she let that philosophy carry over into her personal life. For the most part, the strategy worked well. As far as Kennedy Johnson was concerned, the only reason men were necessary was when her batteries ran out.

Troy touched her hand and she snapped back to attention. Kennedy smiled, knowing that her dimples would flash. Few men could resist them. There was no time to worry about it or any of her other friends showing up. She had to get back to the dating cycle, as she called it, the cycle of things that had to be done to make a date last past dinner. Kennedy prided herself on being able to get it right, and that meant being able to control the direction of the evening. She turned her attention back to her date, nodding again. It was good to look as if you were paying attention to his every word, even if all you heard was *blah, blah, blah*. Her finger absentmindedly circled the rim of her martini glass and she wondered if she could convince him to wear a gag in bed. She chuckled inwardly at the thought. And they said women talked too much. As hard as it was for a single sister, Kennedy had every intention of doing what was necessary to let Mr. Man think he was the one that got to third base on the first date, when truth be told, she would be the one holding the bat. It had been way too long, so long, in fact, that Kennedy was sure that if the wind blew hard enough, dust would fly from underneath her skirt, and she was ready for some spring cleaning.

"Enough about me," he said. "You haven't said a word about you."

Kennedy smiled coyly, then wet her lips just enough to make them shine but not enough to take off her thirty-two-dollar lipstick. "There's not that much to tell really. I'm just not that interesting." That was code for "There is nothing about me that

I want to share with you." And even though he'd said it, Kennedy knew that what he was really interested in required no words.

"C'mon. How can that be, ma? As gorgeous as you are? What do you do again? Tell me about you, Miss Lady." Troy flashed a smile that revealed teeth that Kennedy was sure had been professionally whitened recently. He cared about his hygiene. A good sign. Good enough that she was willing to let him slide for calling her "Miss Lady" and every other nickname for women she hated in one breath. At least he hadn't called her a *dime piece*. Dime piece was game over.

The muscles in her neck tightened but Kennedy forced herself to hold her smile. It was okay to cut him some slack; after all, this was just the first date and it wasn't like she was trying to get married. "I work for G,P,E, and M." She almost hated to tell him. Everybody knew the largest ad agency and one of the largest companies in town by those four letters.

Troy put the martini glass he had been holding down on the table. Hard. "Get out. At that office downtown?"

"One and the same." Here we go, she thought. You would have to live under a rock not to notice that office building and the fifty-foot snowman that sat outside during the sixty-degree-plus holiday season. It was a surprise that Troy didn't mention it. Kennedy knew that what she said next would determine whether she would end the evening with a wild romp in the sack or a friendly peck on the forehead. Tell the truth and a man with a weak ego might run screaming from the building. She sighed. It had happened before.

"That's impressive. With what department?" He didn't even

work in advertising, she thought. Why should it matter? She picked up the toothpick that was perched on her glass and used her own recently whitened teeth to skillfully slide one of the gourmet olives off and into her mouth while he watched, then chewed it slowly. She really, really felt like romping and would be damned if she had purchased almost two hundred dollars' worth of new makeup she didn't need to have a man as fine as this only use his lips to uncover the skillfully concealed frown lines on her forehead.

She couldn't cross her fingers, so Kennedy crossed her legs again instead. "I'm an administrative assistant." Just a little white lie. She could say some "Hail Marys" later. It was better this way, less intimidating. He didn't need to know what she really did, at least not before she knew what type of man he was. She learned a long time ago that women with high earning power intimidated some men. Relationships were hard enough, so why make it any harder by starting out hurting fragile male egos?

He nodded, but didn't stop smiling. "You been there long?"

"Nope. Not too long. How long have you been at your job?" She relaxed a little. He'd just made it easier to flip the script. From the looks of things, she only had to keep him talking about himself just a little while longer. They would be leaving soon. He already had that "I'm just a little tipsy" look in his eyes. She took a small sip of her drink. A little redirection and he would be back to talking about what he did. The dating cycle rules said that most people loved to talk about their work. If they loved their job, they would talk about how good they were at it, and if they hated it, they would use that as an opportunity to gripe. Besides, he didn't need to know anything about her, not really, because in the long run, it just wouldn't matter when all was said and done. The way she saw it, he was good for two, maybe three dates. Any more than that, people got clingy. It was far easier to keep the relationship on the surface.

"Do you think you're interested in dessert?"

Kennedy shook her head. "I don't think so." Did he think she stayed this fine by eating dessert? She wasn't twenty and maintenance had turned into hard work a while ago.

"It won't hurt to look." Troy pushed the menu in her direction anyway.

She sighed, and then opened it. What she had in mind had far fewer calories, she thought, but there was no harm in humoring him. But why the hell couldn't she hook up with a brother who just wanted to get in her panties as opposed to one who wanted to find out all about her then stuff her with food first?

"Is that you?" Kennedy stiffened as a familiar voice came from behind her. She froze, hoping she would just go away and mind her business. What kind of idiot would not be able to see that she was on a date and probably shouldn't be disturbed? Wasn't it written in someone's restaurant rulebook somewhere that if a person looked occupied that the proper thing to do would be to wave from across the room?

"I think a friend of yours is calling your name," Troy said. He looked at the three women that were standing behind her a few feet away.

Kennedy held her menu higher, wishing she could slide under the table. "I think they've mistaken me for someone else."

She froze, refusing to turn around, hoping Marie would take the hint, but of course that would just be too good to be true.

As Kennedy knew they would, Marie Williams and her two friends came right over anyway. "Kennedy, girl, I didn't expect to see *you* here, and you didn't tell me that you had a date."

Kennedy smiled tersely. "I didn't expect you here either." Maybe there was a slim chance that they wouldn't make her do introductions. As soon as she thought it, she knew that those chances were very slim indeed. All three of the women were staring right at Troy and he was returning their questioning gazes with a vengeance.

"So, Kennedy, are these friends from work?" Kennedy pursed her lips. He was trying to make the introductions easier on her, probably thinking that by overlooking the introductions she had just committed a little social faux pas.

Marie said, "I'm a friend of hers. We went to college together. A neighbor actually. Marie Williams." She extended her hand and Kennedy was almost blinded by the shine from the triple-sapphire bling she was sporting. Marie never did anything small. "I didn't catch your name."

"Troy Hughes. It's a pleasure to meet such lovely ladies." He shook her hand gently, smiling that gorgeous smile that had attracted Kennedy in the first place.

Marie giggled like a young kid, ignoring the glaring look that Kennedy was throwing her way. She never could take a hint.

"Well, I certainly haven't heard Kennedy mention you. I'm sure I would have remembered." She paused. "I don't work with her, but she is certainly a star. We heard about her latest coup all the way over at my firm. It was all over the business journal."

Kennedy balked. If she didn't do something soon, her evening would be ruined. "It was no big deal really."

Marie's mouth dropped open and Troy looked at her with curiosity-filled eyes.

"I was just in the right place at the right time. My boss was just lucky that I had forgotten my purse at my desk and needed to come back for it." She turned to Troy. "You see, he was working on a campaign after-hours and went to his car and locked himself out of the building. Wouldn't you know it, I happen to come along right at that minute and was able to let him in. They say it saved his presentation to one national client."

"Secretaries don't get into the business journals often."

She smiled sheepishly. "Small town."

Marie chuckled, then narrowed her eyes. The two women with her looked at one another quizzically. "Is that what they said?"

Kennedy nodded, and then quickly changed the subject. "Troy is a geologist."

"Really. I didn't know they came in brown." Marie and the other women with her all laughed, ignoring Kennedy's frowns.

"I teach geology."

"Are you doing business with Kennedy's agency?"

"Okay, now." Kennedy cut her off. "Enough questions." A thin smile played about her mouth. "Marie, I really would like you to stay and chat, but Troy and I were just enjoying our evening out, you know, a date?"

"Ah. I get ya. Okay, Troy, it was nice meeting you. You two lovebirds take care."

They sat in silence as Marie and the other women left. Kennedy exhaled heavily, then took a drink. "I'm sorry about that."

"Nothing to be sorry about. We were ordering dessert."

From the corner of her eye, Kennedy watched Marie leave her two friends at a table and head toward the restroom. "You know, will you excuse me? I think I need to go to the ladies room."

"I'll be here."

Kennedy practically ran back to the corner of the restaurant and flung open the door. It hit the wall with a loud clang.

Marie jumped and dropped the phone she was holding.

"Dang. You know I can't bend down in this dress." She struggled as she tried to reach her cell phone, but her tight column dress made it difficult.

"Umh. I told you before that Missoni is not for you."

"You are such a bitch."

"Thank you."

"Just get me my phone. Why are you storming up in here anyway? And what in the hell was that all about? You acted like you didn't want to introduce me or something. Don't tell me you are ashamed of me? My dress is a little tight but it's not all that bad. And as much of a hot shot as you are at the office, he didn't seem to know a thing about you."

"We have been mainly talking about him."

"What? You are kidding me, right? Not Miss Braggadocious herself."

"Can you stop mixing your Stanford with your ghetto? It doesn't go well together." Marie had been very cynical lately.

"I'm just keeping it real. Something you don't know anything about." She paused, hoping for more information. "So, is he marriage material or what?"

Kennedy opened her small handbag and took out her Chanel lipstick. "Please. You know how I feel about marriage."

"You are being ridiculous. Look at me."

"Yes, look at you. I think you were faithful for all of two months."

"No need to be nasty." A shadow came over Marie's face. She quickly pointed the conversation back in Kennedy's direction. "You have no idea what you are talking about. This isn't about me, anyway."

"Don't get your panties in a bunch. This is only our first date."

"Thongs don't bunch. And if I know you, it will be your last." She grinned. "Depends on how good he is in bed."

"You really have a problem."

"And you don't? At least I have no illusions about it. Marriage is an antiquated institution that just isn't for me. I have no need for it in my life. I can take care of myself. Besides, men do it all the time." She gave Marie a look that dared her to say anything. "I need some sex, so I'm going to get it."

Marie gave her a disapproving look. "I'm not saying there is anything wrong with that, but at least you can tell the brother where you're coming from. Be honest with him. Men your age start thinking about marriage and settling down as much as women do. It's not fair to them. And you really shouldn't let one bad experience leave you jaded against men the rest of your life."

Kennedy cringed. Marie had to bring up the past. "Whatever. Just like you and your five-hundred-mile-rule isn't fair to your husband. You are forever flirting with other men when you are on the road."

She obviously didn't get it. "Louis and I have a *don't ask, don't tell* understanding. It's just flirting. Damn." She paused. "You'll change your mind one day. What about children? You aren't getting any younger."

"Why should I have kids of my own? I have yours and Mai's. And those I can at least send home when they misbehave."

Marie didn't reply. She and Kennedy had this discussion before. She gave Kennedy a look that spoke a thousand words.

"You can stop lecturing me. I have to get back to my date." Kennedy ran her fingers through her hair, trying to rearrange her curls.

"I still don't understand why you lie about what you do."

She shrugged. "I didn't lie, I just didn't tell him. It's better when men feel like they might be the major breadwinner in a relationship." She lowered her voice. "I told you before, I don't want to intimidate them before they can get to know me."

"Please. You are a psychologist now? Give the man some credit. So, you think they'll like you better if they think you make thirty thousand than if they think you make a six-figure income?"

"Exactly."

Marie shook her head, not believing she was even still friends with this woman. They'd become so different. "That's silly. People who like you are going to like you regardless of what you do or how much you make."

"Maybe on television, but not in real life, and you know it's the truth. How many broke friends have you got?"

"I hear what you are saying, but I still don't understand. Louis likes that I bring home the bacon. He likes that I'm intelligent."

"That's what you say, but you can't tell me that there isn't a strain on your relationship. Louis is pussy-whipped. Let me rephrase my question, how many broke friends have you got, other than your husband?" She waved away Marie's comment. "Most men are into the dumb-blonde syndrome."

Marie couldn't believe what she was hearing. "You are delusional. I'm going to ignore that comment about my husband. He isn't broke. He contributes in a way that we have both deemed acceptable." She applied her lipstick furiously. "And you aren't blond."

"That's true, Stanford, I'm not. But I'm certainly in control."

Marie sighed, shaking her head. "What are you afraid of? You must have had some real issues with your father. And I would've thought you were far too together to be making sweeping generalizations like that." She shrugged. "It's your life. We won't bother you any more."

"I'm glad. And Marie, you really should stop reading *Psychology Today*. Stick to the pharmaceutical business, okay?"

The Trials of a Trophy Wife

Chili's was packed. Mai grabbed her four-year-old's hand and followed the woman guiding her to a table, hopefully one that was off in a corner somewhere. She tried her best to keep an eye on her two other children as they wended their way through the room.

"Is this okay?" The woman was a blond, waifish-looking woman with huge green eyes. Mai couldn't help staring at her obviously collagen-infused lips and tried to answer. Her neighborhood was such a special place. This poor girl had probably grown up right here and had never crossed the bridge to the south side nor the interstate, affectionately known as the other side of the tracks, not that Mai had, but it was the principle that was important.

"This is great." Mai directed the kids in the direction of the table, then turned and whispered to Collagen Girl. "Would you please tell the waiter that it's the big girl's birthday. We need you guys to sing that embarrassing happy birthday song thing you do."

She nodded, then strode away. Mai pulled out her chair.

"Mommy, why do we have to eat here?" Mai's middle child, Sarai, was eight. Her voice was whiny and she looked generally unhappy.

"Because this is your sister's birthday dinner and she gets to choose, that's why."

"Why isn't Daddy here then?"

Mai silently thanked her for mentioning that. She knew and understood that their father worked the hours he needed to so they could live the lifestyle they did. "Just sit down. He's working. You know that. Look at the menu and pick your food. Your Auntie Marie is going to join us instead."

The kids seemed to lighten up a bit when she mentioned her friend Marie. They loved her and Mai was sure it was because she let them have whatever they wanted when she was around. But what else were friends for, right? The kids shuffled a few minutes more and then the younger two began to color happily. The oldest, Lishelle, folded her arms across her chest and sat there with the familiar new-teen scowl on her face. At least she wasn't complaining. Mai flagged down a waiter.

"Can I have a margarita, please? On the rocks. And make it with silver grade so you can leave off the salt." So far, she'd had a rough week and her nerves were frayed. She was going to need all the fortification she could get to make it through dinner, and the last thing she wanted was a bad margarita made with the wrong tequila. It was always tough for her when her husband, Cal, was out of town so long.

"Mom, it's not dark yet." Her oldest was turning thirteen years old. She spoke in that characteristically whiny-preachy voice that only a thirteen-year-old seemed to be able to master. "You can't drink. You won't be able to drive."

Mai rolled her eyes. "Sprite for all the kids, please." She ignored their requests for coke. That would be all she needed, to have to spend the rest of the evening with her kids soaring from a caffeine high. "Marie can drive if you are worried, Miss Thing." One drink wouldn't hurt. Mai was as sure of that as she was of the fact that it wasn't too early to drink. It might not be dark here, but it certainly was somewhere.

"Yes, I can." Marie arrived at the table and made her rounds. She grabbed the face of each child and planted a big kiss in the middle of each of their faces. Even the thirteen-year-old giggled in response.

"I was beginning to think you were going to stand us up."

Her mouth dropped open in fake surprise. "What? And miss my only godchild's birthday celebration? I wouldn't do that." She winked at the birthday girl. "Did you order me a drink?"

"Nope. You're my driver. Your precious godchild is concerned."

"Mom, the billboard says buzzed driving is drunk driving. Do you know how embarrassing it would be for me if my mother was arrested for drunk driving?"

Marie and Mai shared a glance and Mai cursed *Hooked on Phonics* under her breath.

Marie wanted to laugh, but didn't. "You know, it might just be the rest you need." She sat in the chair left for her and picked up her menu. "It sounds like you are having a really rough week."

Mai sat back in her chair. "I can't begin to tell you how tough." The waitress tiptoed around the table, placing glasses of water in front of each of them. Mai immediately sipped hers. "Can I have some lime, please?"

The waitress nodded, then left quietly.

"You know how it is. I had to do my community service for The Links, plus every one of my kids seemed to have extra extracurricular activities. Cal was out of town and you know I have to give that dinner party next weekend. I have been trying to get the house ready for that."

Marie responded with a slight twinge of sarcasm to her voice. "Ah. The trials and tribulations of a trophy wife." She didn't understand how Mai seemed to belong to every group there was, African-American or otherwise and still do all the things she did for her family. She helped other people so much it was almost as if she had no time for herself.

"I'm not a trophy wife. I do a lot of stuff. Did you forget I have *several* degrees?" Although she was a pharmacist, she hadn't worked in many years. After their last corporate move, she and Cal had decided that it was in their best interest if she take the lead in organizing their family life. Her family was her full-time job.

"Call it what you want. I still say it's a nice job if you can get it." She winked at her friend. "Seriously, you shouldn't be so stressed out. If you are doing everything, what does the nanny do?"

"I didn't tell you? She's on vacation this week. And Super-woman me, I thought I could handle it without her."

"That's what makes you super. There is nothing wrong with asking your husband to handle a few things, you know."

"Out of town, remember?"

"I mean generally."

Mai reached over to stop her four-year-old from pouring salt on the table. Marie would never understand anyone's lifestyle but her own. "Never mind." She returned the shaker to its place. "These things are all things *I* do. My jobs. He has his, too. And if I do mine right, then he can do his. Your situation is very unique. I would guess that most women take care of the majority of child-related and household duties. This works for us." Marie was the only woman she knew whose husband did most of the household duties, including cart the kids back and forth to school and day care. But she'd always been a little different.

Marie shrugged. "If you say it does, June Cleaver." Mai sneered at her friend, then took a gulp of her drink.

"Can I take your order?" The waitress was back, still smiling ear to ear. Mai listened as all of her children ordered some variation of macaroni and cheese.

"I'll have the chicken salad," she said.

"Me, too." Marie took a sip of her margarita. "I don't see why we had to come here so you all could order Kraft macaroni and cheese. You do know I could have made that at home for you, right?"

They all answered in unison. "Auntie Ree!"

"You know it's dessert that they're after."

"Speaking of that, I ran into Kennedy last night—"

"Let's not talk about that now. Ears are listening even if they appear not to be. There are some things we would prefer that they not learn about too early." Lishelle smirked at her mother.

"You think that one hasn't heard it all at that fancy private school you send her to? Private school kids are the worst."

Mai jumped suddenly. "Oh—"

"What? What's wrong—"

"Nothing. My phone is on vibrate. It startled me." She dug in her bag and pulled it out. "I just missed a call from some unknown number."

"Don't answer those. They always mean trouble. You know telemarketers call cell phones now."

"I'm saying. Let me just check the messages. Calvin might be trying to call me, although I don't know why he wouldn't use his cell phone. When he's on these trips he gets so busy he only calls like every two days." The phone rang again, buzzing in her hand. Mai flipped it open immediately and her mouth curled into an unconscious smile. She moved it away from her face and mouthed, "It's Cal. Excuse me."

Marie nodded and tried not to listen. She didn't understand how a call from her husband still made Mai gush. She and her husband, Louis, had never been that way. They'd always been very practical about their relationship. Instead she began teasing the kids.

"What? You're where?" The tensing of Mai's jaw betrayed her frustrations. "I don't understand."

Marie paused, studying her friend's face. It was obvious that there was something wrong, and from the looks of things, it was something big. "Everything okay?"

Tears welled up in Mai's eyes. She shook her head slowly, then closed the phone. "Um, I'm going to need a favor."

Marie reached over and took Mai's hand. "Of course. I already told you I would do anything you needed."

"Well, I need you to watch the kids."

Marie looked from Mai over to the kids, who seemed to be happily playing the games on their kids' menu. She swallowed. That hadn't been what she had in mind when she said *anything*. "For how long?"

"A day or so."

Mai had regained most of her composed look, but Marie could feel her hand trembling. Whatever Cal had said, it must have been bad. Mai was always in control. It had been a long time since she had seen her look so disturbed. "No problem. But I have to go out of town Wednesday. I have a trip planned that can't be canceled. But Kennedy and I will take care of whatever you need." She paused, debating whether or not to probe further. "What's wrong? Can you say?"

Mai shook her head, then bit her lower lip, peeling the skin as she did. The tears she was holding back choked her voice. Her words were barely above a whisper. "I have to go to Atlanta. It seems that Mr. Calvin Mott III has landed himself in jail."

The House Husband

"Tell me again why Mai's kids are here?" Louis tried not to glare at his wife. He wasn't expecting to have to take care of extra kids.

"Can we talk about it in the kitchen?" Marie grabbed her husband's shirt sleeve and pushed open the swinging door that led to their gourmet kitchen before he could even answer her. She waited for the door to close completely before she spoke. Something like this could be traumatizing for kids. Hell, it could be traumatizing for anyone.

"Well," she said, "Cal got arrested." She stepped forward to hug her husband from behind. He felt so good to her and they got so few moments alone. With her on the road and him so busy, they rarely had time to be just them, the way they'd been BC, as they called it. *Before Children*. Work and kids seem to take away most of the intimacy in their relationship. Nowadays, their family was run like a business.

"I got that part, but why did they have to come *here*?" Louis started to load the dishwasher. Why was other people's misfortune turning into his responsibility? He wanted to hug her back, but there was just too much that needed doing.

"It's not like they are bad kids or anything."

"I didn't say that. Are we the only friends they have? Why couldn't they stay with Kennedy? She has plenty of room."

"It's not about room. Kennedy is single and has never had children. Would you want our kids to stay with her if there were an alternative?" She paused. "Besides, she has her hands full with her father."

Louis seemed to contemplate his wife's words for a minute. "So, what did he do? What caused the old boy to get thrown in jail? I know Mai must be dying."

Marie shrugged. "I don't know. Mai didn't say. I'm not sure she knows."

"Um-hmm. You mean she didn't tell you."

"What's that supposed to mean?"

"It means just what I said. She doesn't tell you everything."

Marie narrowed her eyes and leaned back on the counter. It was obvious that Louis had something to say, so why didn't he come out and say it? "She does too. We share everything."

"You think you do. You and Kennedy tell her everything and she acts like the momma hen and helps you solve your problems. No one is *that* perfect. I'm telling you that she keeps a lot to herself. A lot. We have been married a long time and I see things."

"You do not. What are you talking about? Things like what?" Louis always acted like he knew so much about her friends.

"Well, I can see that there is no telling what kind of trouble Cal has gotten into."

If she didn't know better, Marie would say that Louis was smirking. "Just what do you know? You are just being mean."

It was Louis's turn to shrug. "If you say so. I'm just saying that things aren't what they seem to be over there. Cal may not be the pillar of the community you think he is."

Marie opened her mouth to answer, but there was a crash in the other room. Marie and Louis both jumped. He gave his wife a look and she went back through the door, yelling, "What is going on in here?"

Louis didn't move, instead choosing to continue what he was doing. She could handle this one alone. He half-listened to the excited voices in the other room, knowing what was happening anyway. The kids would be making up some story about who had not done what, and as usual, Marie would probably not deal with it. He was the disciplinarian in the household and they both knew it, but Louis had learned a long time ago that it was something not worth fighting over. There were a lot of things like that in their relationship and he'd learned to pick his battles.

Louis didn't know how long Mai would be gone, but as soon as Marie left on her business trip, he would be putting out enough fires with five kids to look after. His two were enough, but three extras were going to be a challenge, especially that surly Lishelle. Even though she was so young, that kid was standing on the edge of trouble.

They didn't even get to discuss that Marie had once again committed his services without asking. It wasn't like she would be the one to watch the kids. She might be around to help out for a day or two, but come Wednesday, she would be off on another one of her marathon trips. It was the routine of their lives and somehow things seemed to run more smoothly when she was gone. Sometimes if she was home more than a few days, he almost wanted to ask her if it was time for her to be taking another trip. How had their relationship become a co-parenting agreement? This week was turning into one of those times. They both seemed to be on edge.

His cell phone buzzed and Louis jumped. He'd forgotten that it was in his pocket. He wiped his hands on a dishrag and tried to grab the phone. Just as he looked at it, Marie came back. Her timing was wonderful. He let the phone slip back into its resting place and returned to loading the dishwasher. He could deal with that later. Marie started talking immediately.

"Who was that?"

He ground his teeth. Why was everything an inquisition? She would get all tied up in knots if he did that to her.

"Tenant." It could always be a tenant. Someone in the twenty-unit apartment building they owned always had a problem, especially since the majority of the tenants were UT students.

"Oh." She rolled her eyes. "Your kids—"

"Why do they have to be mine when they are loud?"

Marie smiled and put both hands on her slender hips. "You know what I mean." She paused. "What were we saying? Oh. Yeah. She didn't tell me why he was in jail or what happened. She just asked if we could watch the kids and the birthday lunch was over. But that's not what I need to talk to you about."

Louis felt the cell phone buzz again. "Umh-humph."

"You going to get that?"

He closed the dishwasher. "Get what?"

Marie gave him a quizzical look. "Your phone. It's buzzing."

He shook his head. "No, we're talking. It can wait." Louis always put them first, even if she'd forgotten how to.

"If you say so. Anyway, I have to leave earlier than I thought. I'm leaving in the morning, not Wednesday. Is that okay?"

Too late. Louis weighed his answer. What was he supposed to say? This is what he'd signed up for when he'd agreed to be the one who took primary responsibility for his kids. He smiled warmly, flashing the deep dimples he knew Marie loved. "Of course."

A look of relief flooded Marie's worried face. "I don't want to impose. You sure?"

Louis leaned over and kissed his wife on the lips. They decided a long time ago that since she had better earning potential, he would stay closer to home. She had no idea at all that he was having second thoughts about their arrangement. It wasn't that bad really. He made good money from the building income, maybe not as much as she did, but he got to spend time with his kids that most men never had. Time you couldn't get back. The thing that was getting to him was that Marie seemed to put him last. Her career, first, her kids, her friends, and then if she had anything at all left over, maybe that was for him. "I got this," he said. "You go do your thing." Rather than resort to whining, he found ways to make himself happy. By the way she kissed him back, he knew she was as convinced and comfortable as he needed her to be.

A Hunk in the House

Kennedy rolled over in bed and stretched. She sniffed the air and then smiled. Bacon. She tried to live a good life, but swine was one of her vices. She opened her eyes and looked at the clock. It hit her then. *She smelled bacon.* Where was Troy? After a weekend in, she'd finally managed to learn his name. Was he cooking in her kitchen? He didn't know her like that.

She bounded out of bed and reached for her cashmere robe, tying it tightly around her. *Oh no, he wasn't.* Just because they had a great weekend was no reason for him to think he could cook in her kitchen. It was against the dating cycle rules. Cooking suggested a whole 'nother level of intimacy that she had not agreed to. The weekend would be over in a few hours and that would be that, he'd have to go. Kennedy brushed her teeth and dabbed on some lip gloss, then rushed to the kitchen, her favorite room in the house. Although she had no intention of being a housewife, Kennedy loved everything about her house, including the upgraded kitchen that Mai had helped her design and that she'd forked out a fortune to have. Her kitchen was the heart of her home.

Her feet made a slapping noise on the tiles as she stormed through the house, ready to give the man a piece of her mind. How dare he? She thought. He doesn't know me like that. She pushed open the pocket door that led to the kitchen and opened her mouth to speak. Troy was still as fabulous as he had been the night before, standing over the island stovetop wearing just his boxers. Kennedy hadn't realized just how fabulous his pecs were until that moment. The words got caught in her throat and she closed her mouth instead of shouting the expletives she'd thought of just a minute before. The sight of his chiseled upper body made her change her mind. It was only one day, and that bacon smelled divine. Damn, she chose 'em good. He looked up as she entered and smiled.

"You want coffee?"

"You didn't have to do this." She slid onto a seat. "I actually thought you might be gone or something."

"That would be rude. I was at least going to wait until you woke up, and then I thought I'd make myself useful." Troy smiled, then slid an egg onto a plate. He pushed the plate toward Kennedy.

"I wasn't expecting all this."

"That makes it better then, doesn't it?"

There was an awkward silence. Kennedy contemplated what her next move should be. He was such a nice guy. She just couldn't afford to be involved.

He cleared his throat. "You seemed to be having a tough time or something in your sleep. Bad dream?"

Kennedy's face fell. The dream again. It was always the same. Music playing, her ex, Damon, would be down on one knee in that damned picturesque restaurant, asking her to marry him. She broke into tears, so overcome by emotion that she would be barely able to nod her acceptance. Everyone around them cheered as he slipped the beautiful ring onto her finger, and then they kissed. In the middle of all that, the wife that she never knew he had would rush in screaming, "Get away from my husband!" And just like that, her fairy tale had turned bad. And for some reason, she replayed it over in her dreams every third night or so.

"I'm sorry. I must have been overtired or something. I hope I didn't keep you awake."

"No, you didn't. I was enjoying watching you sleep anyway. You want juice?"

"No thanks." He was too nice. Another reason this had to be the last time they saw each other. They were all nice in the beginning.

"I saw some of your sketches over there. I'm sorry if I was being nosy. You are being underutilized at that place. You would think they could recognize talent when they saw it. From the looks of those, you should certainly be more than a secretary."

"Sketches?" She cringed. Kennedy thought she'd put everything away. And was his tone accusing her of something?

He nodded. "The storyboards." He pointed in the direction of her work corner.

Her face flushed. "Oh. Those. They aren't mine. I just have them here so I can put together the presentation for my boss. You know, administrative stuff."

He nodded again, but Kennedy could tell by the look on his face that he didn't buy her story.

"Look, I have some things I have to do to get ready for work tomorrow. I really appreciate the breakfast and the wonderful date, but I gotta start moving, okay?"

Troy wiped his hands on Kennedy's Williams-Sonoma hand towel and folded it neatly, placing it on the edge of the sink. "I need to be getting home anyway." He walked around the counter and gave her a peck on the cheek. "Maybe we can do this again sometimes, okay?"

A pang of sadness washed over her as she watched him head to the bedroom to get dressed. Kennedy sighed. If this was the right thing to do, then why did she feel so empty about it? It was certainly the safest. If she didn't get involved, she couldn't get hurt. And she didn't want to get serious anyway. It was probably a good thing that Damon had turned out to be such a zero, before she'd made a horrible mistake. Not that he could have married her, at least not legally. After Damon, Kennedy had realized that she really hadn't wanted the complications that marriage would bring anyway. She had a great job, a great house, and her own money. She didn't want to share anything and she certainly wasn't about to get into a situation like the ones Marie and Mai were in. There was no way in hell she was going to be supporting a man, and she certainly wasn't the housewife type. She shook her head. Mai's case was the sadder of the two. She was a pharmacist, for goodness sakes, and all of those skills were going to waste while she was playing at being trophy wife. What if her husband messed it all up? What would Mai have to show for it all other than a big mortgage that she couldn't pay alone?

The phone rang, jarring Kennedy out of her thoughts. She grabbed it just as Troy poked his head back into the kitchen.

"Hello?" Kennedy held her finger up and Troy paused. The person on the other end hesitated. "Marie?" he asked.

Kennedy frowned. Folks really should be more careful dialing, especially on a Sunday morning. "No. I'm sorry. You have the wrong number." She didn't wait for an answer and immediately returned the phone to its base.

"A few friends of mine plan a getaway every year. This year we are going to Cancun. It's next month. Maybe you'd like to go?"

Despite the stirring in her loins, Kennedy groaned inside. It was never that easy. He didn't get it. And they said women were clingy. "Thanks for the offer, but I don't think I'll be able to get away." She shrugged. "I have very limited vacation time." If she went on a vacation with him he would certainly think they were either in or well on their way to a relationship. She couldn't have that.

The phone rang again.

"Hello?"

It was the same voice as before. "Marie Williams?"

Oh shit. Marie had done it again. Kennedy clenched her teeth. "You have the wrong number."

"Everything okay?" Troy asked.

She nodded as the caller repeated the number to her.

"Yes, that's the number you called, but Marie Williams doesn't live here." She hung up the phone, more forcefully this time.

Troy waited patiently. "Isn't your friend's name Marie? The one I met at the restaurant?"

"It is." A prickle of annoyance ran up her back. Not only was he not going to take no for an answer, he was nosy, too. She gave him a look that dared him to ask any more questions and he seemed to take the hint.

Troy looked away, a puzzled look on his face. Kennedy started to explain, but thought better of it. The less he knew about her and her friends, the better.

A door slammed toward the back of the house and Troy jumped. "What was that?"

Kennedy cringed. Her father was up. And things had been going so smoothly. The sound of shuffling came closer. Her father had a distinctive walk. Over the last few months, he seemed to be actually picking up his feet less and less.

"Dad, I told you to give me some warning." Kennedy stepped around the table to pull out a chair for her father. His robe was worn and pulled tightly around him, and his too-long hair was flat on one side. His thin legs were ashen and he wore only one white sock inside his brown fuzzy slippers. She sighed, thankful that he had remembered to put some clothes on this morning. This was a good day for him.

Troy cleared his throat, his arms crossed over his body as if he was trying to hide himself.

"Don't be embarrassed. He won't remember." Kennedy walked over to the counter to get a mug for her father, then filled it with coffee, automatically adding two sugars the way she had been doing ever since she was a girl.

"Why is Damon in your room, Kennedy?"

The name hit her like a slap in the face. "Dad, this isn't my room, it's my house, remember? And this is not Damon."

He seemed to ignore her.

She turned and talked to Troy over her shoulder. "My father lives in my guest house. He doesn't remember things too well."

"Was he here all the time?" Troy's face was filled with confusion.

"Yes, he was. He lives with me. I hope you don't mind if I give him this food. He sometimes doesn't eat too well."

Troy nodded. He didn't want to pry. He knew that Kennedy had been trying to appear distant, but he was moved by the idea that she took care of her father. Underneath all that hard exterior was a tender spot. She obviously needed time alone.

"You know what? It's obvious you have things you have to take care of. I'm going to go so you can get your work done. Just think about Cancun, okay? If only for the weekend."

She had no intention of thinking about anything, but she nodded anyway, then began picking up dishes as if she were going to clean the kitchen.

"Bye, Damon. My Kennedy ain't allowed to entertain in her room. Maybe you can come back another time."

Kennedy gave Troy an apologetic look. If he wasn't scared away before, he certainly would be now. "Just close the door behind you, okay? It will slam lock." Kennedy looked away so she wouldn't have to witness the look on his face. She listened as his footsteps echoed on her stone floors, followed by the sound of her door closing behind him.

Her weekend had been great, but the familiar feeling of emptiness crept over her anyway. Kennedy helped her father finish eating and then went about the motions of putting her prize kitchen back in its normal, pristine order, trying to put thoughts of her weekend and Troy out of her head. As far as she was concerned, he was history as soon as he'd walked through the door.

Troy inhaled, enjoying the smell of the outdoors. It was a beautiful day and he was in a good mood, even if Kennedy hadn't been. She seemed like someone he really wanted to get to know better, but she was really uptight, almost secretive. She obviously felt a strong sense of responsibility toward her family, though, and that was certainly positive. Nowadays, most people put their aging family members into care homes right away. Kennedy had not mentioned any family through their entire date, especially not a peep about her father living with her. He might have thought twice about staying over had he known the situation.

He put his roadster into gear and sped off toward his house. She had so much going for her, she just needed to slow down and appreciate life a little. Many people didn't take the time to do that. Kennedy had damn near thrown him out the door, but that was okay. He wasn't the type to be turned away that easily. Persistence was his middle name. Her head may have been saying no, but her body was sure saying otherwise. It was okay. Caution was good nowadays, but he had a few tricks up his sleeve that should help her let that guard down. Troy knew what a woman liked, especially one as classy as Kennedy was. He picked up his cell phone. Nothing like flowers to let a lady know how much she is appreciated.

Mr. and Mrs. Mott

The room was noisy and full of people, none of whom appeared to be happy. All around her, people were crying, shouting, complaining, or looking generally miserable. Mai sat perched on the bench in the stereotypical-looking police station. She wrinkled her nose. It was a disgusting place, one she never thought she'd see the inside of. The room smelled like wet animals and harsh, industrial disinfectant. An animal whimpered and Mai followed the sound with her eyes. Two German shepherd dogs lay on the floor in the corner. They were beautiful and looked well cared for, but they looked as if they wanted to be there no more than she did.

After her long flight, Mai's back hurt, but she had no intention of sitting back in her seat. There was no telling who'd sat on the filthy-looking bench before her and she had no desire to share even a molecule of dust with her predecessors. A clock loomed overhead. Twenty minutes since she'd signed in. Nineteen and a half since she'd handed over the receipt for the bond

money. It was all too real but felt like she had been thrust into
the middle of a cop show that had not been edited for TV. Mai
felt a pair of eyes on her. She looked up, but couldn't spot the
source of what she'd sensed. Everyone in the room was occupied or seemed to be preoccupied. A couple argued, a few other
people milled around, one or two looked as if they had been
crying. A man sat across the large room reading. His head was
down, intent on his paper. Mai didn't recognize him, but she
recognized the square-toed shoes he was wearing as very expensive.

She fidgeted in her seat. The pain in her back was quickly
becoming excruciating, probably because she was sitting so
stiffly. She relaxed a little, immediately feeling just a little
more comfortable. The longer she waited, the more annoyed
she became at herself. What was she expecting, five-star service? This was a police station, after all. Part of her wanted to
just get up and leave, but she had no intention of leaving yet, at
least not until she got to speak to her husband. He owed her one
hell of an explanation, especially since she'd flown across the
country at the drop of a hat, then ran all over town to find a bail
bondsman. What was that? She hadn't even really known what
bail bondsmen did before this afternoon. Kennedy was the one
who'd told her exactly what she had to do. Although she'd been
afraid to ask her how she knew so much about the workings of
the law, Mai thanked God that one of her best friends was such
a wealth of knowledge.

A woman sat down next to her. From the corner of her eye,
Mai noted her rough appearance. She would never have come
out of her house with her hair in such a state of disarray, no

matter what was going on. Her clothes were a mess, too. They looked well worn and like they hadn't seen clean in quite a long time. *Damn you, Cal.* Mai had no idea yet what he'd gotten mixed up in, but it seemed unfair that she had to suffer too. She slid as far away from the woman as she could. The woman shot her an evil look, then raised her hand to her hair as if she were just a little self-conscious. Mai didn't give a damn. Hell, she wasn't exactly in her element either. Silently, she dared her to say a word to her.

Mr. Square Toes rustled his paper and crossed his legs at the knee. From the corner of her eye, Mai caught him looking this time. She was standing out like a sore thumb. *Maybe she should go to the bathroom and rough up her hair, too. Perhaps she wouldn't be as interesting then.*

Her head throbbed. Mai opened her purse and reached for her small pillbox, quickly slipping one of the small yellow pills under her tongue. She counted off the number in her head. Was this three today? Two? She was usually better than this, but now, everything was a blur. Mai sucked hard on the small pill, feeling the "V" shaped grooves with her tongue. That comforted her a little. In just a manner of minutes, familiar warmth would spread through her body and her nerves would be calmed. Things would be better then and she would handle anything Calvin would tell her when she finally got to see him.

The trill of her cell phone rang through the waiting area, causing several of the other people standing near her to check theirs. Mai flinched at the intrusion, but no else one seemed to mind the noise above the din. She snatched it open almost gratefully. Sitting in the police station was like riding on the

Greyhound bus. If she were occupied, there was a better chance of her being left alone. The only thing that would make it better was if she could fall asleep and drool from the side of her mouth. Maybe she wouldn't look so nervous if she had something else to think about.

"This is Mai." A warm feeling floated through Mai's stomach as the Valium began to do its job. Some of the tension in her body began to float away.

"Hey, Mai. It's Louis. You hanging in there?" Her face burned. By now she was sure that he knew why she had to go to Atlanta. What in the hell had her dumb husband been thinking? She forced a smile into her voice.

"I'm doing the best I can. I'm waiting for him to be released now. The kids okay?"

"Let me know if you need anything." He paused. "I needed to check in with you. Lishelle says that you forgot to tell us that she was having a sleepover at a friend's tonight."

Tension gripped Mai's neck. This was all she needed right now. "Did she? I said no such thing. She knows we don't allow sleepovers during the week. Uh-uh." Lishelle had just officially made teenager and she was already trying Mai's nerves.

"That's what I thought, but I wanted to double check."

"Well she—" Her response left her brain. Mai barely recognized her husband as he shuffled into the room. His clothes looked dirty and wrinkled and he had what looked like several days' growth of facial hair. *Just how long had he been in there?* Mai wondered when Calvin had aged so much; he certainly looked a good five years older than he had just a few days earlier. Her voice was barely a whisper as she continued to speak into her phone. "I'm going to have to call you back, Louis." She clicked the phone shut without waiting for his reply.

Mai was overcome with emotion as Calvin came toward her. All the annoyance and anger she'd been feeling earlier left her and her eyes welled up with tears. Calvin, her immaculate-looking spouse, looked a mess. His usually crisp, clean white shirt was dirty and missing its monogrammed pocket. His face was even bruised in several places. She stood up, letting both her bag and phone slide to the floor. She wrapped herself around him as the tears ran down her face.

"I'm okay," Calvin said, pushing her off. "Get your bag, Mai." His voice was stern instead of relieved. Calvin's eyes quickly darted around the room.

"I didn't know what happened to you." Mai sobbed in between her words. "I was terrified when you called me."

Cal's mouth was set in a straight line. "I didn't mean to frighten you. I'm exhausted. Let's just go." Calvin shoved his hands into his pockets and quickly sidled away. He walked as if he were trying to get out of the police station as quickly as possible. Mai snatched up her belongings and hurried to follow him. Was he limping? Pangs of annoyance were returning. Had he even thanked her?

They waited until they were in the car to speak. Mai slid behind the wheel and started the engine. Calvin stared out of the side window, his face turned away from her.

Mai said nothing, waiting for her husband to initiate a conversation and an explanation. Being arrested was so far out of character for Calvin that Mai's mind was blank for what seemed like a long time. She tried to be patient, but once the car left the parking garage and hit daylight, the words just seemed to explode from her. She couldn't wait any longer.

"So, are you going to tell me what happened? I had to leave the kids with my friends and you know how trying Lishelle is right now. Who knows about this?" She took a breath and wet her lips. She needed to get all the details so she would know how to deal with it when people asked questions later. And she was positive there would be lots of questions. There was no way this would stay a secret and their friends and neighbors would certainly ask. They probably wouldn't be kind about it either.

"This was all a big misunderstanding."

Her mouth dropped open. "Really? Isn't that what they all say? Please don't let the next sentence out of your mouth be that you didn't do it. Jails are full of innocent people. Isn't that what they say?" She didn't mean to sound so sarcastic, but she couldn't help it.

Calvin reached into his jacket pocket and pulled out his sunglasses. He slipped them on, then leaned his head back on the headrest.

"I know you have something to say. I understood the charges quite well. Public misconduct? Assault? What happened?"

"You wouldn't understand." His voice sounded heavy.

Mai's mouth dropped open. "Oh? Try me. I think I have been pretty understanding up until now. Why don't you just break it down for me? Tell me the events that led up to me having to fly all the way to Atlanta."

Looking out of the window, Calvin swallowed hard. It would be too much to think his wife would be able to understand everything that had happened, but he certainly wasn't in the mood for attitude. "Mai, it has been a hectic twenty-four hours." He reached over and put his hand in her hair while she drove. "It's totally my fault. Sort of dumb. You know I'm embarrassed."

Mai tried to keep her eyes on the road as she listened to her husband's words.

"I didn't see those damned motorcycles. They parked weird. Of course now that I think about it, I saw the guys when they came in. You know it was Black Biker weekend in Atlanta."

Mai knew she should be feeling some type of alarm. The Valium was having its full effect. Instead of being worried, she was filled with a calmness that she had come to be known for. "Black Biker? You don't ride a bike. Are you having one of those mid-life crises or something?"

"No, I'm not. I was in Atlanta for a business meeting. You know that. This group of bikers parked behind me at a restaurant and I knocked one of the bikes pulling out of my spot. Unfortunately, that caused a whole row of bikes to just fall over."

"So they put you in jail for that?"

Calvin rubbed his temple. "No, they put me in jail for the fight that followed. Let's just say that a couple of the fellas were a little upset about their bikes. That and I'd had two drinks."

Mai's stomach sank. "So, you were under the influence? What were you thinking?" She paused. Everybody made mistakes sometimes. Maybe this was Calvin's time. "We are absolutely going to need a lawyer. Don't worry though, I know just who to call."

Small beads of sweat had formed on his brow. She might not

understand or appreciate the whole story, but Calvin had no doubt that he could count on his wife. She was capable in a way most people couldn't begin to approach. Mai usually found a way to handle most things that life threw at her, for herself and for other people. This latest hiccup didn't look like it would be any exception.

Thousands of questions ran through Mai's mind as she checked into the hotel. Getting into fights was not like Calvin. He was usually very calm about most things. Being able to talk himself out of even the toughest situations was one of the things he was known for. If she were any other wife, she would probably hound him to death to find out the rest of the story, but they had been married long enough for her to realize that was not going to work. If Calvin wanted her to know, he would tell her in his own time. They had that kind of understanding. Everybody knew that Mai and Calvin Mott were a team, and that wasn't about to change now. He handled the financial end of things and made sure that Mai's life ran smoothly and was free of unpleasantness. She took care of everything else, and liked doing it, no matter what her friends thought. Mai fought hard to resist the temptation to question her husband further. Calvin didn't need a lecture. He needed a hot bath and some TLC, the way only she could provide it.

"Here's your room number." The clerk pointed to the small folder that held the keys. He'd written their room number almost illegibly. Mai smiled pleasantly anyway, nodding her thanks. She fumbled with her bag and her keys and headed back to the car where Calvin was waiting for her. From inside the hotel, she could see the car where she'd left it, not far from the door. Calvin appeared to be talking to someone. Mai hadn't planned on making nice with anyone, but she put on her best smile anyway. As she got closer, he looked almost like the man she'd caught staring at her back at the police station. That was strange. Maybe he'd been staring at her because he'd recognized her or knew Calvin from somewhere. The man looked up as Mai's heels sounded on the pavement, then hurried away from the car.

Calvin rolled up the window as Mai got back in the car. He jumped when she slammed the door. "That was fast."

"Was it?" She put on her seat belt. "Who was that? I thought you might have fallen asleep in the car."

He rubbed his face. "It's been a rough twenty-four, baby. I got a lot on my mind."

"That man I saw you talking to. Was he in the police station?"

Calvin shrugged, looking away. "He was asking for directions."

"Oh. He looked just like a man that was sitting in the police station. I would have sworn it was him." She started the car. "Our room is in the back. You should be careful talking to people. We don't live here. He could've carjacked us or something."

"No one wants this rental car, honey. Besides, he was too well dressed to be a carjacker."

Mai smiled warmly. "If you say so. I hope a shower will perk you up. I got something that will take care of that headache and anything else that ails you. How many times do we get a night away from the kids like this?"

Any other day, Mai's statement would have made him smile,

too. Today, he was just tired. He knew in his gut that he wouldn't be able to keep secrets long. Mai would find out the truth, all of the truth soon enough. They might as well enjoy their bliss as long as possible. Instead of answering her questions, he just leaned over and kissed his wife. He felt better when she began to kiss him back.

Peanuts, Coffee, and a Little Something Extra

They called her group number and Marie boarded the plane. She swore under her breath. What in the hell had she been thinking when she agreed to be booked on such an early flight? She did the same thing for every trip and cursed herself anyway. It was a small price to pay for being able to spend an extra night in your own bed. She glanced out the terminal window. It was still dark, for Christ sakes. Still groggy from the lack of sleep, Marie stumbled, then filed along with her fellow passengers. They went through the normal door, but then turned and headed down some metal steps toward an emergency exit. Marie groaned. It was never a good sign when boarding a plane required a walk on the tarmac.

She was seated mid-plane about halfway back. Window seat, as requested. Marie ducked her head to get into her row, barely missing the overhead compartment. This was a small plane. No business class. It would be all peanuts and coffee. With the new security rules, there hadn't even been a chance for her to get coffee, and she'd already searched her bag thoroughly for any remnant of anything edible. All she had come up with was fuzz. Usually she kept a protein bar or a piece of gum with her, but her kids had apparently gotten hold of whatever might have been there. She would just have to get by with airplane peanuts today.

Marie placed her bag under the seat in front of her, missing the days of airplane meals. She could vaguely remember flying with her parents when she was a kid. There was a full meal on every flight for every passenger, even those not in first class. She'd gotten out of bed at the last possible moment and tried to be as quiet as she could. It wouldn't have done any good to wake the rest of the family up by making breakfast at 4 A.M. Her stomach was already growling and she was starting to regret not grabbing something.

A large presence seemed to close her in and Marie looked up, right into the eyes of a very huge, very handsome man. She swept his body quickly, then felt herself blush. He was certainly a fine specimen. At least there was one pleasant thing about the morning. She tensed and every molecule in her body was awake. He wasn't even sitting down and the musky smell of his cologne was filling her row.

He swung his heavy bag up and into the overhead bin without too much effort. Marie watched from the corner of her eye. The way that bag looked, it should have been more difficult than that. Marie watched his chiseled face, her eyes now locked on to his well-defined, square chin. What were the chances that he was going to be sitting next to her? Probably slim to none? She looked toward the front of the airplane quickly.

Where was the mother with the screaming lap child? Or the three-hundred-pound man with bad body odor? That is who she would normally get.

Mr. Big made eye contact, then smiled as he slid into the seat next to Marie. Her stomach flip-flopped. The fates were smiling on her today. Maybe it was going to be a good day after all.

His seat belt made a loud click as he closed it around his trim waist. Marie swallowed, flustered. So many men her age were already victims of middle-age spread. Not this one. He shuffled his feet back and forth to get comfortable, his knees almost touching the back of the seat in front of him.

Marie enjoyed the warmth of his body as he sat down. His thighs were muscular enough that she could feel them next to hers. What did she do to deserve to be so lucky?

"Hey, I'm Darren. If I'm too big, I can move." He leaned into the aisle and glanced toward the back of the plane. "It doesn't look like the flight is full."

Her heart pounded in her ears. Marie wondered if he found her as attractive as she found him? She fingered the ends of her shoulder-length hair, a warm tingling replacing the hunger pangs she'd been feeling a few minutes ago. "No, you're good." The sensation of his thigh against hers felt good, real good. Marie tried to hold back her smile. Early morning might not be so bad after all.

"I wouldn't want to make someone as fine as you uncomfortable."

Umph, there was the signal. That one statement told her what she needed to know. Mr. Big was interested in her too. Marie cocked her head to the side, licked her lips and took a deep breath. It's just a little harmless flirting, she thought. "Now, how could you possibly do that?" Her eyelashes fluttered. It was as if someone had flipped her switch and her body was now on flirt-o-matic.

He smiled, and Marie felt warmth spread through her.

"Nice ring." He pointed his little finger in the direction of the two-carat engagement ring that she had personally upgraded last year.

"Thanks."

"You have kids?" he asked.

"I do." Marie licked her lips.

"That's real nice." He paused. "Can I buy you a drink?"

Marie chuckled. "We're on a plane."

"I know that. But I could still get you a Bloody Mary. Or a coffee." Darren raised one eyebrow, a mischievous look on his face.

"Coffee is free."

"All the better. It's a start. And maybe I can get you a real drink later."

She still had it. His comment was a challenge, and she was feeling a little mischievous today herself.

Louis let the stack of weights fall to resting position with a clang, then took a big inhale. Midday at the gym was quiet, his favorite time to come. Working out with a minimum of interruptions helped him to get his head right. After the kids were in school, before he did anything else, he headed for his workout. Over the years, his routine had remained constant, even after he'd lost his favorite workout partner. He and Marie used to be a fixture in the gym, but that was before they'd taken the leap to parenthood.

The smell of antiseptic sprays melded with that of sweat. Noise was limited to the clang or hum of machines. There was soft music playing and the televisions that hung suspended from the ceiling were muted. Few people spoke, those that were on machines were wearing headphones, most staring intently at one television or another.

Usually, there were just a handful of other people milling around; today was no exception. He spotted the regulars, some he knew to be housewives and there was always a stripper or two with bad boob jobs. And then there were two or three other men who were self-employed like him.

He was used to being outnumbered in the gym, and it didn't bother him. For the most part, he minded his business, and almost everyone else seemed to mind theirs too, leaving him to complete his workout in peace.

"You gonna lay there and look at the weight or can I work in?"

Louis felt a pang of annoyance as the familiar voice pierced the silence. He liked being alone with his thoughts. He certainly didn't feel like messing around with Maxfield Walters today, but he sat up on the bench anyway. "Hey Max," he said. "Of course you can work in." Maxfield was a lawyer turned lobbyist, so if the legislature wasn't in session, he sometimes worked out midday, too.

They gave each other daps and Louis moved aside so Maxfield could get to the bench. "This weight okay?"

"Nah, man, this is a little sissy weight. Throw on two more twenty-fives for me."

Maxfield was the old-fashioned gym showoff type, always tried to do more than was safe if other people were around. Louis guessed that it was a good thing that the gym was light on the women or Maxfield would ask for even more weight. What a kid. If he wanted to kill himself, that was his business, Louis thought. He lifted the steel plates and slid one onto each end of the bar.

"How's my favorite kept man?"

Louis sighed, remembering why he didn't like Max. "Hate. So early in the morning."

Max laughed. "Not hate. You are made of better stuff than I am, man. Better stuff than most of us. I know for a fact that I couldn't do half the shit my girl does during the day and I wouldn't even try. And then I think of you, holding it down just as good as most sisters, if not better."

Louis folded his arms. With his archaic ideas, it was a wonder Maxfield even had anyone in his life. "I need to get my next set in. Just lift."

"I see. You don't want to talk. I understand. Some people are like that while they work out. Concentration is necessary in the gym." Maxfield paused to push the weight away from his body and into the air. "But, what I want to know is, how the hell do you handle it?"

"What are you talking about?" Louis clenched his teeth together. This was not something he wanted to discuss with anyone, much less some gym rat he didn't even like or respect.

"Your woman, man. Doesn't she travel all the time? Ain't you worried that someone might try to move in on your territory?"

A heavy sigh escaped Louis's lips. "Women aren't territory,

Max. And if it was going to happen, I'm sure all she had to do
was walk around the corner. Marie and I have an understanding."

Max let out a series of grunts as he lifted and lowered the
weights. "If. You. Say. So." He replaced the bar back on the
stand. "Okay. If not her, then you. I know there are things a
man needs. How do you stay away from temptation?" He sat up,
and then wiped his forehead. "Let me just finish and then I will
give you back your bench."

Leave it to a guy like Max to just blatantly disregard the rules
of the gym. He'd said work in, not take over. Louis decided he
wasn't worth his time, so he nodded, hoping that Max would
just finish up and then go away.

As soon as he laid back down on the bench, he started talking again. "You see that dime piece over there?"

Louis looked in the direction he indicated. "You mean that
young woman?" He hated the term dime piece. Max was juve-
nile, plain and simple.

"Does she do anything for you? She's hot, man. Think about
it, your wife is gone half the week every week. That girl has
been checking you out since I came over here. You could have
that keeping you warm at night if you wanted to."

"What the hell are you talking about? That girl is too busy
gyrating on top of tables at night to keep anyone warm. I'm married. With children. I have responsibilities. You know what, I'm
done here." Louis walked away and left Max staring after him.
He'd spoiled the mood. The workout was over. Louis headed for
the shower.

The warm water cascaded over Louis's body, calming him

down. Why had he been so irritated with Max? He was just being himself. It's not like what he was saying wasn't true. Although he was used to the way he and Marie lived, there were certainly days when he wished it was some other way, wished that she had a normal job that didn't take her out of town so much. And although he loved the freedom that managing the apartment building gave him, there were times when he missed the fast pace of his old office environment.

And then there was Josie. Louis stepped further inside the stream of water, letting it hit him in the face full force. He had to admit that woman was something else. Ever since she'd moved into the building, she called him three and four times a day for every little problem she imagined in her apartment. And that last time, sheesh. He'd gone over there because she was complaining of knocking in the walls. He could only stand at the door speechless when she'd opened it with some kind of negligee on, something so see-through, she might as well have come to the door naked. Josie had body and damn, he couldn't take his eyes off her.

Louis closed his eyes and saw her standing before him in all her purple-ness as if she were right in front of him now. Ever since that day, Josie had intensified her calls and he couldn't get her out of his mind. When was the last time Marie had worn anything like that for him?

He rinsed the rest of the soap from his body and tried to ignore the heaviness between his legs. His dick was reaching for the sky like a felon stopped by the SAPD. He ran his hand down its length and then turned off the water and wrapped his towel around him. He would bet she'd left a few messages for him while he was working out. Damn, she was as fine as hell. And willing, too. A deadly combination. Hopefully, she wouldn't be a tenant that stayed long; that way, she wouldn't be a temptation. He had responsibilities to take care of and had no plans on being distracted. Maxfield would never understand that, he was sure.

Kennedy

The lights were low in the huge lobby. Kennedy arrived earlier than most people that worked in the massive building. She was used to the dim lighting in the morning. Both the lighting and the air conditioning systems were on a timer, so it would be a full hour before the rest of the vestibule was lit up and the stuffiness left the air. Downtown would be flooded with sunlight and teeming with early-morning commuter traffic.

She rang the small doorbell to the right of the doorway, then waited to hear the click that told her that security had unlocked the doors. She inhaled, taking in the freshness of the morning air and turned just enough so that security could see her badge through the closed-circuit monitors. The click was almost imperceptible. The door shifted just a little in response to being released. Kennedy swung it open and hurried inside. She needed some peace and quiet before everyone else got in, special time she planned to use to put the finishing touches on her project.

They grinned as she walked by. Kennedy thought nothing of

it. Security at G, P, E, & M was always friendly in the morning. Certainly paid to be that way, they were probably told to greet everyone that walked through the door with a hello. Kennedy nodded in return, then looked back down at the marble tile gliding under her feet, listening to the sounds her shoes made as she made her way to the elevator. Her thoughts were already on her day.

She stepped out of the elevator onto the dark blue carpet, straightening her pencil skirt as she did. It wasn't even seven o'clock and the darn thing was already twisting around her body. She pursed her lips as she pulled it back into place. A full day of skirt-straightening was sure to be annoying, and Kennedy wasn't looking forward to it. She sighed. Why did she never think of these things while she was getting dressed in the mornings? She tried to be an optimist and look on the brighter side of things. The skirt might be annoying but at least her suit looked good, or at least it did when the skirt acted right.

Her office was on the third floor. Although she was early, she wasn't the first to arrive. As always, the receptionist was there and appeared to be busy already. It was almost as if she'd slept there or something. She waved at Kennedy before she opened the door, then chimed out her chipper good morning as soon as Kennedy swung open the heavy glass door separating the vestibule and the office area. *How was it that some people were always so happy in the morning?* Kennedy eked out a smile. She was as close to being addicted to coffee as possible and she had yet to have her morning cup. Coffee was a prerequisite to starting her day. She often wished that there was a way for her to inject the caffeine into her veins. It would be faster that way.

"You must have had a great weekend." The receptionist said, smiling.

Kennedy paused. This woman was absolutely the happiest person she knew, even on a Monday morning. Her face was plastered with the biggest grin Kennedy had ever seen. *How did that even happen?* "I did. It was restful. How about you?"

"Mine was the same as always."

Kennedy nodded. "Thanks for asking." She didn't think anything else of it as the woman handed her the slips of paper that contained her early-morning messages. She sifted through them and headed back to her office, but then stopped short at the door.

Her normally pristine office appeared to be overflowing with flowers. Kennedy's mouth dropped open in shock. She made it her business to leave it clean, with nothing on her desk when she left every day. She stood at the door and looked around at bunches and bunches of flowers. She counted five huge arrangements, and not one had a daisy in it. Kennedy had never even seen half of the species of flowers before. She quickly recovered from her surprise and walked toward her desk, suddenly knowing what all the grins were about. The security guards and the receptionist had all known about the flowers.

She removed the card from the bouquet of flowers in front and a nervous feeling ran through her stomach.

Thank you.

She turned the card over. That was all it said, no signature, no nothing. Without thinking further, she knew who the flowers were from, and although she wanted to be annoyed, she couldn't. Despite herself, a small smile played across her face.

What woman didn't like getting flowers? She began to remove them from her desk so she could work. Even if she didn't want to be involved in a serious relationship, she was flattered, she couldn't help but be. Still, this amount of flowers meant Troy wouldn't be going away that easy.

"So, are you going to tell?"

Kennedy looked up to discover that the receptionist had followed her to her office. "Excuse me?"

"I only know of a few reasons why a woman would get flowers like this."

"None of which is your business." She winked. "Can I help you with something?"

She held out a slip of paper. "Here, you dropped one of your messages."

Kennedy took it. "Thanks."

"You really aren't going to spill it?" She looked on expectantly.

"Nothing to tell."

"Okay. Well, don't forget that you are supposed to take your father to the doctor this afternoon. I blocked that off on your calendar."

Kennedy sat down in her chair. She *had* forgotten. She clicked her computer keyboard to bring her schedule up, then remembered that the receptionist was still there. "Thanks." The flowers forgotten, her brow was creased with worry. The appointment had somehow slipped through the cracks. She would have to do some creative rearranging. Her schedule was packed, but it wasn't like she could let her father go to the doctor alone. The doctor said he might get lost, or worse. She could

worry about Troy and his flowers later. Right now she had a slew
of work to do before she could leave and get her father to where
he needed to be. She pulled a few storyboards out of her desk
and propped them up on the easel near her desk. As it was, she
might have to come back to the office later in the day.

Kennedy rushed into her house, leaving the door open. She
dropped her bag on the floor, then headed out the side door that
led to the guest house her father stayed in. More of a detached
bedroom than a guesthouse, it was only a few steps from the
main house, across a small portico. If the shades were open,
she could normally see right into the room from her own living
room, making it easy for her to keep an eye on her father. The
arrangement was one of the reasons she'd bought the house in
the first place. She could have her privacy and her father could
still have his without her being too far away if he needed help.
The door to the main house slammed beside her as she stepped
through it. In her haste, she'd forgotten to hold the door. The
loud slamming sound made her jump. She hated to rush around
like this, but it seemed to be the story of her life lately. Her last
meeting had run over, so now she was on the brink of running
late for her father's appointment.

The shades were drawn, blocking the view into the room.
Kennedy knocked gently, then waited for her father's answer.
He might be sick, but he still deserved his privacy. After she
knocked again, she turned the knob and stepped into the one-
room suite. It was dark and it took her eyes a minute to adjust.
The smell of mustiness mingled with that of her father's ar-
thritis balm. Did he bathe in that stuff? She thought. With the

shades drawn, it was as if it were midnight as opposed to mid-day. As soon as her eyes started to focus, Kennedy walked around the room opening the shades. She squinted as light began to fill the room.

Her father was sitting on the couch. She didn't doubt that he'd been there all day. He was covering his eyes with one hand.

"Dad." Kennedy's heart sank. It would have been too good to be true for her to come home and find him sitting by the door, dressed and ready to go.

"It's too bright in here."

Kennedy paused. "You were supposed to be ready."

"Why aren't you at school, Kennedy?" He dropped his hands from his eyes, resting them on his knees. "You playing hooky again?" He looked at her as if he were surprised to see her, even though she'd called and reminded him of his appointment right after she'd gotten to the office.

Kennedy sighed. Although she had educated herself to the hazards of her father's condition, it never became any easier to face. Lately, he rarely referred to her as an adult anymore. It was as if his mind was stuck in a time twenty or so years earlier, leaving Kennedy a perpetual teenager in his world. "Let's get ready, Dad, we don't want to be late."

"Where's that boy? He's not here, is he? You know you ain't supposed to be entertaining in your room."

"I know, Dad." It was sometimes best to just go with the flow instead of trying to correct him. She carefully guided her father toward the bathroom to help him finish getting dressed. He was still wearing the robe he'd had on when she left. She clenched her teeth together hard. How was it possible that she hated that robe so much? As soon as the opportunity presented itself, Kennedy planned to replace it with a new one when he wasn't paying too much attention. It seemed almost as if he started wearing it when he was diagnosed.

"Where are we going?"

Kennedy handed him the mouthwash. "To see the principal."

"You in trouble?"

She paused. He seemed to ask her that question a lot and it always confused her. Sure, she had her time when she was a teenager, but she didn't think she'd been in any more trouble than the average kid. Why was it that her father only seemed to be able to remember those bad times? Kennedy was sure that the "boys in your room" comment that he kept bringing up had to do with the one time she'd snuck a boy into her room. Bad decision, but she'd been seventeen then and about to go off to college. Although she regretted the decision now, it'd made sense to her then-seventeen-year-old mind. What didn't make sense is the way that one thing seemed to stick with her father. He couldn't remember to change his clothes, but he could remember the details of something that happened almost twenty years ago like it was yesterday. "No, Dad, I'm not in trouble. I'm on the honor roll."

That seemed to calm him. She tried her best to rush him the rest of the way through getting dressed, and then ushered him into the car. Kennedy closed her door, then slipped her Blackberry into its dashboard holster, so she could glimpse the screen while she drove. She contemplated her father's condition, noting the irony in the way he was now, all alone with only his daughter.

In his youth, her father had been very handsome and quite the playboy. She'd heard all the stories about how he'd given them all hell, even her mother. Kennedy had been a child, so of course she couldn't remember everything, but she did remember her mother and father arguing over where he'd been and with whom many times. Back then, it seemed like women were always vying for his attention, even in front of his mother's face. After her mother died when Kennedy was in college, there were plenty of them around, wanting to play house with him or cook for him, trying hard to be the next wife, but her father didn't stay with any one of them too long. Kennedy remembered a long string of women all vying for her and her father's attention, right up until he started to get sick. Where were those people now when he needed them? Life was a funny thing.

Kennedy looked at her father from the corner of her eye. He seemed to be much smaller than just a few years ago. There had to be something the doctor could do for him, something to help him remember just a little better. Her father used to be an immaculate dresser, priding himself on his grooming. Now, it was a good day if he remembered to brush his teeth. She'd been told time and time again that there was no cure, but a girl had to hope. There had to be something that could at least help her father's quality of life.

The Blackberry's screen flashed, catching her eye. Tension crept up Kennedy's neck. She hoped that it wasn't the office. She didn't want to deal with them now. She glanced at the screen and relaxed a little. It was nothing more than an email notification that she had a phone message at home, so it couldn't be too important. Anyone who really needed to reach her would know how to do it, so they wouldn't have to leave a message at her house. She knew this, but touched the button on her earpiece to dial her voicemail anyway. It was probably a doctor's appointment reminder or something.

She listened to the message while she looked for a parking place.

"This doesn't sound like you, but I know I dialed the right number. I'm looking at it on my screen. I just wanted you to know that I really enjoyed meeting you. Maybe we can get together again and get to know each other better. Give me a call back. I want to get together with you while I am in town next week. Here's my number. 678-453-8978. Thank you, Marie. It was such a breath of fresh air to meet you."

"Girl, watch where you're driving. You could kill us both!"

She'd been so busy listening to the message that she bumped the curb in front of the parking space. "I'm sorry, Dad. I'm sorry." She couldn't believe her ears. She knew exactly what Marie had done. She tried to hide the rage she was feeling. It wasn't the first time Marie had given some man she met out of town her phone number. The last time it happened, she'd promised that she wouldn't do it again. Eventually, they all stopped calling. Kennedy knew that Marie wanted her to take messages for her, but she refused. She wasn't a dating service and she didn't approve of her behavior, even if she claimed that it was all right with Louis. That was crap. Kennedy had always liked him, and he seemed to be a great husband and father. It was a shame the way Marie treated him. It was a miracle that they'd stayed married this long. Marie's running around might as well be running Louis off. Enough was enough. It was time for them to talk. Sure, Marie had stood by her through thick and thin, including the whole Damon debacle. She owed her, but there was only so far that could go. Kennedy turned off the car and gathered her things. "While she is saying 'Scat! Scat!' somebody out there is saying 'Here kitty, kitty.'"

"Your mother used to say that."

Kennedy jumped. She hadn't meant to say that out loud, but Marie made her so angry. "You know, Dad, that's right, she did." She smiled and looked at the emotion in her father's face. His eyes were clear for the first time today. Her lapse had given him a moment of clarity. That had been one of her mother's favorite sayings.

Once inside, her father slipped back into his funk, barely speaking to the doctor. Kennedy walked her father into the examination room, then took a seat by the door. By now she was used to the routine. She was patient as the doctor completed his exam, then slowly helped her father get his clothes back on as she waited for the doctor to return. He cleared his throat as he walked in, then smiled weakly at Kennedy while he spoke.

"Well, he seems to be doing fine. Not too many changes."

"That's good, I guess. But is there something we can give him to help him a little? I was reading about some new drug on the Internet. Lately, he doesn't even get dressed. He forgets."

The doctor paused. "Well, we can try, but we have had this conversation before. This is how this disease goes. You might consider moving him—"

"Moving him where? My father belongs with me." Her jaw

tightened. There was no way in hell she was abandoning her father. Families stick together.

The doctor held up his hands. "I'm not suggesting that he doesn't. All I'm saying is that it is only going to get more difficult. You're a relatively young woman and you deserve to have a life too."

Her face burned. "I have a life." She swallowed, trying to choke back the lump she felt growing in her throat. She rubbed her father's back as the doctor wrote a prescription. He ripped it off and handed it to her, but he didn't look at her again.

"The nurse will give you a sheet that has instructions on how to give this to him."

Kennedy nodded. He probably gave this speech several times a week, something he was taught to do in medical school. She'd already tuned him out. It wasn't like he really knew the best thing for her family. If he couldn't help her father, she would find a doctor who could. She hated the way he looked at her anyway, like she was helpless or something.

"I'll see you back in three weeks, to see how he's doing." He paused, scribbling on his notes. "Keep an eye on him."

Dirty Little Secrets

"Thank you so much for doing this, Louis. We owe you a big one." Mai held her phone between her head and her shoulder as she pulled on her hose. Calvin was in the bathroom, still showering, it seemed. "We're headed to the airport in a few minutes." She felt slightly guilty at leaving her children with her friends, but this was certainly an unusual situation.

"You know this is no big deal. We know you would do the same for us, too. Our kids' schedule is very similar, so it should all work."

Marie married a gem, she thought. If the shoe were on the other foot, there was no way Calvin could take care of their kids *and* someone else's. He would lose his mind. "Now. Lishelle has cheerleading after school. Her session is right after your daughter's, but if it's a problem to wait for her I can have one of the other mothers bring her home."

"Don't worry about it. I'm not as organized as you are, but we got this. It's going to be fine, Mai."

"And Sarai has Brownies. That's right at the school. I usually just pick her up after I get Lishelle from cheerleading." She slipped her foot into her pumps. "Are you sure this is okay? Missing one time won't kill them, especially Sarai. She's only eight, it won't be the end of the world."

"You have enough to worry about," Louis said. "I promise the kids will be fine."

Mai hung up her phone and paused. Deep down, she knew they would be fine, but that didn't stop the control freak part of her from worrying. Louis was right about one thing, she was concerned that her kids would suffer because she wasn't there. The sooner they got home the better.

Atlanta's Hartsfield airport could be a mess, so she had planned to arrive for their flight about two hours early. As usual, things took longer when you had more time. Mai stepped up her dressing, throwing last-minute toiletries into her bag. "Cal? Honey?" She called out to her husband, planning to remind him of their flight time.

He didn't answer. Mai paused, thinking. What in the world was taking Calvin so long in the restroom? Had he grown new parts to wash or something? He was definitely taking the longest shower in history at a time when they couldn't afford to be leisurely. They still had to return the rental car first and heaven knows that could be a disaster.

She stepped closer to the door and raised her hand to knock. The muffled sound of Calvin's voice made her stop short. What in the world was he doing? She tapped on the door lightly and tried hard not to sound as annoyed as she felt. "Calvin, we have to catch our flight. Will you be out soon?"

"In a minute." Mai could hear him clear his throat, then resume his conversation. She glanced at her watch, annoyed. There was no way in hell she was missing her flight and rushing him would only cause her to be more stressed. Calvin was grown and a frequent traveler. He knew what had to be done. She put on the last of her makeup and returned it to its case, then threw the bag into her suitcase.

Finally, the water sounds stopped coming from the bathroom and the door swung open. The warmth of the shower steam poured into the small hotel room. Mai turned around smiling, but what she saw stopped her smile in its tracks.

Not only was Calvin not dressed, but he was still in the underwear that he'd slept in. His white tee shirt was as disheveled looking as it had been when he'd gotten out of bed. His hair looked as if it hadn't seen a good brushing in days.

She halted, shocked. "We're going to miss our flight. Do you know what time it is?" Her eyes widened.

Calvin looked past his wife. "There's a problem. I can't get on the flight." He spoke tentatively, as if he were testing the idea of staying behind.

"What do you mean? We've got to get home. The kids—"

"You go without me." He paused. "I need to tie up some loose ends. I'll come on a later flight."

"You're kidding me, right?" She didn't try to hide the irritation in her voice. "What am I going to tell the kids?"

He stepped toward her and tried to comfort her, but Mai stepped away. "You don't have to tell them anything. I'll be home before they go to bed. There's another flight that's four hours later. I'll take that one."

"I wish you'd said something." She paused, thinking. "It's only four hours. Why don't I stay here and take the flight with you?"

"No, you go ahead. I won't be long."

She narrowed her eyes. *What the hell was going on?* "So, are you going to tell me what it is that's so important that you can't take the flight that we paid a premium to get on?"

"Lovee, please don't be that way." He called her by her pet name and tried to step closer to his wife again. This time she let him and he wrapped his arms around her, burying his nose in her hair. "I have to finish the business meeting I came to have. With the whole incident that happened, I didn't get a chance to meet with my client, that's all. My boss is going to be pissed as it is, the least I can do is to go back home with the job accomplished."

Mai's body betrayed her and she softened, melting into her husband. She wanted him home. With her and the kids. And she wanted to stay angry with him for this disastrous trip, but she found herself giving in. There was a flicker of apprehension. "I have to get home. The kids—"

He kissed her on the forehead. "You go. I promise it will be all right."

"I'm not bailing you out again." Mai released her husband and turned around to grab her purse. She opened it quickly without looking, letting her fingers feel the contents. Where in the world had the pillbox gotten to? She located it but didn't pull it out, instead she ran her fingers over the jewel-encrusted top for reassurance.

Calvin chuckled. "I promise, you won't have to. I'm scared straight."

"I hope so, Calvin, because I'm not kidding, okay? I need to use the little girl's room." Mai stepped into the bathroom, not believing that he would even try to make jokes. "You can drop me off, then return the rental car." She closed the door behind her, opening her pillbox at the same time.

Hartsfield Atlanta airport bustled. Calvin knew that his wife was pissed, but his hands were tied. He was a man that handled his business, and this was no different. He hopped out of the car and popped the trunk to remove her bag.

Mai was already stepping from the car when he made it around to her side. He forced a thin smile as they made eye contact. At least she was much calmer than earlier. As usual, Mai had taken the bad news with as much decorum as possible. He expected nothing less. Calvin placed her bag up on the curb and closed her door. They hugged, and he kissed her, inhaling her scent. She smelled clean and fresh.

"I love you, Lovee. I'll call with my arrival time."

She nodded. "Don't forget, you know—" An airport cop interrupted then. She tapped on the hood, then pointed at the couple. Calvin bristled, but stepped backward toward the car anyway. A ticket from an airport cop would certainly be the icing on the cake.

"I gotta go. Kiss the kids for me." Walking the few steps back to the car felt like a death march. How the hell had he done something so stupid? The worst part was, he couldn't remember all the details. Calvin slid into his seat and clicked his seat belt shut, watching Mai as she walked away. He admired the sway of her backside as she rolled her small bag behind her.

He left the airport, careful to drive no more than the posted speed limit. From now on, he crossed his *i*'s and dotted all *t*'s. The meeting place was only a few minutes away, right at the next exit. If things kept up the way they were, he would make it to his meeting early.

Calvin glanced at the dashboard clock. He would need every extra minute possible to get himself together so he could think rationally. Normally, figuring out the next step was easy, but this time, he was at a loss. There was just no way that he could see to get out of this one.

Luckily, there were only a few people at the Waffle House. This particular location was newer and larger than most of the Waffle Houses he'd ever been in. He walked through the door and was overwhelmed by the smells of things frying. His mouth immediately started to water. Memories of Waffle Houses past bombarded him. When he was a teenager, Waffle House used to be the stop after a late night out. They'd only recently built one in San Antonio, and he and Mai had never been in it, although he'd suggested it. She'd thought he was crazy when he'd brought it up. She was the family health police, and a fried anything breakfast was out of the question for them.

The waitress pointed toward a booth with her head and Calvin headed that way. He slid into it and sighed, thankful that it was toward the rear of the small building. Not that it mattered. Who would see or even care about his predicament? He picked up the menu, just as the man he was waiting for joined him.

Calvin could smell him even before he looked up. Just as he was yesterday, Davon was wearing strong, musky perfume. His heavy shoes clicked on the tile as he stepped into place near the booth. He was as well dressed as he had been last time they'd met. He didn't speak as he sat across from Calvin.

"What can I get ya?" The waitress stopped, poised with her pen, barely looking at the two men.

"Coffee." They both spoke at the same time. She nodded and scurried away.

"I see you made it." Davon snarled, baring teeth covered by a gold grille in the front. "I told you I'd be waiting when you got out."

Calvin felt his palms get hot. He needed coffee more than he had in a long time. "I'm sorry about your friend. I didn't mean to—"

"He'll be fine. You gonna have to pay for the bike though. He loved it."

Calvin nodded. "I was surprised. Very surprised."

"I can understand that. But what we gon' do about our problem?"

The waitress was back. She slid two white mugs in front of the men. They paused as she filled it with coffee. Davon reached down and Calvin tensed. He wouldn't shoot him or anything in public, would he?

"Just be cool, man. I want to show you something." He produced a wrinkled photo, handing it to Calvin. It looked as if it had been riding in someone's wallet a long time.

Calvin stared at the small image. Sure enough, there he was, with a bottle of malt liquor in one hand, his other hand on a woman's chest. They were both laughing. He looked like a different person in the photo. Hell. He had been a different person then. Those were the days. He'd been so crazy and carefree.

"You 'member that?"

He nodded. He couldn't deny that this was a picture of him.

"And her? You remember her, right?" Davon pointed at the woman in the photo.

Calvin searched his memory. He remembered his bachelor party well. His frat brothers from Morehouse had hooked him up that night. Three days before his wedding. He remembered the cake and he remembered the woman. They told her that she was an exotic dancer and she'd gladly accepted the cash to dance at his party. By the time she and her friends arrived, he'd been pretty drunk, so time and alcohol had erased the rest.

"Look. That was a long time ago."

"Not that long. Thirteen years." Davon paused. "That girl you don't remember? She was my baby sister."

"Was?"

"She dead now. Died a year ago. From the HIV." Calvin felt his stomach jump. He was going to die. "What? HIV? How long—"

"She contracted it well after you, my brother. At least we think so."

Calvin relaxed a little, but the sinking feeling at the bottom of his stomach didn't go away. "You said—"

"Don't worry, there was a child. The two of you, you got busy that night in your hotel room. Right down there on Peachtree." He pointed over his shoulder with his thumb, then looked down at his hands, twisting a paper napkin.

"I don't remember that. How do I know that—"

Davon's face darkened. "Look, I ain't gonna let you do this twice. They took your sididdy ass to jail before. You won't make it there again. Baby Sis would never lie. She told me all about it. We were close. She told me as soon as she knew, then wouldn't let us contact you. She didn't want anything from you then."

"Okay, okay." Anger wasn't going to help him get to the bottom of this. "Why am I just hearing about this now? Thirteen years? You think about it. How would you react? It could be a scam."

"This ain't no bullshit. You have a little girl. She thirteen now. Born in May of the following year."

Calvin did the math. Three months before his own Lishelle. "Wait, I thought you said—"

"I did. You think I'm stupid? She was a preemie." He slammed his fist on the table. "Look, my sister is dead and we need you to take some responsibility. We ain't a rich family. I saw your fancy wife. That the same one you was marrying? My sister never asked you for nothing but now—"

"She never told me. I didn't even know her name."

"Whatever. Just like you rich niggas not to care about something like that. All she was to you was a piece of ass. We just needs some cash. We don't need to be part of your happy life."

Calvin paused, thinking. He had a lot to lose, either way. Questions reeled through his brain. What if he was HIV positive? What about his wife and kids? He had no idea how much these people wanted, but how was he going to explain paying cash out to a miscellaneous person? Mai wasn't going to stand for that. And if he told her, his marriage might be over. A baby was one thing, but HIV was something else. His life might be over. He rubbed his hands together under the table. "Can I think about it?"

"Mothafucka, what's to think about? This ain't about you and me. This is about a child. My niece. You supposed to be so successful and upstanding and all. I woulda thought you would just do the right thing. You moved on up and all that, but you still an ordinary nigga." He paused. "That's right. I know all about your nice, cushy life. Your picket fence. All that fake TV shit."

"I never said I wouldn't do my duty. But it's a delicate situation. There are other people involved."

"The only people I'm concerned about is mine, you know what I'm saying?" Davon's mouth set into a tight line. "We think about ten thousand dollars a year."

Calvin's mouth dropped open. "Until she's eighteen?" Sweat dropped onto his brow.

"Naw, man. Ten thousand a year from birth. We thought we'd go easy on you seeing as you had no idea."

"That's over one hundred thousand dollars."

"And? The state of Georgia would give us more. How much you make? Eighty grand a year? More? If you want us to go that way, we will."

Calvin thought quickly. There was no way in hell he could just hand that kind of cash over without Mai knowing, even if they had it sitting in the bank, which they didn't. He made good money, but they lived good too.

"Okay. Let me talk to my lawyer. He's probably going to want a paternity test."

"You saying my sister was a liar?"

"I'm not saying that at all. I'm just saying that we need to make sure we do the right thing, for all involved."

Davon visibly relaxed.

"We just need to figure out a plan of action."

"I got your plan of action. You do what you supposed to. You ain't gotta meet her, but you *will* take care of her. That's the right thing to do." He grabbed a toothpick, putting it in his mouth.

"We'll do what we have to." He paused. "My life at home is going to be hell."

Davon laughed. He pointed the toothpick at Calvin. "It's gonna be hell either way, my man. 'Cause if you don't handle your business, we gonna wreck your fairy tale in ways you ain't never imagined." He threw a card onto the table and stood up. "You got the coffee, right?"

Calvin nodded.

"Don't make me come looking for you. Trust me, I *do* know where you live."

White Picket Fences
and Hot Grits

Marie stuffed her bag into the gym locker and then slammed it shut. The locker room smelled wet and was packed with the after-work crowd. She put her earbuds on just as another woman bumped into her. Marie cursed under her breath. She hated coming to the gym at this time of day, but it was the best she could do. The only saving grace was that her friends would be here too. Hopefully, they had been able to commandeer a machine for her. After a few days on the road, she needed to get her cardio on. Flying always made her feel as if her clothes were just a little tighter than they were when she'd left, and it had been a long week. Marie tugged at her shirt, willing it to come just a bit further down. The way she felt, she needed to stay on some machine for at least an hour.

In the aerobics area, a herd of people panted as they ran, cycled, and stepped their way to nowhere, most in their own world, with headphones on and eyes glued to various television sets. As soon as she stepped into the main exercise area, Marie spotted Mai on the elliptical machine, working hard. From across the room, it looked like sweat had made her clothes almost transparent in a few places. The water bottle on the front of her machine gently rocked back and forth in rhythm with her steps as she stared straight ahead at the television screens above her. Marie waved in her direction and made her way over. She wanted to catch up and couldn't wait to ask her about what had happened with Calvin. His arrest was more drama than any of them had had in their lives in a while.

The machine made a humming sound as Mai rode it. Marie pushed the newspapers on the floor to the side with her foot and then slipped into the space between the machine and the wall to wait for the machine next to her. "How long have you been here?" she asked.

"Awhile. I've been on here for forty-five minutes." Mai huffed in between words.

"Stop. What're you trying to do? That's a long time."

"At my age, I need every minute I can stand. Got a formal coming up in a couple of weeks, and I refuse to buy anything new, so I gotta make my body fit into the old." Mai wiped her forehead with a towel that had been draped over the console of the machine. "Besides, I gotta keep up with you young things."

"Girl, you crazy. You are only a few years older than I am." Marie cut her eyes at the woman on the machine next to Mai and glanced at her watch. Hopefully she would get the picture and move on. "Where's Kennedy?" She looked around the gym to try and spot her.

Mai cleared her throat. "You know, patience is a virtue. I suppose she will be along soon. Had to get her father situated."

"Whatever, Mama Lovee. I gotta get done here and take my narrow behind home. The kids will be coming in from various places soon and it's rent night. You know Louis has got to make his rounds. If we waited for some of those tenants to mail their checks, we would never get paid."

"I'm done." The woman used her towel to wipe off her console and then stepped down from her machine. She gathered the newspapers from the floor.

"I didn't know those were yours, sorry. Didn't mean to kick them." Marie said.

"No problem. I shouldn't have put them there, but there isn't a trash can nearby."

"I'll take them off your hands if you're done with them." Marie held out her hand. "I could use some reading material."

The woman paused, then shrugged and handed the papers to Marie. She took them, stepped onto the machine, and pressed the *quick start* button. She pushed the pedals hard, not talking as she arranged the newspaper in front of her.

"I think I should warn you that Kennedy is pissed at you." Mai paused and took a drink from her water bottle, then started pedaling again. "I'm kinda pissed at you too."

"Really?" They were always pissed at her about something.

"She's mad because you gave some guy her phone number. Again."

Marie fumbled with her paper. "And you?" She knew that there was more to the story. After being friends for years, she knew that there were always layers of meaning to most things that Mai said.

"I don't understand you. Can you help me to understand

why you do it?" Mai remembered when Marie and Louis met;
they'd been so in love although they both denied it at first.
That made her friend's behavior lately even more unbelievable. What had happened to make her so disenchanted with
her marriage?

"Do what?" She already had an idea what she was talking
about, but she wasn't about to make it easy. They had no right to
judge her.

"Why do you even get into situations where you feel you have
to give out your number or Kennedy's number? You are a married woman, you are not supposed to be dating. Heaven knows
what else you do." Mai huffed, but kept pedaling. "Am I missing
something?"

"None of us are saints, and I think I resent what you are implying. I'll have you know I have done nothing wrong. I haven't
had sex with anyone outside my marriage, although it's not like
I haven't wanted to." Why was she rationalizing her behavior?
She and Louis were the only people who needed to be concerned
with what she did or didn't do. And there was only so much any
woman needed to admit to anyway.

"So, what the hell are you doing?"

Marie pedaled harder, a lump forming in her throat. Each
time she met someone on the road, she felt a quick sense of
guilt that she would always push to the back of her mind. This
last time was no different. Something always stopped her
before it got sexual. She just never had the guts to actually
go there, to that place she couldn't take back. "I like to feel
wanted. What woman doesn't? Especially when you feel so

unappreciated at home? It feels good to me and it's lonely on the road."

"But why give any number at all? Do the men even know that you are married?"

"Of course they do. I don't hide anything. I guess I'm just saving up for the rainy day. What if there is something better out there?" She paused.

Was this the same woman who'd been so sure that her husband was her soul mate? Her one and only? How did this happen to people?
"Girl, there is nothing better. It's all the same shit, different day. Marriage is what you make it. And you ain't making yours anything good at all."

Marie's face darkened. "Don't judge me. Your marriage isn't perfect. No marriage is."

"You're right. It's not. But I at least try not to disrespect my husband publicly."

The women were silent as both tried to concentrate on their workouts. Marie stared at her paper and got lost in the music in her earbuds and Mai resumed watching television.

As she pedaled, Marie tried hard to fight the resentment she was feeling. What the hell did any of them know anyway? Other than this latest hiccup, Mai seemed to have the picture-perfect marriage. Her husband had a good job and worked hard. He took care of her the old-fashioned way. The fairy tale that rarely existed anymore. Truth of the matter was, if she didn't bust her ass at her job, they might not eat. Marie loved her friends, but she couldn't help but feel just a little angry. Someone had sold her a bag of goods. Why in the hell did her

friend turn up with the white picket fence and all she'd gotten
was chain link?

Early evening was the best time to collect rent. Mostly everyone
was at home. Louis drove around his building's parking lot, finally finding himself a space. Gaps in the asphalt leered at him
like a sinister grin. The lot would have to be repaved soon. He
sighed. That would certainly be a major expense, but a necessary one. If the building looked good, it was an easier sell to
students and their parents, his preferred tenants. Right now,
forty percent of the inhabitants in the buildings were college
students. If he had his way, he would raise that number as high
as he could get it, and that couldn't be too difficult considering
the number of universities in San Antonio. That type of tenant
usually paid in full for the entire year, and that was absolutely a
bonus. The more of them that did that, the fewer rents he had to
go and collect in person. Fewer nights he felt like people were
hiding from him to avoid paying up.

Louis took the rear entrance. It was almost 7 P.M. and he had
to knock on at least ten doors. He knew that many of them
wouldn't answer. That was just part of being a landlord. One in
particular would probably be waiting for him. Josie. Louis
planned to collect her money first and get it over with. Josie had
been blowing up his phone just about every other day for two
weeks, since the last time he'd seen her, then today nothing.
Not a good sign. It was like the calm before the storm.

He walked up the four flights to her apartment, then slowed
down as he neared her door. Not hearing from her meant that
Josie probably had something up her sleeve. He felt ill at ease as

he wondered how she could possibly top last time. He hadn't answered many of her calls and was slow to call her back when he did, but deep inside, he knew that Josie was not the type to be easily discouraged. That scared him a little. There was only so much a man could take.

The door was slightly ajar. Louis closed his eyes, took a deep breath, then knocked gently. He waited. Just as he thought, she didn't answer. His thoughts raced. The open door meant Josie wanted him to come in, but he didn't want to play her game. That could only mean trouble. He'd barely escaped last time. Although he fought hard to resist, he felt his penis get heavy. Why in the world couldn't she have been ugly?

"Josie?" Louis called out without entering the apartment. "I need to pick up your check." The seconds ticked away in his head. He could skip her and come back later, but he somehow knew that wouldn't help matters any. He knocked again.

"I'll be right there. I'm grabbing my checkbook. You can come in if you like."

Exactly. Louis stood where he was, riveted to the spot. The head on his shoulders was screaming at him not to move. Stay put. The one between his legs was a different story. For several years, all he'd had was married sex. Planned sex. Sex when the kids were sleeping. A lot about his relationship with his wife had become routine, and most of the time, she had dictated the shots both inside and outside the bedroom. *If he liked.* Music was playing inside the apartment. Al Green. Of course. This was a scene from a movie if he'd ever seen one. The movie where the unsuspecting or unwilling man was seduced.

The door swung open. Louis held his breath, half-expecting

a near-naked woman to be standing in front of him like last time. To his surprise, Josie was fully clothed this time. Jeans and a tee shirt. He exhaled slowly. She even looked delicious in a simple pair of jeans and a white tee shirt. Damn. *I can do this. This is about simple lust and I am bigger than that.*

"I said you can step inside. I was cooking. I need to get my checkbook." Josie wiped her hands with a dish towel. "I ain't gonna bite you. Not this time." Josie smiled at him and looked almost as sweet as a siren on the rocks calling to a passing ship.

Louis peered over her shoulder into the semi-dark apartment. Sure enough, he could smell the savory smell of something cooking. Josie motioned toward him with her head, and for some reason, he followed. Alarm bells were still going off in his head, although much quieter than they had been earlier. He stopped just inside the room, automatically closing the door behind him. It closed with a thud, the sound reminiscent of a prison door clanging shut.

Josie disappeared back into the apartment while Louis stood in one spot, looking around the room and wondering why in the hell he'd closed the door. He'd been in and out of the place several times over the past three months, but he'd never really looked around. A big brown television in the corner. An old stereo. Even Josie's furniture looked much older than she could possibly have been.

"Most of it came from my folks."

Louis jumped. He hadn't expected her to come back so quickly. Her bare feet made almost no sound on the carpet. "Its nice." Her small apartment was a stark contrast to his house.

Things didn't quite match but they somehow all went together perfectly. Nothing planned, but it all fit.

"You lie." She chuckled lightly. "I took it to college and then it ended up here. No use in throwing stuff out if it ain't broken, know what I mean? Since you're here, can you take a look at that radiator over there? I was hearing those knocking sounds again."

He sighed. "I don't think anything is wrong with it. This is an old building. It creaks."

"Seems like you oughta fix that, all the money we pay." Josie stepped closer to him.

Louis could feel her breath on his neck. He stepped back and stumbled. She smelled like baby powder. "We're working on it. Um, I need the check."

"I have it." She paused, then chuckled. "I make you nervous, Louis?"

He wasn't nervous. At least not that he was going to admit. Louis shook his head. Josie was so close he could smell her. She wore a soft, flowery scent. Every lick of sense he had told him he should move again, possibly run from the apartment, but his legs weren't willing. Josie was rare. Dangerous. She was a young woman, but she recognized her power the way a much older woman might, and seemed to be taking pleasure in watching him squirm. She stepped in, closer to him, and the heat from their bodies made Louis begin to sweat. He leaned in and just then, the music changed. More Al Green. Love and Happiness.

"You like Al Green? They don't make music like this anymore." Josie's husky voice was barely above a whisper. She sang along with the words, her almond-shaped eyes closed for a minute. "People all over the world make love to Al Green."

Damn. This was one sexy woman, he thought. Every neuron, every muscle in his body was responding to her the way he should only be responding to his wife, but he was powerless to move. His penis was so hard it was like he'd looked Medusa herself in the face. Louis had forgotten what being this excited felt like.

Josie wrapped her arms around his waist and brushed her lips on his. "I think this is my favorite Al Green song," she said.

A shock went through Louis like an electric current, and somewhere in his head, a switch flipped. He was old enough to remember what Josie didn't know. Al Green cheated on his lover, wrote this song, and then was almost killed with hot grits.

Second Chances

"How did you get this number?" Kennedy stood in the locker room with her phone pressed to her ear. As she strained to hear the voice on the other end, her emotions vacillated between twinges of happiness and excitement and feelings of annoyance. It hadn't been an oversight that she hadn't given Troy her cell phone number.

"Your secretary gave it to me." He emphasized the word *secretary* as if to let Kennedy know that her secret was out in the open. If she had a secretary, she couldn't possibly be one, could she?

She paused, then swallowed. "She did?" What else was there left to say? She was busted. He surely knew by now that her whole story about being an admin at the advertising agency was a crock, a thinly constructed one at that. And he'd been so good in bed.

"I can't believe she did that."

"Don't punish her or anything. I had her convinced that you

wanted to hear from me directly. It really wasn't her fault. I told her I kept transposing numbers or something and couldn't get it right, but that I wanted to follow up about the flowers."

Kennedy sat on the end of the wooden bench. "Okay, so, to what do we owe this honor?"

"I thought maybe I could take you out or something. Give you a chance to explain yourself."

She drummed her fingers on the wood, looking down at the floor. The rules were explicit. Troy was at the *cut him off* point, after only one date and one night together. Too bad. They usually lasted at least three. And he was pushy. "Well—"

"Look, no pressure. I just really enjoyed myself and wanted to see you again."

He didn't even sound angry. What kind of man didn't get angry at being lied to? Kennedy felt her body betray her as her stomach tingled. Instead of wanting to run, she was even more intrigued. "You know, my dad—"

"Look, I know you want me, but I can feel you letting the fear of the unknown get in the way of what you know you need to find out."

Kennedy opened her mouth and then closed it again. What, exactly, do you say to something like that? Sure, he was arrogant, but she almost had to admire the man for being so direct. Damn. And she thought she had game. Here was a serious player.

The silence was heavy. She was running out of excuses. He knew all about her job, and seemed savvy enough to have already figured out what ballpark her salary was in, and he didn't seem even the tiniest bit concerned. He'd even met her father and wasn't scared away, and hadn't asked any questions yet about the strange name her father had called him. Still, she knew that those problems could pop up any time. She sighed. He might act like it was okay that she made more, but as soon as they got a little more serious, he would have a problem. She'd seen it time and time again, the man constantly feeling as if he had to prove how manly he was, one way or the other. On the other hand, she had to admit she was kinda relieved that the truth was all out in the open. It was like a weight had been lifted from her shoulders. Here was a man who knew all about her and wanted to date her anyway. "Well, I could leave him for a couple of hours."

"It won't be too late, I promise. We could start again and I could find out about the *real* Kennedy. The one who went to Stanford and is a hot shot ad exec."

Wow, he'd certainly done his research, she thought.

"Before you ask, any idiot can use Google. I do my homework, too. How's Saturday?"

"That's fine." Kennedy couldn't stop herself from grinning from ear to ear. She snapped her phone shut and stood up, stretching. Sometimes you just had to throw caution to the wind and go for it, she thought. She glanced at the big clock on the wall. It was getting late and she was going to have to cut her workout short. As it was, Mai and Marie had probably left already and she was going to have to sweat through it alone. Although she'd left some food for her father to eat, she wasn't quite sure that he would actually eat it if she wasn't there. He seemed to be having a tough week. He'd been unusually sad after his doctor's appointment.

Just as she was about to reach for the locker-room door, it

swung open. She stepped to the side to let people pass her, then grabbed it and slid through. Noise from the exercise room floor assaulted her immediately and she walked almost directly into her two friends. Both showed obvious signs of having really worked out. Mai's workout clothes were covered with sweat. Her now-empty water bottle was in one hand and a small towel in the other, while Marie's normally perfect hair was all over her head. A newspaper was folded under her arm. Her iPod was strapped to her biceps and the earbuds trailed over her shoulder.

"I guess I'm real late, huh?" Kennedy spoke to Mai first, still grinning from her earlier conversation with Troy.

Mai wiped her face with her towel. "So, why are you so happy? That's a real switch for you, isn't it? I don't think I have ever seen you glad to be so off your schedule. And the gym has never made you particularly happy." Kennedy was the one of the three that always whined through her workout, preferring instead to socialize more than sweat.

"Nothing," she lied. "I'm trying to make up for lost ground. I had to take my father to a doctor's appointment the other day and I'm still trying to catch up." She held her hand out toward Marie in a silent request for her newspaper. Marie nodded and handed it to her as both she and Mai raised their eyebrows. They were both used to their friend using her father as an excuse for everything that went wrong with her day, whether he was responsible or not.

"I haven't seen you grin like that since I watched you across the restaurant the other night." Marie picked at her fingernails, searching for dirt only she seemed to be able to see. "You know, since you were out with what's-his-name. Troy." She paused. "If I didn't know better, I would guess that you had a date lined up. Or have you kicked him to the curb already?"

Kennedy's face darkened. Leave it to Marie to put a damper on her feelings. When had she become the mean one? "I guess you would know. About dating, I mean. Seeing as how you seem to be married-but-still-dating." She glared at her friend. "You wanna tell me what the deal is about giving out my phone number? I've asked you not to do that. Some guy keeps calling me, looking for you, and he doesn't seem to believe that you don't reside at my address. What is that about?" She snapped at Marie in a bigger way than she had intended, but her answering machine had at least four messages from that very same guy today.

"No need to make a scene." As usual, Mai was concerned with what people would think. She stepped in between the two women, trying to get Kennedy to calm down. This animosity was new. The three of them had been great friends for ages, ever since Mai had been the Dean of Pledges and Marie and Kennedy were line sisters, pledging Alpha Kappa Alpha Sorority. The three had been thicker than thieves ever since, standing by each other and holding secrets and confidences.

Marie moved closer, lowering her voice. "I thought I might be doing you a favor." Her voice had a saccharine ring. "Let's just say I'm screening them for you. You aren't getting any younger and seem to be having a problem holding onto a man. I thought I'd round them up so you could choose."

For the second time in fifteen minutes, Kennedy was speechless. What in the hell was she talking about? She was not judging her or pointing fingers. If she wanted to cheat on her husband, that was her business, but did she have to involve her friends? "For a smart woman, you have a lot of issues." Kennedy's mouth felt dry. "You need to talk to someone about them. I was trying to be your friend. I'm just asking that you don't give out my number." She paused. "What's wrong with your cell phone? Or better yet, just don't give them any number at all. Walk away."

"You know I can't give out my cell number. Louis might see the bill."

Kennedy shrugged. "Well, you can't have everything." She had nothing else to say to Marie. Her logic was so twisted it was unbelievable. "Damn. It's getting late. I got to go work out." She turned her back to Marie, her arms crossed across her body. "Mai, I don't know how you deal with her. I'll see you later." Kennedy walked off leaving her two friends, Marie with a smirk on her face, and Mai with an "I told you so" glare in her eyes.

Disorderly Conduct

Mai silenced the alarm and rolled over toward her husband. He lay very still in the bed beside her, his chest rising and falling softly. He'd tossed and turned so much throughout the night, she was glad to see him finally get some rest. She spooned him and smiled, pulling the down covers over them as she snuggled as close to him as possible. For the nearly fourteen years that they had been married, morning was their favorite time of day.

It was still dark outside. The clock had been set early on purpose, giving them just enough time for their morning sex before she would have to wake the kids. The sun wouldn't be up for at least another forty-five minutes, but Mai didn't need light for what she had in mind. She and Calvin had always had a very healthy sex life and knew the intricacies of each other's bodies very well. He enjoyed sex and even if she wasn't always too crazy about the idea of sex, she enjoyed pleasing him. Her mother always had very clear ideas of a woman's role in a marriage, and although some might consider them very old-fashioned, that is what she'd been taught to do if she didn't want to become one of those women on Lifetime TV whose husbands no longer found them sexually interesting. Mai never wanted to give her man reason to have to look elsewhere.

Her hand slid down her husband's front. Mai loved the feel of him close to her and even after being married so long, she still enjoyed the feel of him in her hands. She closed her eyes and snuggled in close, smiling as she found her target.

Normally, that was all it took. Calvin would take over from there. Mai waited, and instead of turning over, kissing her passionately and then pulling her to him the way she expected, she felt her husband stiffen. He was awake. Calvin's breathing changed, but not in a good way. He wasn't welcoming her in; he was clearly shutting her out. He didn't get hard, nothing.

"Calvin?"

He grunted.

"You okay?"

He paused, then answered. "I'm fine. Just not in the mood this morning."

Mai didn't know what to say. What in the hell did that mean? The Calvin she knew was always in the mood and had never turned her down once in all the time they'd been together. That was something they joked about. The only thing she'd ever had to work hard at was not running away from him. Although she did enjoy pleasing him, she didn't necessarily enjoy sex. It was something that needed to happen to maintain their married lives together. Yes, she liked him close, but didn't necessarily like him that close, at least not as often as he wanted to be. "Did I do something wrong?"

"No," he said. "No, you didn't." Calvin sat up suddenly, swinging his feet to the floor. "I'm stressed. I gotta get to the office early." He stood up, stretched and walked toward the bathroom. Mai lay there for a minute, flabbergasted. She sniffed at her underarms. Did she smell or something? That wasn't it, but Calvin was obviously serious about what he'd said. The next thing Mai heard was the sound of the shower filtering through into the bedroom.

Feet shuffled by the bedroom door, then paused. One of the kids was up. Mai lifted her head. "Yes? You should be getting dressed for school. You don't want to be late."

Mai already knew it was Lishelle. She often woke up before anyone else in the house, to her own alarm clock. Right on cue, she poked her head through the door. She was still in her pajamas and her hair was flat on one side, plastered to her head.

"Can I use your bathroom?" Her voice was groggy.

"Why? Daddy's getting dressed."

"Sarai went in and locked the door." She whined. "I really gotta go." Lishelle put her hand between her legs and shuffled back and forth from one foot to the other.

For a second, Mai longed for the day when she'd been a small girl. She'd been so sweet and trusting. She lay back down on her bed and sighed. The kids did this to each other every morning. A Jack and Jill bathroom seemed a good idea when they were younger, but now all it'd done was cause morning fights. "Okay, but make it quick. You guys have to get moving."

She watched as her daughter scooted through their room toward the bathroom. Mai could tell that she paused near their vanity and she hoped that Cal had closed the door to the shower area. She swung her legs out of bed and paused on the side of her bed, just as the shower stopped. Mai listened as Louis and Lishelle exchanged a few words. He even sounded grim with her. What in the world was wrong with him? Normally, Lishelle was the apple of Calvin's eye, and, even when she was wrong, she was always right. Daddy's little girl.

Lishelle ran back through the bedroom without pausing. Was she upset? The bedside clock said that it was time to get moving. Another day in the life of a mother. Not only was she going to have to rush the girl, now she was going to have to assuage her hurt feelings, too.

Cal appeared from his shower, a towel wrapped around his waist. He was still dripping. Mai glared at him. Why in the hell did he have to make things worse?

"What?"

"You didn't have to be so mean to her."

"Yes, I did. She was messing with my phone."

He looked at her, clueless, then disappeared into the closet. This was new. There had never been a time when Calvin didn't at least have time for a quickie or a kind word for his daughter. Now he seemed to have time for neither. Whatever was bothering him, he needed to get over it. Fast.

Sunlight streamed in through the picture window. Mai sat at her desk and sucked on her bottom lip, one hand on her lukewarm cup of tea, the other on the stack of bills piled in front of her. Paying the bills was her least favorite part of her week, but she was glad to be back to her normal routine after returning from Atlanta. It had been a hectic weekend, but she refused to dwell on Cal and his drama for any longer than was necessary, even if he had been distant since they returned.

Normally, early morning after the kids had gone off to school was her peaceful time. It was too early for folks to call and she usually had a little time to herself before she had to start running errands or cooking or helping with homework.

Anyone looking on would think she had the perfect life as a lady of leisure, but lately, between the kids and whatever was going on in their lives, Mai felt as if she had no time to herself at all. She was always running from this place to that. She could normally find a few minutes of respite on a weekend, but this past weekend left her feeling particularly frazzled, more than she was used to for the beginning of the week.

The phone rang and she glanced at the caller ID, one of the century's better inventions. It made it easier to screen out almost all calls from salesmen and begging relatives without too much trouble. At this hour, she was sure it would certainly be one of the two. Mai had every intention of not answering the phone, but she jumped when she read the screen. The initials HCES flashed at her. Hill Country Episcopal School.

Mai grasped at the handset and knocked over her tea, immediately flooding her desk and her stack of bills.

"Everything is okay, no one is hurt or sick." The booming voice of the headmaster of the school immediately calmed her nerves and Mai reached for the roll of paper towels she kept in her drawer. At least they knew how to start the call. Whenever a

parent got a call from the school, the first reaction was that
something was wrong; at least that was the way it was for Mai
each and every time it happened. And God forbid that something was wrong. Mai would always blame herself, even if she
in no way could have prevented whatever it was. Somehow each
call was an accusation.

Mai dabbed at the soggy papers, trying to save as many as
she could.

"If possible, I would like to set up a meeting with you and
your husband. We have some concerns about Lishelle."

Mai's mind whirled. What kind of concerns could they possibly have? All of her kids were fine, or at least they had been
when they'd left this morning. All of the homework had been
done and everyone was dressed properly. Suddenly, she had a
million questions she wanted to ask, but she couldn't manage
to find words, only panic.

"Okay," she said. "When did you want to meet?"

"I know your schedules must be very busy, so many of our
parents are, but I was thinking that this afternoon might be
best."

The feeling in Mai's stomach intensified. Whatever it was, it
was serious. "Both of us?" How often did they ask for both parents?

"I think so."

Mai paused, thinking. What had Calvin told her about his
day? She pursed her lips in determination. He was just going
to have to clear his schedule for this. He'd be annoyed, but
his daughter was certainly the most important thing on his
agenda.

Mai hung up the phone and dialed her husband's number. She didn't get him, but that was no surprise. Calvin often didn't answer his phone if he was in a meeting or something. The bills would have to wait.

Butterflies danced in her stomach as Mai's kitten heels clicked on the floor of the school hallway. Why the hell did some medications work so slowly? She taken her last pill before she'd even started the car, and if she didn't know better, the Valium was taking longer and longer to calm her nerves. A blanket of calmness should've enveloped her by now. Where in the hell was it? Mai's fingers gripped so tightly at her cell phone that her knuckles were losing their color as she strode toward the headmaster's office. What in the world had Lishelle gotten herself into? Sure, she'd been surly and withdrawn lately but what teenager wasn't?

Every few seconds, Mai forced herself not to bite her lips. Both she and Kennedy had the same habit, always had. If she didn't pay attention, they'd end up sore and bruised looking and heaven knows that would be an ugly way to greet the headmaster. What kind of impression would that make, especially after their daughter had done something that made them summon her parents to school for an immediate conference?

Mai stopped just outside the office and pressed redial on her phone. She hadn't heard anything from Calvin yet and still had no idea if he'd even gotten her earlier message. Not being in touch was so unlike him. At the very least, he could have called her back and told her that he was too busy. Damn him. Why was she always left to deal with things like this? She'd even sent a few text messages just for good measure and he'd apparently ignored those too. Just as she snapped her phone shut, the headmaster stepped into the hallway, a toothless smile plastered to her face. Her lips were so tight, they almost disappeared into her face.

Dr. Greeley was known for her stern ways, and her austere clothing reflected it. Her face was almost without makeup, save a coat of neutral lipstick. Her hair was pulled back from her face and knotted in a stereotypical teacher's bun, causing her angular nose to look as if it stuck further out from her face than it did. Her man-cut dark blue pantsuit was expertly tailored, but even so it somehow served to neutralize her sexuality. Looking at her now, Mai couldn't recall if she'd ever seen the woman in a skirt or a dress of any type. Put a hat on her, and you might be looking a man.

"Mrs. Mott, so glad you were able to make it." She looked behind Mai expectantly. "Is Mr. Mott on the way?"

Mai nodded, embarrassed. She was being scolded again. "It's sometimes hard for him to get away. I left him a message. I'm sure he'll be here as soon as he can. His office is way south." She smiled weakly, hating to make excuses for Calvin. At times like this, she hated her husband's job and the hours it demanded. Sure, she loved control and loved that she took care of most aspects of their family life, but it was tough when he needed to get away on a moment's notice. Calvin was so dedicated to his work, he just couldn't or wouldn't do it. But he'd been that way when they got married, right? It was dedication that made him so successful and it was that same dedication that had attracted her in the first place.

Dr. Greeley glanced at her watch. "So, should we wait, you think?"

Mai bit her lip again, then winced and looked away from what she thought was a look of disapproval. She shook her head. "I know you must have a full schedule. Why don't we go ahead and get started?" She let the headmaster guide her into her office and slid quietly into a chair as Dr. Greeley closed the door behind her. The room seemed unnaturally silent as she waited for the woman to take her seat. Every sound was magnified. Mai was acutely aware of the ticking of the clock on her wall, the crunching sound Dr. Greeley's loafers made on the carpet, and the muffled sounds of the rest of the campus on the other side of the door. She took a deep breath, trying hard to remain calm.

The panic she felt really wasn't about Lishelle and she knew it. She was having her own mini flashbacks of her childhood. Her parents were stern and if they'd been called to school for any reason, Mai knew that she might be two seconds from a public beating, right in front of the class if need be. Once was all it took and Mai made sure her parents were never called for anything ever again. She shivered at the memory of that humiliation, but she hadn't been alone. Many kids her age could probably tell the same story.

The headmaster planted herself firmly in her chair, then swung it around. There were no pleasantries as she opened her drawer and pulled out a folder, then cleared her throat loudly. "So," she said. "How are things?"

Mai paused confused, knowing that she was being asked a loaded question. How were things where? With Lishelle? With her husband? Was she asking if they were the stereotypical broken family or what? What was it she wanted to know? "Fine." She spoke tentatively, knowing that her daughter would have to go to school in the shadow of anything that was said in this meeting.

"Uh-huh." She put her elbows on the desk and pressed her fingertips together in a *v.* "At home, I mean."

"Excuse me? What does this have to do with Lishelle? Where is she? Is there something you want to say?" It was getting harder to keep her calm. Mai felt as if she was under some kind of microscope.

"Well, we've found that in cases like these—"

"Cases like what?" Calvin strode into the room. "What'd I miss?"

Mai sighed, relieved that her husband had not embarrassed them by blowing her off. He'd been doing so many things that were out of character lately, she couldn't be sure.

Mrs. Greeley stood up and extended her hand. "Like this. As I was just about to tell your wife, Lishelle's grades have been slipping and she seems distracted in class. We have found that this almost never occurs in isolation. I just wanted to ascertain what else was going on in her life. At home, I mean."

Calvin and Mai exchanged glances as he took a seat. "I'm not, I mean, *we're* not sure what you mean. Things are as they always have been at our house." Calvin smiled at his wife, although she was obviously glaring at him.

Mai tried to hide her annoyance. Where in the hell had he been? Cal continued. "Even good students can't be perfect all the time. She seems like any other thirteen-year-old. She is on the cusp of becoming a young woman and you know how they sometimes feel themselves a little bit."

The headmaster paused, looking first at Mai, then at her husband. She didn't appear to believe a word of what Calvin had just said. "Okay," she said, opening her desk drawer. "As you know, we like to take a participatory approach to education here. We like to think we are partners with families in fostering positive growth in children."

Mai tried to remain calm. Was all the mumbo-jumbo necessary? When in the world was she going to get to the point?

Dr. Greeley cleared her throat as she produced several plastic bracelets and placed them on the desk. "Lishelle had these." She waited again.

Mai looked at her husband and shrugged. "And? They're just bracelets. All the kids have them."

"Not exactly. Aside from being a violation of the uniform code, they have meaning."

"Yeah, save the troops or something like that, right?" Cal played with the wheel on his Blackberry.

"I wish it was that simple." Mrs. Greeley picked up a bracelet and held it in the air by two fingers. "You see, this purple one means your daughter is okay with kissing."

Calvin's head snapped up, and both his and Mai's mouth dropped open.

She placed it back on the desk and picked up another. "And this blue one," she paused, "this means that your daughter will perform oral sex."

"What?" Mai yelled, jumping to her feet. "That's ridiculous, she's just a child!"

Calvin dropped his phone.

"Please sit down." She swept the bracelets back inside her desk. "But that is what they mean nonetheless. We've banned these from campus as many other schools have done." She spoke slowly. "Furthermore, we confiscated them from her while she was inside the boy's restroom." Everyone was silent. Mai and Cal were both frozen in place, stunned. Mai blushed, turning her normally rubicund skin an unnatural beet red.

Dr. Greeley leaned forward, over her desk. "Now, in cases like this, we like to look a little deeper. She is your oldest, correct, so there are no teens in the household for her to pick this up from. Has she been exposed to any inappropriate television, anything like that? Sometimes things like this are a cry for attention—"

"I don't know what you are suggesting, but I assure you our household is quite normal." Calvin was seething with anger, using the voice that Mai'd only heard him use with business colleagues before. "Lishelle is not allowed to watch much television, especially nothing that would teach her anything like this. And she gets plenty of attention." He looked at his wife. "All of our children do." Calvin snapped to action. His face was hard, his temples pulsing. "We'll handle this. I promise you." He stood and began pacing the room. "I don't know what is going on, but we will get to the bottom of it."

"We don't want to alarm her. She's at an impressionable age—"

"Impressionable. My ass!"

"Please, Mr. Mott, keep your voice down."

Mai's voice shook. "So, is she in trouble at school?"

"She'll get detention for being in the boy's bathroom, but I wanted to speak to you first. I thought it important to make you aware of what was going on in your daughter's life. We were confident that you'd handle it."

"You damn right."

"Calvin, please calm down." Mai composed herself, automatically smoothing the imaginary wrinkles in her skirt. For a second, she caught a glimpse of the Calvin she'd met in college, the one from a single-parent family in the hood. Knowing Calvin, he was probably reading all sorts of things into the headmaster's comments. "We'll handle it."

Dr. Greeley paused again, then flipped open a manila folder and wrote a few lines. When she was done she put her pen in its holder and looked up, smiling again, as if none of the past few minutes had ever happened. "Okay then. That's done. Painless. We won't speak of this again." She nodded, then walked over to the door and opened it, ushering both Calvin and Mai out.

The couple left the school silently, neither wanting to utter a word until they were well clear of the building. Calvin walked his wife to her car, opening her door for her. "You gonna handle this? We have to clamp down on that girl."

"You know I'll talk to her." Part of her resented what her husband was implying, that somehow this thing that their daughter had done was her fault, that she'd been the one to let some little detail slip through the cracks, and now it was coming back to bite them in the ass. Mai did feel guilty, but she still resented the accusation.

"Talk? Our parents would have whipped our natural asses

for some shit like this." All of his proper talk was gone. He rubbed his forehead. "Are there any all-girl schools in town? Maybe we ought to try that."

Mai ignored his reference to beating her child. That was out of the question as far as she was concerned, and Calvin knew it. He might be old school when it came to discipline, but she was not. What had spanking made her but afraid of her own mother to this day? She didn't want her children to be afraid of her, she wanted them to respect her and feel comfortable that they could come to her with anything. Isn't that what most of her friends did? Why shouldn't her children be able to do that too?

"I think moving her to another school is too drastic. Lishelle would hate us for that. And I don't think it's really about the boys. You heard what the headmaster said. Maybe she needs something we aren't giving her."

"I don't know about all that. We give our kids everything they need." Calvin was calmer now. "Besides, our parents didn't know about any of that fancy shit that woman was talking about but we didn't do anything like this. Especially at her age."

"Maybe. We don't know that she did anything yet. And we had our share of drama, you know that."

"She was in the goddamn boy's bathroom."

"Still. I've been in the men's room before."

Calvin stared at his wife as if she were a stranger. "This isn't about you."

"I'll talk to her. You coming home now?" Mai knew that he probably wasn't, but she still hoped he might consider it.

"No. I've got to go back to the office. I'll be late again." He looked away.

Mai's breath caught in her throat. Normally, Calvin being late wasn't a problem, but she'd had a weird feeling ever since she'd returned from Atlanta, and then the sex thing this morning happened. That weird feeling had turned to a voice in the back of her head, nagging her, and it sounded alarmingly like her mother. "Sex," she would say, "is a necessary evil. It's something only nasty girls do, and we ain't nasty in this family. Keep your legs together until you get married, and then do it when you have to keep your man in line." Well, she'd done all that and then some and she still felt as if there were things in her husband's life she didn't understand, even after almost fourteen years and three kids. Something wasn't right and it almost felt as if he'd even been avoiding coming home early.

Calvin held the door for her as she got into her car, then closed it behind her. He stood there with his hands in his pockets as she started the car, waiting as she rolled the window down. She looked at him expectantly and he leaned in and kissed his wife on the side of her mouth.

Mai looked into his eyes, searching for information. The meeting with the headmaster had been upsetting, but she got the feeling that there was something else he wanted to tell her.

He knew what she was thinking. Mai had an active imagination and there was a good chance he had added fuel to the fire by not returning her calls, but he needed to think. He'd known that she was more than capable of handling any emergency that might have come up and she hadn't disappointed. Mai was like that, always thinking that she was the root of everything wrong or that she could fix anything if you'd let her. But this thing with the kid, this was something he had to fix himself, or at least figure out a game plan. Davon had called him first thing in the morning to remind him of their conversation, as if he'd forgotten. What married man would? All of these things were a big deal, life changing.

Calvin dropped his cigarette butt on the pavement and snuffed it out with his toe. He was a nervous wreck. He hadn't smoked in ten years, then this morning, boom, it was like the cigarettes assaulted him and forced their way between his lips. It would only be a matter of time before Mai picked up on the scent and got on his case about that too. As if he needed to risk her ire with something else.

Sex with her this morning had been out of the question, at least until he got himself checked out. He could see the accusations in her eyes, even if she didn't say anything. She probably thought he was angry with her or that he had a girlfriend on the side or something, but it would kill him if he had anything and had passed it on to his family. Years had passed and chances are she had anything he did, but he wanted to make sure he'd covered all possibilities and had done the responsible thing where he could. Calvin rubbed his forehead. What in the world had he been thinking that night? Why couldn't he remember more? He'd dreamed about the possibilities and none of them were good.

The morning had been filled with planning. He'd taken some time to himself to figure out what the hell he was supposed to do. It wasn't like he could walk up to his family physician and say, "Hey Mac, can I get an AIDS test?" Not only was the man his doctor, but he was Mai's doctor too and a family friend. Their kids played together. They were all in the same social circles, for Christ's sakes. That alone would kill Mai. And if he knew what Calvin was worried about he would forevermore feel as if the man was accusing and pitying him whenever he looked his way. Sure, things were supposed to be confidential, but were they ever really? Didn't it all get mucked up where friendships were concerned? It was just too much of a risk.

Calvin slid behind the wheel of his car and started the engine. His head throbbed. He leaned on his steering wheel a moment to think. It'd been a helluva morning. First thing, his boss was waiting for him in his office. His talk with Davon had already set the tone for the day. As soon as he walked into the office, he'd felt the chill that was permeating the air. Everyone sat tight-lipped without looking up when he'd walked in. There were none of the usual smiles or warm hellos he usually received in the morning. That could only mean one thing: bad news that he was the last to hear. Something was up. He should have expected it, but with all that was going on, he didn't even think about the possible impact on his job.

There'd been a visitor in his office. His boss was there with a grim look on his face. Apparently there was some concern that his arrest could tarnish the company image. Something about a morals clause in his contract, one he'd skimmed over and forgotten about years ago. He'd walked to HR with a grim look on his face, like a dead man walking.

He was suspended pending an investigation, but he didn't have time to even think about that, with everything that was going on. He'd left the office and went straight to the library, where he could search the Internet in relative privacy. Disorderly conduct was the least of his worries. It wasn't like he could look up what he needed at home and certainly not at the office. He would deal with the suspension thing later.

That miracle he was hoping for might be on the way and maybe, just maybe, he would never have to discuss what happened in detail with his wife. She was so unusually calm about everything, she was probably ready to blow at any moment. Mai didn't fool him, there was only so much one human being could take. Besides, there probably wasn't a woman on earth who could be calm when she found out that her husband conceived a child during a one-night stand with a stripper whose name he didn't even know.

Calvin reached into his pocket and pulled out the address he'd scribbled on a sliver of paper. He stared at it, then swallowed deep. His stomach felt sick. How was it that things done years ago always came back to haunt you? A car drove by and he jumped, then calmed himself. He was on edge, but had to keep it together so he could handle his business. It would only be a matter of time before old boy was on a bus to Texas and he needed to have it all figured out by then. He hadn't even called his lawyer yet, but he had found a clinic that would give him an anonymous AIDS test, and it was way out of town. It was better that way.

Crazy in the Blood

arie was lost in steam so thick she couldn't see the shower door three feet ahead of her. She closed her eyes and let the water from the shower cascade over her face and body, washing away the dirt and the baggage from the work week. She savored the last few minutes of her weekend morning ritual. Her kids would be up in a few minutes, and as always she would enjoy her time with them. They would demand pancakes and then need to be whisked off to various places. After being gone almost all week, she usually spent most of Saturday with the family if she could. The rest of the day would belong to them, but the next few moments belonged to her.

The first bit of daylight streamed through the bathroom window and Marie turned the chrome knobs and stopped the water, then pressed the steam LED readout that screamed ninety-nine degrees. The pipes ceased their knocking and the air cleared slightly. Marie took one last deep breath, then pushed open the swinging door that led to the rest of her bathroom.

She grabbed an oversized towel and wrapped it around her. The phone was ringing. Marie listened for the sound of someone else picking up the phone, knowing that it wasn't coming. Louis avoided answering the phone when he could and the kids would ignore it. She hesitated, then made a dash into the bedroom, grabbing at the receiver. It slipped from her hands and hit the floor with a thud and she reached for it, huffing slightly.

"Hello?"

Her voice met dead air on the other end.

"Hello?" Marie listened intently. Someone cleared his throat and then the line went dead. A feeling of annoyance crept over her. How rude was it that a wrong number couldn't even apologize for disturbing her morning, especially since they'd damn near called in the middle of the night?

The sounds of muffled music floated into her room. The kids were up. Even at six years old, her son loved to crank up the sound, no matter what time of day it was. If she didn't hurry, he would be firmly planted in front of the Playstation. She quickly lotioned up, skipped the makeup, and pulled on her favorite pair of jeans. Her three-year-old padded into her room just as she finished brushing her teeth, the feet in her pajamas making soft scrubbing sounds as she dragged her feet on the wood floor.

"Hungry, Mommy."

Marie smiled. Her children were truly the joy of her life. No matter how her week had been, they always made her feel better. She bent down to kiss Walani on the forehead. "You want pancakes?"

She nodded without removing her favorite finger from her mouth.

"Where's Daddy?" If she was making pancakes, she might as well make them for everyone. Between her son and her husband, they could eat a boatload. She didn't know where they put it. Neither one of them seemed to gain a pound and they ate like horses.

Walani shrugged and leaned into Marie's legs.

Marie kissed her again and headed for her son's room, her daughter padding behind her.

The music was even louder than she thought it was. Walani held her ears as Marie walked over to her son's stereo and started pushing buttons. She'd been the one against him having anything more than a simple radio, but Louis insisted that he needed an elaborate setup for his iPod. She'd been against that too. Louis Jr. was just too young.

"Mom!" Junior spun around as soon as Marie lowered the volume to what she thought was a more acceptable level.

"Where's your dad?"

Louis shrugged too. Didn't kids use words anymore?

"Breakfast. Come downstairs."

Marie left him there, knowing that he would turn the sound back up as soon as she left. She helped her daughter get dressed, listening as she chatted with her about the things that happened to her at preschool. A familiar twinge of remorse hit her. She loved her job, but as she listened to her daughter's jumbled stories, she felt like she'd missed a whole lot this week.

By the time she went downstairs, Louis Jr was already seated at the table. He had his iPod on and turned up so loud that Marie could hear the beat of the music he was listening to. He bopped his head to the music and played with his Gameboy at the same time. Marie shook her head, then headed into the pantry to gather what she needed. Junior warbled every other word of a Disney Channel tune. With his earphones on, he was loud and off-key. Marie chuckled. The boy was just like his dad. Neither he nor Louis could carry a tune in a bucket. He would probably be switching from the wholesome-sounding lyrics to rap in a year or so. She decided not to say anything, turning instead to the refrigerator. A girl had to pick her battles.

Louis had left a note in his usual place, taped to the refrigerator door, in between spelling tests and three-year-old artwork. Marie squinted to read the sprawling marks. The grocery store. She frowned, then glanced at the clock. He was out early. It wasn't even nine o'clock. Marie removed the note, then opened the large door to get the milk and eggs. She let Walani act as if she were helping, enjoying the time with her kids. They sang their own songs and banged pots. Junior couldn't stand it anymore and finally got tired of acting like he was too old and joined in, too.

It took a while, but finally everyone had their special pancakes. Marie pursed her mouth with satisfaction and looked around the kitchen. As usual, she'd left it a wreck, covered with flour and other debris.

"Mom, you made a mess." Walani grinned, her face dotted with batter.

"We made a mess." Marie couldn't help grinning back. "That means they are going to be extra good." She piled up some pancakes on her kids' plates, then turned her attention back to the kitchen. Louis was sure to have a conniption when he saw the mess they made. Marie grabbed a sponge and tried to put things back in order.

As she admired her handiwork, the doorbell rang. Both Walani and Junior jumped to their feet and raced to the door.

"Don't you open that door!" Marie yelled after them, wiping her hands on a dishtowel. They usually listened, but she followed them quickly just to make sure. Walani would be fine but her son was sometimes overeager, and there was no telling who was at the door.

The kids stood behind her. The woman at the door was unfamiliar. Marie immediately noticed her high cheekbones and eyes that hinted at Asian ancestry. She had a pleasant look on her face and was nicely dressed in a well-cared-for pair of jeans, ankle boots, and a sweater that Marie recognized as high-quality cashmere. Better dressed than most salespeople would be.

"Yes?"

"Oh, hi. I'm sorry to bother you. I'm Josie Jennings." She hesitated, then began again. "You're Marie, right? I live in your building."

It took a moment for what the woman was saying to register. Marie couldn't place her. "Oh, yeah, I'm sorry. How can I help you?" Marie really had no idea who the woman was at all. She usually let Louis handle all the details of their real estate.

"Your husband was at my place the other day—fixing the pipes." She paused a minute, seeming to realize that Marie had no idea who she was. "I keep hearing this knocking sound. Well, anyway, he left some stuff. Some tools. I brought them back." She presented a long screwdriver and a drill.

"You didn't have to do that. You could have left them downstairs in the maintenance room." Marie reached for the screwdriver. It was nice of her to take a trip across town to bring

Louis's things back. In all the years they had owned the apartment building, she'd interacted with the tenants very little. This was the first time one of them had actually been to their house. Truth be told, it made Marie just a tad uncomfortable. In general, where they lived was not public knowledge; they used a business address for all of the correspondence and rent payments. Had Louis given this person their address? Then again, the address probably wouldn't be that hard to obtain if someone knew their names.

"I thought he might need them. To fix stuff for other people." Her pause was awkward. "I left him a few messages but I haven't been able to reach him." She paused her halting speech, trying to peer around Marie and into the house. "He left his driver's license too. It slid down behind my radiator and I finally got it out."

"Really?" That was unusual. How in the world had Louis's driver's license gotten out of his wallet? "I guess you couldn't have left that in the maintenance room."

Marie felt a tap on her leg. Walani stood next to her, waving her down like she did when she wanted to tell her a secret, the latest three-year-old craze. "Just a minute, sweetie, let me finish."

Josie looked surprised. "I'm sorry, I didn't mean to interrupt."

"No worries. We were just having breakfast. Louis is at the store. Matter of fact, would you like to join us?"

"I couldn't do that. I just wanted to drop these things off."

Josie paused there, but didn't seem to be leaving. It was awkward, but Marie felt suddenly hospitable as she stared at her daughter's grinning face. Walani loved company, and company for breakfast would surely make her day. "Louis will be back in a few. It's no problem. You drink coffee?" She waved the visitor in.

Josie grinned from ear to ear, showing her impossibly white teeth. "I sure do." She licked her rose-colored lips and stepped inside the house.

The supermarket was nearly empty so early in the morning. Louis had slipped out of bed just past dawn, throwing on some jeans and a tee shirt. They needed a few things to get through the weekend, but more than that, he needed some time to think before his household got going.

He'd taken a drive around town before finally ending up at the supermarket. As soon as he'd left the house, he dialed Maxfield's number and left a message on his cell phone to return the call. The man was annoying, but he needed some legal advice.

Over an hour had passed and Marie and the kids were surely up already. Halfway through the supermarket, Louis realized he'd been walking around on automatic, placing things in the basket. What in the hell had he been thinking? He reviewed the week's events in his head, playing the moments right before he'd stepped inside Josie's apartment. He couldn't deny that he'd known what she was up to the minute he'd seen the door slightly ajar, but he'd blatantly ignored the little warning voice inside his head. He would have to be both blind and dumb not to see that the woman intended to wear him down until he'd caved. She'd laid the trap and he'd stepped right in.

They needed paper towels. He scanned the aisle for the brand they liked best, sighing to himself. Maxfield had better call him back soon. There was only so much shopping he could do. And every time he thought about Josie and that seductive body, his stomach trembled. Damn, she was fine. Louis knew it was wrong, but her lips had felt so damn good on his. And she smelled like a fresh shower.

He grabbed a few rolls, trying to shake the memory from his mind. He wasn't the cheating type. At least he was going to try not to be the cheating type, but women like Josie, damn, they made it hard. And it didn't help that Marie worked in a job that kept her away so many nights. A vacant bed and a willing substitute; shit, was Maxfield right? He shuddered at the thought. If he was anything like Maxfield was, he'd be jumping at the chance to get with Josie. She took good care of herself and was more than eager. Hell, if he were anything like he'd been in college, he would be paying her a regular visit. Once he met Marie, he'd been cured of all that, just plain sprung. She'd been so fine then. They'd met at an icebreaker, a step-show competition. He'd been blinded by her pink and green, and he had been a good boy ever since she'd worked her mojo on him.

Those days were behind him now. He was a family man. It wasn't worth giving up what he and Marie had built for a few minutes of fun, right? And Josie'd been calling him regularly, too. He'd stopped answering his phone and was trying to ignore the endless text messages. He refused to let himself be duped into going over to her place again. He'd done his homework. He was not under any legal obligation to fix the minor things that were wrong with her apartment, not unless they were a health hazard, he knew that much. Josie was going to have to do better than the knocking in the pipes she'd been complaining about. It was obvious that the only knocking she was interested in was the knocking of the boots, his boots, and he wasn't up with that.

He was in the cereal aisle when his phone rang. Maxfield's number appeared on his screen. A sense of relief washed over him, as if whatever Maxfield had to say might solve his problem.

"What you need, man?"

Louis stepped to the side of the aisle and wet his lips. "I need some help."

"It's Saturday, I don't do manual moving or anything like that."

"No, professional advice. You gotta tell me how to evict a tenant."

"Shit. You know I'm not a real estate lawyer. What, is the tenant not paying rent? What?"

"No, she pays."

"Then as far as I know, you can't evict her. You can't just throw people out on the street in this state. What did she do?"

Louis took a moment to think about just how much he wanted to tell Max. He couldn't have his private life becoming locker room gossip. He was cut from a different cloth and would probably want to take advantage of the situation rather than end it. He turned his back to the aisle and lowered his voice. "Well, she is just making life very difficult for me. Every time I have to go there, she damn near tries to jump my bones—"

Maxfield guffawed on the other end of the phone line. "So, you're feeling the heat. Is she old and ugly?"

"No. The opposite." His face was grim.

"I don't see what the problem is then, man. Smack that ass, no one will know. Many men would love to be in your shoes—"

Why did he have to be so crass? "Max, be serious. I don't feel like this is some ordinary come-on. This woman has crazy in her blood. I can smell it."

"All right, all right. There is a simple solution to the problem, a logical one, and you didn't need to call me to figure it out. Just don't go there. You don't have to unless she has no heat or water and not even then. Call a damn repairman. Easy. Better yet, don't call one and then maybe she won't pay her rent. Then you would be fully within your rights to evict her."

Louis closed his eyes and leaned on the cart, feeling utterly miserable. "You know you're right."

"I always am. But you should consider—"

"No."

He paused. "Okay. On the serious tip there's one other thing." Maxfield lowered his voice and took on a more serious tone. "You should tell your wife about it. She'll want to know."

A Moment of Clarity

Kennedy stubbed her toe, then tripped into her father's room. She grimaced, then placed the tray she'd prepared onto the small bistro table in the corner. "Dad, this should hold you. I'm going to call to check on you. Please answer the phone."

He nodded, but didn't take his eyes off the Gene Kelly movie that played on the television. Old movies were his favorite. He seemed clearer today than he had been lately, more focused.

Kennedy was glad of that, but she still was nervous about leaving him alone in the middle of the afternoon on a Saturday. There was something that made her want to stick close lately, a feeling in her gut. "You sure you're going to be okay? Can I bring you anything else?" She bit her lip. Maybe she ought to give serious consideration to getting a caretaker for him, someone who could come in midday. Usually when she went out like this, it was at night and he was either asleep or well on his way to bed.

He grunted.

"Dad, look over here. Remember the panic button, okay?" Kennedy pointed to a large red button by the side of the bed. "If you feel any distress, you press this."

"I'm not a child, Kennedy, and I'm certainly not hard of hearing. You don't have to talk so loud." His mouth was set into a straight line and he gave her a withering stare. For a second, Kennedy could see a flicker of the stern father she remembered him being.

Yup, he is very clear today. Her feelings were a little hurt by his tone, but she let it go. She picked up his jacket, which had slid onto the floor. She felt the inside pocket before hanging it back up on its hook. Just in case, she'd slipped her contact information into his pocket a while ago. It made her feel better. Taking care of him was hard sometimes. There were so few glimpses of any gratitude from him, just anger at everyone and everything around him, and lately, it seemed worse. She tried her best to be understanding about it, but it was hard. It had to be frustrating not to be able to remember and not to be able to express yourself, especially for someone like her father. He'd been so outgoing and surrounded by friends. Now it was just the two of them most of the time.

Kennedy closed the door behind her as she left, leaving her father alone in the guesthouse. Even though he'd been short with her, she still felt the tiniest bit better that he was so much more himself today.

Troy had told her to dress casually, so she ran upstairs to finally put on her shoes. Her toe still smarted each time she put it down from where she'd hit it. She rubbed it as she sat on the small chair in her bedroom and surveyed her choices. He'd said *comfortable*, but there was no reason why she couldn't be cute. She chose a pair of white Coach sneakers and gingerly slipped them on, then stood up to admire her handiwork in the full-length mirror. Her Nike sweat suit looked sporty, but classy, too. Kennedy turned around to do one last booty check, smiling at what she saw in the mirror. As far as she could tell, things were all good.

The doorbell rang and she froze, staring at the clock on her dresser. He was exactly on time. There was still a nagging feeling in the pit of her stomach. Was she going out with him again too fast, too soon? The doorbell rang again and she grabbed her handbag, then started back down the steps, pausing at the front door to check her reflection one last time.

He had flowers. She'd planned to play it cool, but it was kinda corny that Troy was hiding behind a huge bunch of daisies. She tried hard to suppress a grin as he peered from behind the bouquet. Did he have stock in a florist or what? On their last date, she'd had a one-track mind and hadn't allowed him to be very romantic at all. They'd been playing cat and mouse, and she'd been the one doing the chasing, even if he hadn't realized it then. Kennedy hated to admit it, but it was somewhat of a relief to just relax and let a date be normal for a change.

"Looks like you're ready." He lowered the bouquet, handing her a newspaper with the other hand. "I retrieved your paper from the bushes. I see you have one of those joker paperboys, too, trying to put the paper out of the way on purpose." He paused, attempting to rub his back with one hand. The flowers leaned dangerously to one side. "You might want to take it with you. We have about a forty-minute drive."

"You want to tell me where we're going?"

"Nope, not yet." A mischievous smile played across his face and he reached into her house, placing the flowers on the console table just inside the door.

He smelled wonderful, a tiny hint of spice. How could she complain when he smelled as good as he did? Troy looked great too. His deep-red shirt was obviously well ironed and crisp and hugged him in all the right places. Something about a well-ironed shirt was incredibly sexy. He was still fine, that was for sure. Although the thought of not knowing where they were going was a little disconcerting at first, especially for someone who was as used to being in control as Kennedy was. Being surprised held a certain charm. All the mystery had certainly piqued her interest. She'd already quelled the urge to fight. "All righty then. Let me grab my stuff." She went back into the kitchen to grab her keys and glanced through the house in the direction of her father's room, pushing her uncertainties to the back of her mind. "You are going to have a great day." She spoke to no one in particular, then headed back to the front of her house where Troy was waiting. Her gym bag was on the floor, still where she had dropped it when she'd come in from the gym the other day. Kennedy grabbed the newspaper that was sitting on top of it. Forty minutes would be more than enough time to catch up on all the news. She tucked the newspaper snugly under her arm and took a deep breath. Troy smiled at her from the door and she had a flash of the weekend they'd spent together. Her insides tingled. He was hot and had already proven he knew his way around a bedroom. The date could only end positively, right?

Kennedy didn't read the paper. Troy didn't mention any-thing about the lies she'd told, instead she found him watching her intently from the corner of his eye as he drove. She tried to ignored his stares and they spoke in quips and jests. His voice held a hint of laughter the entire ride. Things were different this time than they had been on their first date. Easier, more relaxed. Kennedy was still guarded, but it'd been a long time since she let anyone get to know her this way. Troy was still sexy and still smelled good, but Kennedy found that she was able to actually concentrate on his words once she stopped trying to manipulate things to go the way she wanted. She only thought about The Rules one time, and then she pushed the thought right out of her head. A feeling of relief washed over her. *Sometimes it feels good just to let go and let someone else be in control.*

The time flew by like it was just a few minutes. Troy turned off the road and headed down a long and narrow unpaved trail that was lined with trees on both sides. He laughed as Kennedy was thrown from side to side inside the car. Her eyes opened wide and she grabbed the handrail. "So, is this where you take me into the woods and kill me or something?"

Troy chuckled, but didn't answer her directly. He slowed down as he approached a small stone building that didn't look unlike a tollbooth. A park ranger appeared and Kennedy was silent as Troy handed him a few dollars and received a parking permit in return. He placed it on his dashboard, then rolled up the window. "We're sort of camping."

"You're kidding, right?" Kennedy had only been camping once in her life, and she didn't remember it being good, either.

After the trip was over, she'd been covered with bug bites, forty-two of them to be exact. She'd suffered for days and was positive that there was still at least one permanent scar on her legs from the ordeal. She didn't consider herself to be the rustic type. When Troy had said be casual, she'd thought maybe they would be doing a lot of walking or something, but camping had never crossed her mind.

"No. But don't worry, you'll be fine. It's more like a picnic with a twist."

"I kinda have a hate-hate relationship with nature. Bugs." They hadn't even gotten out of the car yet, and Kennedy could already feel the beginnings of an itch.

"I thought you were a nature-loving type."

"I am. It's just that I love nature when it's outside my window, not when I am out in it."

Troy covered her hand with his. "I promise you, it'll be fine." The paved road ended and they continued down another curving gravel road, until Kennedy could see water from her window. They drove along a river so slow it looked like a pond, the surface disturbed only by a few intermittent ripples. He pulled the car to a stop in front of a small wooden and brick building with a picnic table by its side. It sat under a large tree, about ten feet back from the quiet river. The building was enclosed only by a screen on three sides, the fourth was a solid wall. Kennedy was skeptical, but she followed Troy's lead anyway and carefully stepped out of the car. An amazing quiet immediately surrounded her. It was hard to believe they'd been roaring down the interstate not ten minutes before.

"I wouldn't have thought that you were into this type of thing at all."

He tilted his head to the side, his eyebrows arched. "Just because I am a geologist doesn't mean I can't appreciate natural resources. My job is to learn how to harness them."

"Harness them? Your job is to find oil."

"And you fabricate realities to sell products. What's your point?" He winked at Kennedy, then walked to the rear of his car and produced a large, old-fashioned picnic basket and a small black cooler, which he carried to the picnic table.

"Can I interest you in some wine?"

Kennedy walked slowly over to join him. So far, so good, but she wasn't quite sure about all the nature. Anything could happen. She nodded anyway and Troy unzipped the cooler.

The cooler held a surprise of its own. It was made especially for wine. He removed two wine glasses, followed by a bottle of merlot.

On a good day, Kennedy prided herself on being able to see most things coming, but she hadn't anticipated anything like this. So far, she had to admit, this date was unlike any other she'd ever been on. Kennedy smiled. "I've never been camping like this."

"I said we were camping, not roughing it. I'm not so into that. I figured we wouldn't be interrupted by nosy friends or anything like that out here." Troy paused to fill their wine glasses. "I have a few surprises in store for you. Why don't you go get your reading material? It's all about you today. We came here to relax and just be."

How could anyone not appreciate what Troy was trying to do, even if the idea of relaxing was a foreign one? Did she actually remember how to do that? She wasn't sure. There wasn't a time in her recent memory where she had actually done nothing for more than a half-hour stretch at a time. Kennedy was used to going full speed all day, every day. She watched as he continued to pull things from his basket. Just how much did he have in there?

"It'll take me a few minutes to get my smorgasbord prepared." Troy gave Kennedy a mischievous wink.

She sipped the wine, smiling. "A smorgasbord, huh?"

"Well, you already know I've got skills in the kitchen. You're about to find out that I've got skills that extend far beyond breakfast. Go."

Kennedy got her papers and returned to the picnic table to find that Troy had set up a full-blown spread, complete with tablecloth and all. "This doesn't look like any picnic I've ever been to."

Troy admired his handiwork. "Not camping like you're used to. No picnic like you're used to. And you thought I was just a pretty face." He winked at her and she blushed. "I wasn't too sure what you'd like, so I tried to bring an assortment. And you didn't exactly look like the paper-plate type, so I wanted to make sure you were comfortable."

The table was neatly set for two, complete with china and battery-powered candles in the center. "I'm impressed."

"I wasn't trying to impress you, just feed you. I made a couple of different things for you to try. I hope outside is going to be okay. If not, we can go inside." Troy gestured toward the hut. "This is ours for the day, too."

"Wow. You were prepared."

"I try to be." He smiled, then pulled Kennedy closer.

She hugged him back, enjoying the strength in his arms. It was like they were the only two people in the world. All she could hear was the sound of birds and there was not a bug in sight. It was starting to feel like she'd made a good choice. The date had really just begun, and she was reveling in having someone take care of her for a change.

Troy kissed her lightly on her cheek. "If you think this is something, just wait until you see what I have planned for dessert."

Kennedy couldn't help but enjoy herself. She gave up fighting after the second glass of wine. By the third, she wasn't drunk, just tipsy enough not to care at all when Troy spread his sleeping bag on the concrete floor inside their camping hut. She tripped over the edge of it and then giggled as Troy helped her down to the ground.

He pushed her hair back from her face and then kissed her gently at first, and then deeper. The only sound was their breathing and that of acorns dropping onto the metal roof of the hut. Troy sucked her bottom lip, and her hips rose to meet his body. The firmness of his penis pressed into her through his jeans. The combination of the wine and the almost vacuum-like soundlessness of the park was magic for Kennedy. Normally, she would be the one giving orders, but today, all she wanted to do was follow Troy's lead as he pressed into her.

The thought that someone might get close enough to see inside the hut occurred to her, then flitted away as quickly as it

had come. She didn't hesitate as he covered them with other
blankets, then began to undress her slowly, first removing her
blouse, then her bra. He flicked his tongue first across one nip-
ple then the other. They were already hard as rocks and she
moaned at the gentle sensation. A familiar wetness started in
her underwear. Kennedy reached for his penis and he stopped
her. He was still fully clothed. "Today is about you," he said,
then kissed her softly.

Kennedy was on fire. Troy worked magic with his mouth and
hands, setting small fires on her skin wherever he touched.
Her bottoms came off between kisses and Troy moved his ex-
plorations further down, flicking his tongue on her navel. She
didn't have to give orders, his body seemed to speak to hers as
he moved with pure instinct. For the first time in a long while,
Kennedy was not in control. She had no idea what time it was
and didn't care.

Troy worked his tongue like it was a finger, alternating
touching her softly with a long, flicking motion that he moved
across her hypersensitive skin. The ache in her nipples seemed
to be connected to the wanting in her clitoris, and she found
herself arching her back, wishing he would get there quickly.
His fingertips teased the top of her neatly shaven pubic hair.
If he was trying to make her beg, he was damn close to suc-
ceeding.

He looked up and smiled at her, then flicked her clitoris gently with his tongue. Kennedy gasped. It was if something inside
of her came out of hiding. She was no stranger to sex, but this
was different. Troy wasn't having sex with her, he was showing
her how she needed to be loved.

He moved his tongue, slowly at first, then more rapidly, alternating between licking motions, then sucking her in other places. Kennedy shuddered. Soon Troy's movements became indistinguishable from each other and the roaring in her head drowned the acorn sounds out. Kennedy quivered, then exploded.

Troy pushed his face deeper into her, and unable to take it anymore, she tried to push his head away. He resisted and continued to probe deeper, until Kennedy screamed. He stopped finally and pulled her close, wrapping them both up in the blanket.

"I hope that means it was good."

She was breathless and hot all over, but wasn't able to respond. Kennedy curled her body into his as she slowly came back to the present. That was the most unselfish sex she'd ever experienced. Troy didn't seem to care that they hadn't had actual intercourse. How was she supposed to act in the face of such selflessness?

Leaves rustled outside the hut and she jumped.

"Relax," he said. "It's fall and this place is teeming with squirrels."

She licked the dryness from her lips. It was hard for her to resist the urge to make nut jokes, but she restrained herself. "What time do you think it is? I probably should check on my father."

"We should head out of here soon. I'm going to pack up our stuff and get rid of the trash so you can get dressed."

Troy leaned in and Kennedy closed her eyes as their lips met. Her head swam and Kennedy had to steady herself even though she was still lying down. There just may be something to this letting-go thing. This had been a good day, the best she'd had in a long time. Sure, they'd had sex on their last date, but she felt more relaxed than last time, more free, as if she and Troy had shared more than before. He stood, and Kennedy admired his toned butt as he put his pants back on. *When had he even removed those?*

Troy glanced back at her over his shoulder and winked, then leaned down to make sure that the blanket was still covering her. He straightened it a little, then left the hut. The door banged shut behind him. Kennedy waited until he was clear of the hut, then gathered her clothes and dressed under the cover of the blanket.

She found him outside, putting their trash into a plastic bag that he'd obviously brought with him. "You thought of everything, didn't you? Can I help?"

"Nope, you can't. Why don't you read those papers so we can get rid of them, too?" He motioned toward her newspapers.

Kennedy'd lost interest in the news by now, but she took the papers anyway and parked herself at the picnic table. She unfolded them and flipped to the business section, scanning the page. Her eye was drawn to a small sidebar and she gasped, covering her hand with her mouth.

"What's wrong?" Troy stopped packing the picnic basket and looked up at her.

Why hadn't Mai mentioned this? "My best friend's husband has been suspended from his job. It made the business section." She held the paper up for him to see.

"Let me see," he said. "If he made the paper, someone thinks

it's a big deal." Troy came around behind her to read the head-
line.

LOCAL EXECUTIVE, CALVIN MOTT III, SUSPENDED AFTER ARREST

"Funny thing is, she didn't mention it to me. Or to our other
friend, Marie, the one you met. If she had, Marie would have
certainly told me about it."

Troy didn't speak as he continued reading. He placed the
paper back down onto the table. "You two real close?"

"The three of us have been friends since our college days."
Kennedy exhaled, unable to believe that Mai had kept something
so big from her. She'd thought they talked about everything.

"Maybe she was embarrassed."

Kennedy shrugged. That would not be unlike Mai. Between
the three of them, she was as close to June Cleaver as it could
get. News like this would certainly ruin her façade of being the
perfect wife in the perfect family. Calvin's arrest was one thing.
That she could easily sweep under the rug or pass off as a
wrongful arrest for some noble purpose, especially since it'd
happened out of town. Losing his job was another thing. How
long could she hide that? She and Calvin appeared to be doing
okay financially, but not many families could stand the loss of
major income for too long, not even perfect ones like hers. And
Mai wasn't exactly the cut-back-on-things type. Just say the
word *budget* and she would break out in hives.

"Maybe."

"That or maybe she doesn't know."

Good Girls and Good Drugs

Her life was falling apart. Mai was sure of it. Calvin was once again not answering either of his phones and her kids had gone stone-cold crazy. She stood, fuming, at the bottom of the steps, so angry that the walls on either side of her stairwell appeared to be rippling. She wanted to pinch herself or hit replay or something.

Lishelle's behavior was beyond belief. The girl had just yelled at her and told her to stay out of her life, then stormed upstairs. Mai was still paralyzed from shock.

Terror and anger gripped her body. Mai had a flash of herself, mimicking the very same words her own mother used to say to her and the thought had terrified her. Everyone always said that you become your parents but she'd worked hard to avoid that. How could it be happening to her? Her head throbbed so hard that she was sure that her blood pressure had risen off the charts.

Mai's hand had been in the air, ready to slap her thirteen-year-old across her surly little face, but she caught herself.

"If you hit me I'm going to call child protective services on you." Mai still couldn't believe a child that had come from her loins had the gall to even suggest anything like that. And then she stood there with her fist balled up, as if she was going to return a punch if Mai had slapped her. Hit your mother? That was surely as much of a death sentence today as it had been when she was a child, an even bigger travesty than threatening to call CPS.

"And you might as well call the morgue too because you will be dead before they even arrive." Fuming, she stopped herself. If she'd hit Lishelle then, it would have been much more than a spanking, more like slapping a grown woman down. Didn't her mama say that if you talked like a grown-ass woman, you could get a grown-ass woman's beating? But this was now and she wasn't her mother. "Wait until your father gets home," she'd yelled instead.

"Why? It's not like he would care." The mention of her father was enough to bring the belligerent child to her knees, crushing the stony appearance she was trying to project. Lishelle burst into tears and Mai had that terrifying instant where she and her mother were the same person. She'd let her daughter go storming up the stairs while she held her ground, followed by a door slamming that had shaken the entire house. Perhaps it was her father's spirit that kept her rooted to the spot in disbelief, and it was a good thing, too. She'd do her other children nor her husband any good if she went to jail for child abuse.

Her anger slowly dissipated and the shades of red and green she was seeing returned to normal. Sometimes it was better just to leave well enough alone. Both of them would only regret any action she took now. It was best to calm down first, then deal with Lishelle.

Mai went to her kitchen to find her purse and make a cup of tea. *When had things gotten so out of hand?* It was almost as if the girl's birthday had come and someone flipped her evil switch. Lishelle had just been a sweet eleven-year-old and her mother had been her best friend. How did they go from sweet and cuddly to needing an exorcist in the blink of an eye? What next? Lishelle was too young to wear black lipstick and pierce herself, or at least Mai hoped she was.

Mai put the kettle on and pulled down her teapot and her favorite loose tea. She needed all the help she could get to shake the uneasy feeling she was having. Thank goodness the other kids were with friends today. She was too flustered to be bothered sifting through her handbag, so she grabbed it and began to remove the contents, throwing everything she pulled out onto the granite countertop. Mai moved slowly at first, removing things carefully, then more quickly as it emptied. Where in the hell was it? Panic rose in her chest and she became less careful. She reached the bottom of her bag and gasped. What the hell? Mai opened it wide, searching through the bag's nooks and crannies. Finally, she found what she'd been looking for, stuffed into a side pocket of her bag. Of course what you were looking for was always the absolute last thing you'd find.

A sense of relief washed over her when her fingers wrapped around her pillbox, Mai grasped it tightly. She needed more than just an iron will to deal with Lishelle and her nonsense. Mai shook the pillbox. There was no rattle.

"Fuck!"

Empty.

It was 3:15. This was not a problem, it could be handled. She grabbed the phone. Her fingers trembled as she dialed the pharmacy. As soon as the computer picked up, she punched in her prescription number from the label of the pill bottle, which she kept in a kitchen cabinet. She could have a refill within the hour and everything would be back to normal.

The phone made several clicks and there was no voice confirming her refill. "Please wait," was all the machine said. The hair on the back of her neck bristled. *What the hell?* This had never happened before.

"Walgreen's Pharmacy. How can I help you?"

Dumbfounded, she paused for a minute. "I, uh. I was trying to get a refill on my prescription." Mai let out a nervous chuckle. Maybe the computer was down today or something.

"Prescription number?"

Mai knew the number by heart. She repeated the six-digit number like the woman on the other end was hard of hearing.

"I'm sorry. It says here that you are out of refills."

She was sinking through the floor. *What the hell—?* "No, that's not right." Mai's voice cracked. She knew that it was right, but she didn't want to face the truth. She held the bottle in her hand and there it was, right next to the skull and crossbones. Refills left: a big fat zero.

"I'm sorry, you're going to have to call your doctor."

"Wait, I just need a few. I'll call the doctor right away."

"Sorry, Mrs. Mott. You'll need to call your doctor *first*. This is a controlled substance. We can't even give you a few." The silence on the phone was enormous.

She was holding her breath. Mai's mind whirled and she exhaled. What in the hell was she going to do? She needed those pills.

They helped her think, cleared her head so she could just deal. "Thanks." Her hand trembled and Mai feverishly pressed the flash button on the phone, then listened for the dial tone. It was getting close to 4 P.M., and her doctor's office closed early on a lot of days. Mai cleared her voice and tried to sound cheerful, like this was no big deal. The receptionist transferred her to the nurse.

"Hey Lisa, it's Mai Mott. I have a problem. I seem to be out of my prescription with no refills, the pharmacist said I needed a new script. You think Dr. Day can call one in?'

"Let me check your chart."

Mai silently grit her teeth. She'd only been going to the same doctor for umpteen years, you would think they knew who she was.

Muzak played Michael Jackson.

A simple *yes* would suffice. She leaned on the counter and tapped her fingers on the marble as she waited.

"I'm sorry, Mrs. Mott. You'll have to come in."

Panic filled her. "Did you talk to the doctor? She knows me."

The woman repeated herself, sounding indifferent. "I have no doubt that she does. You'll have to come in."

Mai slammed the phone down and tears sprung to her eyes. This was not a good time for them to be pulling this on her. The kettle hissed and she jumped, startled.

Tea seemed like an even better idea than it had a few minutes ago. Anything to quell the panic that was rising in her gut, keep her rational. Mai wiped her hand across her face, pressing her fingers firmly into the space between her eyes. If she could just talk to her husband, she would feel better. She was going to have to pull it together somehow. It was girls' night tonight.

Kennedy and Marie were meeting her for dinner, and she needed to be calm to deal with Lishelle. There were ten thousand other things she had to do today and there was no way she could do them if she weren't calm enough to think.

Her hand trembled as she poured the water over her tea leaves, then returned the kettle to its resting place on her stovetop. The click it made when it made contact with the metal stove grates sounding more like a bang to her, not unlike the sound of a gun being cocked. Mai snatched the phone from its cradle and punched in her husband's number at work.

Voicemail.

She called his cell.

Voicemail.

Her nose flared. How was it that the very things that were supposed to make your life so much easier could become the targets of so much hate? Mai slammed the phone down on the counter. It slid across the smooth surface, then bounced on the floor, the battery and back going in one direction, the phone going in the other. Damn him! It seemed like the only way to contact him lately was to email him. What next? Would she have to make an appointment just to talk to him soon?

Mai went to her desk and sat her tea down, then wiggled her mouse to make her screen come alive. She paused, and then instead of opening her email program, she opened a browser window. She was a smart woman, she should have thought of this before. Anything she wanted could be found on the Internet. She typed the words "Internet pharmacy" in her search window. Pages of listings came up. Didn't her mother used to tell her that there was more than one road to the square? There had to be a

way for her to find what she needed online. Everything else was
there.

She rolled her chair closer. "Thousands of reliable drugs
from Canada." A smile found its way through her mask of panic.
This was certainly as good a place as any to start. Mai felt better
already, and if this didn't work, she could get in her car and
drive to Nuevo Laredo. Dammit, this was Texas and she'd driven
longer than two hours to get to a mall before, so a drive to Mexico would feel like a small errand.

Lishelle slammed her door and locked it behind her, although
she doubted her mother would even bother to follow her. She
pressed the button on her iPod and her iDog jumped to life,
blaring the music of Chris Brown. She put on a good act, trying
to behave as if she cared when she really didn't. No one did. Did
they think she was stupid? This family life thing was bullshit,
especially when everyone had so many secrets. Her mother was
always trying to act like everything was so perfect up in their
house, when it was all phony, and she was the only one who knew
the real deal. What was the point in even following their stupid
rules if they weren't being straight with her, with any of them?

She mouthed the words to "Excuse me, Miss" along with the
music as she pointed her browser to the Hill Country chat room
that she and some of the kids from school had set up. This was
the only place where she was real. Her friends knew all about
her and didn't even care if her mother was a fucking drug ad-
dict. She wasn't blind. Every chance she got, Mai was popping
those damn pills, taking far too many. Lishelle knew, she'd read
the pill bottle and looked it up on the Internet. Her mother had

gone over that "not to exceed" warning many months ago. And her father, he was a joke, too. Lishelle was an expert hacker, and come to find out, he had a whole other life. She'd went into his cellular account a long time ago and read all of the old text messages. Tears sprang to her eyes as she thought about it. Lishelle wiped them away with her fingertips. All this time, she'd been thinking she was his "special girl," and he had another special kid somewhere that he'd been hiding all this time. Had he been hiding her and her sisters, too? Was he ashamed of them, too? And they acted like everything was all normal.

There already were two other people in the chat room, her two best friends. The names they used online glared at her. Lishelle glanced over her shoulder, double-checking to make sure her door was still locked, then she caught herself. Her mother was probably downstairs popping more pills, anyway. She logged on.

GOODGIRL93: HEY
SK8TR: WASSUP. BOUT TIME YOU GOT HERE.
STARGZ6: HEY
GOODGIRL93: DRAMA AT HOME
STARGZ6: WE WERE JUST PLANNING OUR SHIT. YOU WITH US OR WHAT? A BUNCH OF US R CUTTING OUT NEXT WEEK. WE'RE GOING OVER TO THE PILOT STOP ON I-10.

Lishelle caught her breath. She paused at the keyboard, her fingers tense. What in the world would they do at a truck stop? Both her friends had always been a little more daring than she was. They were the ones who gave her those damn bracelets in the first place. She knew they cut school whenever they wanted to, but she never went with them. Butterflies tickled her stomach. They always seemed like they had a good time, and never got in trouble. At least not too much. If they did, they kept it quiet and their parents made a donation to the school or did whatever it was they had to do so their kids were covered. Thanks to the two of them, Hill Country Episcopal School had a wonderful computer center. They joked about it all the time.

SK8TR: C'MON. YOU KNOW SHE DON'T GET DOWN LIKE THAT. YOU SEE HER NAME, RIGHT? WE DON'T CALL HER THAT FOR NOTHING.
GOODGIRL93: YOU NEVER KNOW WHAT I'LL DO.

Lishelle's heart pounded in her ears. They didn't know, and neither did she. Why should she be the only one in her house without any secrets?

Cal slipped into the small clinic, not bothering to remove his sunglasses. The door closed behind him, bouncing on its hinges, and a tinny-sounding bell announced his entry. He looked around quickly, his eyes darting around the room. The shadows cast by the dim fluorescent lighting gave the room a dingy feeling and Cal had a sudden urge to shower. The walls were lined with various health-related posters in both English and Spanish, but they didn't register with Calvin. He walked with his head down, slowly approaching a smoked sliding window. A large, hand-drawn arrow pointed down toward the counter, directing all who entered to sign in on a curling list taped to the small counter. The window slid open as he neared and a pair of green eyes appeared from behind it.

A woman looked up at him and smiled as she raked her eyes across his body. He felt naked. A slender hand pushed a clip-board toward him. "Sign in here," she pointed, "and if you have any insurance at all, indicate that here."

He nodded, taking the forms she was handing him. Cal cleared his throat but didn't speak. He was a little annoyed by looking through sunglasses indoors, but not so annoyed that he wanted to remove them. They were a barrier between him and the rest of the people in the room, a place he could hide. He licked his lips and quickly found a chair in the corner of the room, as far away from the rest of the people as he could get. His mood was far from social, so he didn't want to give anyone the impression that he might welcome a conversation or even casual eye contact. This visit wasn't about making friends. It was about taking care of business.

It took a few minutes to skim the forms. Privacy forms. In-come forms. It looked like pretty standard stuff. Cal licked his lips, then looked up at a sign he'd walked past. *Confidentiality guaranteed*, it read. The reason he'd picked this place. He needed his business kept quiet, no matter what the outcome. Even if the results were negative, just being seen in a place like this one could be bad for him, and there would be no way for him to explain it. He had enough problems right now and didn't need to compound them. People like him didn't go to free clinics, they went to fancy doctors on the other side of town.

Calvin filled out the forms, remembering to sign the name he'd chosen. He was now James Cowley. Unemployed and sin-gle. No insurance. The seeds of nervousness gnawed at his stomach. It would be a miracle if he didn't develop an ulcer before all was said and done. He'd tried his best to take a note from his wife. Tackle the problem one step at a time, and this test was the first step. Cal wiped his sweaty palms on the knees of his trousers, then stood up and walked back to the window. A few people turned their eyes to him as he moved, but Cal looked straight ahead and most of their gazes turned back to the television that was suspended from the corner of the room.

It didn't slide open this time, and Cal knocked gently. He looked down at the sign-in sheet, noticing that there were at least twenty names ahead of him. It didn't even look as if there were twenty people in the room. Finally, the window opened and the same eyes and forehead appeared. He handed his clipboard back through the window.

"Please have a seat and someone will be with you soon." She started to slide the window shut and Cal stopped her.

"How long is the wait?" he asked.

She looked down at his forms, flipping through them.

"No insurance?"

Cal shook his head.

"Unemployed?"

"Right now." His palms were sweating again.

The eyes surveyed him, then looked him straight in the eye.

Although he was nervous, Calvin knew it wouldn't show in his face. Years of corporate meetings had taught him how to conceal his thoughts.

"Okay," she said. "It might be a while. The doctor actually hasn't gotten here yet." She looked at his hand, still blocking the window. "Could you move your hand, sir?"

His cell phone trilled in his pocket.

"And you're going to have to turn that off, Mr. Unemployed." The chill in her voice was startling.

"I apologize." He lowered his voice, trying to appear as casual as possible. "Will I have to come back in for results?"

The eyes narrowed. "Depends on what you need. For some things, you just call in. We'll assign you a number so you can identify yourself on the phone. The nurse will fill you in on all that."

Satisfied, he nodded, then slowly removed his hand from the window. His stomach churned as the woman slammed the window shut. Calvin made his way back to his seat, wishing he'd had the foresight to bring a newspaper or something with him. He tripped on a little girl's toy and her mother glared at him.

"Sorry," he mumbled.

Her face was hard and weathered by time, although she couldn't have been more than twenty-five or twenty-six. Hard life, hard times. How different was this woman's life from the dead woman's, Davon's sister? She wore an acrylic sweater that obviously had seen better days. It was tan and had pilled and was stained on the right shoulder. Shame burned Cal's face as he stared at the girl. Anger glittered in her eyes and he looked away. She was obviously from a different world than he was, but they ended up sitting right next to each other in the free clinic. Supposedly, he had all the privileges and he could afford the best doctors, yet here he was, not even giving his real name. The irony of the situation was disturbing.

A pair of white-coated technicians walked in, wheeling a cart with various-sized artificial breasts on it. Apparently, they were going to demonstrate how to look for breast lumps. Calvin looked for a magazine to read, then hunkered down to wait.

Our Kind of People

"Who was that?" Louis's head throbbed as a sliver of panic raced though him.

Marie looked at her husband. "Who?"

"In the car I saw pulling away from the house? Who was it?"

"Is there a reason why you sound so angry?" She turned off the water in the sink, then grabbed a dishtowel to finish drying the last of the breakfast dishes.

Louis leaned on the leather kitchen chair with one hand, trying to steady himself. *Men don't faint.* "I'm not angry," he said too quickly, then flashed his wife a smile. "I was just wondering who'd visit us so early in the morning." Louis put the newspaper he was carrying down on the table, then pulled the chair out. He looked away from Marie. His mind raced. If that had been who he'd thought it was, all hell was about to break loose.

"One of our tenants. She was rather nice."

"Really? Who was it?" He already knew the answer, although *nice* hadn't been what he expected. *What in the world was she doing here? At his house, for Christ's sake?* Louis inhaled deeply and pretended to flip through the paper. There was no reason to get all worked up. He hadn't done anything. No one had ever been convicted because they'd thought about committing a crime. *That was all he'd done, was thought about it. Other than that damned kiss. And she'd kissed him, so all was good, right? I can't even convince myself.* Louis knew he was innocent of any wrongdoing, but he couldn't stop the prayer that he began to hear in his head.

"Josie Jennings. She was kind enough to bring back the tools you left at her place." Marie wiped her hands on a dishtowel, then came up behind her husband. She rested her hands on his shoulders. He jumped, then froze as she leaned down and kissed him gently on his cheek.

"Why so tense, Louis? It's Saturday, you should relax some." She kneaded his shoulders with her fingers. "She brought your driver's license, too. You really have to be more careful about that. Thank goodness she found it."

Louis's voice was quiet. "Josie was here? That was nice of her. What else did she say?" His voice was too high. It was inconceivable that that woman had actually been inside his house. The one he shared with his wife. What had they talked about?

Please God, Please help me. Please don't let Josie have been in here, telling my wife about the way I undress her with my eyes every time I see her. Puh-lease tell me she didn't mention how my dick was standing at attention when she came to the door damn near naked, or the way I don't look away when she looks at me with that look that says she wants to get buck naked and I don't look away 'cause I want to get buck naked, too. Dear God, please don't let her have mentioned anything about Al Green and the way I let her kiss me and how attracted

I was when she did, or how she had me running out the door like a
fifteen-year-old with no self-control.

He didn't remember leaving any tools, and as for his license, she'd pickpocketed him for all he knew. If he hadn't left her place as fast as he had, he might have left something far more incriminating.

"Nothing. Why? She was very nice. Had breakfast with me and the kids." She paused. "By the way, you missed it, but I might be persuaded to make you something else if you want."

Louis's expression was still and serious. "No reason. It's just odd that she would come here and even stranger that you would invite her in for breakfast. She didn't strike me as your type of person."

Marie's fingers stopped massaging. "And what kind of person is that? What is that supposed to mean?" Her voice had an edge to it.

Louis didn't want to get into a debate. "Nothing, honey. You're just so refined. You know what I mean. Josie didn't seem like to type of person you'd get along with normally."

"I think I'm insulted, Louis. Are you trying to say that I'm bourgie or something? I get along with anyone and you know it." Marie crossed her arms in front of her.

"Not what I meant." He floundered, searching for the right words, but was thankful at the turn that the conversation had taken. If anything worth noting had gone on with Josie, Marie would have surely called him on it by now. "You should be careful about who you let into the house, especially around the kids. We don't know anything about that woman, okay?"

"We know where she lives. She seemed really nice."

"People are not always what they seem." Louis forced a smile. "That may be true, but other than that, what do we *really* know about those people?"

"These people? Who's bourgie now?" she chuckled.

"Marie. I'm serious. That one calls me all the time. If you could put a tenant out for being annoying, her apartment would already be for rent. She makes me uncomfortable. She didn't have to come here and you know it." Louis's dark eyebrows slanted in a frown. "If you would just listen to me for once—"

"If I would just listen? I'm not one of the kids." Marie sighed. "Louis, if you have something to say you should say it. What in the hell is going on?"

Louis's stomach churned. How could he say what he needed to say without alarming her? He swallowed his despair, then tried to calm himself. "I want my family to be safe, that's all. It was a very purposeful thing to keep our private information private. Please think twice about opening the door to strangers, that's all I'm saying. I feel it would be safer for us that way, that's all."

Louis got up and went to Marie. She stood a few feet behind him, her mouth still open as she tried to figure out how a perfect morning could come so close to being ruined. He touched her face with his large hand, cupping her chin in his palm, then pulled her gently to him and held her snugly.

Marie stood frozen in disbelief for a minute, and then hugged him back. They were all entitled to a bad day, and Louis was certainly having his.

Louis Jr. raced down the field. Marie smiled, happy for him. A woman sitting next to her was hopping up and down, shouting for her son, and her elbow poked Marie in the side of her face. "Shit!" The word had flown from her mouth before she had time to think about it and the parents around her glared at her as if her words would pollute their kids for life, even if their young ears hadn't heard. She rubbed her cheek and blushed, trying to look apologetic. Not that she was. Kids were smart enough to know that they couldn't say everything their parents could. At least hers did.

"I'm sorry. I didn't mean to—"

"No worries." That was going to bruise. Marie opened and closed her jaw, wincing at the pain. She hated this. Why she'd agreed to taking Junior instead of Walani was beyond her. Louis liked soccer more, and dance was at least inside a climate-controlled building with comfortable seats and civilized parents who weren't screaming at the tops of their lungs.

"Can I go sit in the car?" Lishelle hadn't stopped pouting since she'd picked her up.

Marie shook her head, not taking her eyes off the game. She might not particularly enjoy being at the game, but she loved to watch her son. "You can read right here," she said. There was no way in hell she was letting Lishelle out of her sight. Not in this park. There was no telling what she'd end up doing.

Mai had called as she was leaving, complaining of being under the weather, and like a dummy, Marie agreed to take her son to soccer, too. She'd even volunteered to take Lishelle and Sarai so their mother could rest. What had she been thinking? Lishelle had made it clear that she was very unhappy with being at a kiddie soccer game. Marie was trying to be the nice "Auntie Ree" that she was known for being, but it was hard. She really wanted to tell her to put on her big-girl panties and suck it up, but she didn't, choosing instead to ignore her.

Junior's team scored a field goal and the crowd roared. Marie even yelled a little, watching the crazed antics of some of the other parents. These folks were serious about their kid sports. From the size of the crowd and the way the parents were acting, you would think that this wasn't a bunch of little kids at all, but some professional team in the soccer finals or something.

Putting Junior on a soccer team had been Louis's idea. He was the one that was the sports fan and thought that their son needed to be more active when he really wanted to be at home, reading or something. Marie had to admit it had been a good choice. Junior had only whined through the first two games and seemed to be okay now. The team ran down the field again and Louis Jr. caught her eye and waved. Marie smiled. He did seem to enjoy himself when he played. It was hard not to be caught up in his enthusiasm.

"Marie, I have to go pee." Lishelle sighed and rolled her eyes, poking Marie in the arm to get her attention.

It was evident to everyone around her that she was not enjoying herself at all, but that was no excuse for disrespect. "I'm still Auntie Ree to you."

"Whatever. You're not even my real aunt." Lishelle jutted her chin out in front of her, and Marie caught a glimpse of hardness that she hadn't realized was there before.

The look of enjoyment suddenly left Marie's face. Had she heard correctly? What in the hell had gotten into this girl? "That may be, but you still are not old enough to call me by my first name, Miss Thing. I'm the closest thing you have to a *real aunt*, so you'd better change your tone." Marie gave her a withering gaze. Neither Mai nor Calvin had any sisters. "Do you need me to take you to the bathroom?"

"I can go alone. I'm not a little kid, you know." Lishelle stood up, tossing her hair in a gesture of defiance.

"Like hell you can. Not in a public park. You just hold on." The mother of one of her son's teammates was behind her. Marie turned around and tapped her on the knee. "Listen, I have to take this one to the bathroom. Would you mind keeping an eye on Sarai and the boys for me? My boy and the Mott kid?" The woman nodded. Satisfied, Marie led Lishelle from the bleachers and across the field toward the restrooms.

They didn't talk as they walked. Marie remembered being thirteen, the age where little girls seemed to turn into monsters. She'd started to feel herself, as her mother would say, the same way Lishelle seemed to be doing now. All it took was one case of surliness and her mother had back-handed her right across the mouth so hard that Marie was convinced she'd been trying to get her to swallow her teeth. After that, she might have thought about it, but she never talked back to either one of her parents again. She'd been the smart preteen, putting on the pretense of being above all that acting-out, so her parents had never questioned. She'd gotten away with murder because she was labeled a good girl. Apparently Lishelle hadn't wisened up to that yet, or Mai hadn't slapped her hard enough for her head to spin around on her neck.

Where had those days gone? Parents didn't spank their children anymore, at least not out in the open. It wasn't PC. Marie shook her head as she watched Lishelle marching across the field. She tried hard to stay just in front or just behind Marie, like she was suddenly ashamed to be seen with the woman she'd adored just six months ago. The child thought she was going to the restroom, but as far as Marie could see, she was headed straight for a butt whipping, or at least she should be, but she doubted that Mai or Calvin would give her one. They didn't believe in that type of thing. Of course it was easy for her to think that. Her kids were still little and adoring. The dark cloud of hormones wasn't hanging over their heads yet.

Lishelle entered the bathroom first and Marie stood outside, leaning against the building, trying to watch her son play soccer. With a pang she realized that one day she and her kids would be going through the same thing Mai was with Lishelle, but she hoped not. She hoped that they would stay angels for many more years to come. It was doubtful, though, given all the quiet hell she'd raised. How many times had her own mother told her that her turn was coming?

The crowd of onlookers watching the game jumped to their feet and screamed, cheering on the team. Junior's team was really doing it up. *Where was Lishelle?* How long did it take, exactly, to use the bathroom these days? Marie glanced at her watch, then a quick and disturbing thought hit her. What if something had happened to her in the bathroom? Marie would never forgive herself. She should've taken a minute to check the restroom before the girl had gone in. There was no telling who might have been inside.

It took a few seconds for her eyes to adjust to the dimmer light inside the bathroom. The room smelled of disinfectant. Marie could hear male voices and she quickly looked up alarmed, then realized that they were coming from a vent, high on the wall. It must lead to the other side of the building where the men's restroom was located. She exhaled, thankful.

Lishelle was just inside the door with her back against the wall. Marie squinted, then cocked her head in disbelief. What in the world was the girl doing? "We're missing the game—"

Tears were streaming down Lishelle's face. She stood completely still, leaning against the wall and holding her stomach. Marie opened her mouth to speak and then realized that Lishelle wasn't hurt, she was listening. The voices registered. "I heard that they didn't even let him take his things out. They just escorted him from the building. No work, no pay until the investigation is finished."

They laughed. It sounded like two people. "I wonder what he told his wife. If I know Mai, she probably beat his ass all up and down the street when she found out."

Found out? Found out what? They were talking about Calvin. Mai's Calvin. Mai hadn't mentioned that Calvin was suspended or fired. The shock of discovery hit her, making Marie gasp.

Lishelle was crying. She'd heard them talking about her father, and from the looks of things, she was as surprised about the news as Marie was.

Marie slammed open a stall door. The sound it made reverberated through the building. It had the effect she intended because the men stopped talking. Marie turned on the water and grabbed a handful of the brown recycled paper towels and wet it. "C'mon," she said. "Let's wash your face. The game is almost over. We can go soon."

Lishelle sniffled as Marie wiped her face.

"Uh-uh. You hold your head up. You didn't do anything. Whatever they are talking about, it has nothing to do with you." She finished cleaning her up and tossed the crumpled towels into the trash. Marie looked Lishelle in her eyes. The haughtiness she'd spied earlier was gone, replaced now by a mask of uncertainty. Poor kid was having one hell of a day already.

"Auntie Ree?"

"Yes?" Marie pushed her questions to the back of her mind and tried her best to smile.

"Did my father lose his job? What are we going to do?"

Marie rubbed Lishelle's back. "I don't know, baby, but that's for your parents to worry about, not you. And I'm sure everything will be fine."

Her words seemed to make her feel better because Lishelle smiled tentatively for the first time since she'd picked her up. Marie told her the truth when she'd said she had no idea what was going on. She really didn't have a clue. As far as she could tell, everything was as it always was in the Mott household. It was unusual for Mai to keep something like this to herself. Marie thought that the three of them shared everything, but it occurred to her that maybe Mai wasn't the one that'd been doing the sharing over the years. Perhaps her life wasn't as perfect as it always seemed. Maybe Mai was just better at keeping her problems to herself than she and Kennedy were.

A Taste of the Truth

Swig was a breath of modern smack in the middle of downtown. Kennedy was pleased that they'd agreed on the location, but confused. They'd always eaten dinner on ladies' night out, and unless things had changed, the only food on the menu at Swig would be appetizers. She hadn't even gotten there yet and her stomach was growling up a storm.

Kennedy paused as a gentleman swung the door open for her. She flashed a smile, then continued her sashay into the martini bar. Her leather skirt fit her like a glove and flared out just above her knee; the confidence in her walk sent it swaying with every step. It wasn't yet seven o'clock but the place was already packed. Conversation buzzed beneath the sound of a four-piece jazz group that played in the corner. The hostess looked at her expectantly.

"Meeting friends," she said and immediately scanned the crowd with her eyes. Hopefully Marie and Mai had arrived already and gotten a table. It was a warmish evening, and even though she'd lived in San Antonio many years, Kennedy couldn't resist the charm of the water that lay just outside the rear doors of the bar. Swig was on the west bank of the city's famous River Walk, and although it was sure to be teaming with tourists, it was still the best spot to watch people. If her friends had done it right, they would have already secured a seat there.

They were going to have a lot to talk about. She'd made a promise to herself that she would push her disagreement with Marie to the side. After what she'd read in the paper and then online in the business journal, their tiff was small news. Mai had a lot to tell them about or at least talk through and Kennedy planned to be there for her if need be. Kennedy wasn't sure yet what had happened, but the girl was sure to be stressed whatever the case, even if she was the Queen of Cool.

Only Marie was waiting. She sat at the very corner of the patio, nearest the water. As usual, there was a crowd of people around her. Marie was that way. No matter where she went, she made friends. Folks just liked her. That was certainly one of the reasons neither she nor Mai could stay angry with her for long. She was so charismatic that Kennedy was sure she had missed her one true calling. That woman should have been in politics or on the stage. It wouldn't be a surprise if that is where she ended up. How one person could always be a party all by herself was amazing.

Kennedy paused to take in the scene. It had just gotten dark and the River Walk was ablaze with lights hanging from the ancient trees towering overhead. Everything was all lit up for the holiday season, even though it was almost sixty degrees.

Every table had several glasses on it and the mood out here

was as festive as that inside. Laughter mingled with the sounds of the upbeat jazz music from the inside. Small speakers were strategically placed so the band sounded almost as good on the patio as it did everywhere else in the bar. Beyond where Marie was sitting, a gondola filled with gawking tourists floated past and the people on the patio waved.

"Hey, woman," Kennedy said.

Three of the people talking to Marie chorused their hellos.

"Hey, sweetie. I was beginning to think I was on my own. Let me introduce you to my new friends." Marie grinned. "Everybody, this is my friend Kennedy. She's here for the ladies' night I was telling you about."

Kennedy smiled sheepishly and shook the hands she was offered. More than one of the men devoured her with their eyes.

"Does that mean we have to go?" one of the men asked.

"I'm afraid so." Kennedy winked at him, giving him her Miss America smile. "Ladies' night is for ladies. It was good meeting you though."

Kennedy waited while they said their good-byes. She watched and tried not to be critical as two of the men pressed their business cards into Marie's hand. She was silent as she waited for them to move away. "I don't know how Louis does it. It must be hard to be married to you. You just attract people."

"He's not worried and neither am I. Louis knows where he stands. He knows that I am married to the best man for me."

"If you say so. Where's Mai?"

Marie smiled. "Not here yet. I think she's having a rough day."

"Tell me about it. A rough few days is more like it. Did you order?"

Marie shook her head and Kennedy pulled out the heavy wrought-iron chair and sat down. She waved at the waitress who was across the patio scribbling on her pad while she laughed with other customers. "I'm so hungry. I have got to eat something or I'll be drunk as a skunk before we're done. And I do think I need to stay sober tonight. You look good."

"Thanks. You too." Marie answered her tentatively, as if she were afraid of what was to come next.

"How was your week? You were gone, right?" Kennedy cleared her throat.

The waitress interrupted them before she could answer.

"I think I need your appetizer sampler. Plus I'd like a Swig." She turned to Marie. "Have you tried those? They're the best thing here. The favorites."

"Uh, what's in them?" Marie stared at the small menu.

"What do you care? It's all alcohol. She'll have one too."

The waitress shrugged, then walked away, leaving Marie staring at Kennedy with an open mouth.

"You're sort of presumptuous, don't you think?"

Kennedy counted to three. *She isn't worth the fight.* Although she'd told herself that everything was water under the bridge, she obviously still carried some resentment. She exhaled heavily. "You want me to get her back? I apologize."

She shook her head again. "Hey, have you heard anything about Calvin? I overheard the strangest thing at the park. It sounded like they were talking about him and I just hope not. Bad part is Lishelle was with me and she heard them, too."

Kennedy's eyes widened. People were already talking, she

wasn't surprised. "It was in the paper. Believe it. I wonder why Mai hasn't said anything?"

"I'm not sure. But she never really tells us anything, does she?"

Marie was right. Mai never told them anything really personal, at least not bad things. It was like she wanted them to think she was perfect or something. Hearing Marie give voice to her thoughts left her feeling disappointed.

How had their friendship become so one-sided? And why hadn't they noticed it before? She'd hate to think that the two of them had been so wrapped up in their own lives that they couldn't see what their friend needed. "I thought the same thing. It's kind of sad. That makes me feel like she doesn't trust us or something."

Marie shook her head in disagreement. "I don't think it's about us at all." The two women sat in silence for several minutes. The waitress finally bought their drinks and left. Kennedy immediately sipped hers.

Marie looked at hers questioningly, then gingerly lifted her martini glass for a sip, and then smiled. She carefully returned it to the table, trying her best not to spill any. "Okay, you were right. This is pretty good."

Kennedy smiled. "I would never steer you wrong. This is the signature drink here." The alcohol quickly warmed both her insides and her disposition. "Food'd better come soon." They both were soon laughing as they sipped at their drinks. Kennedy's head was already starting to swim. "So, tell me." She couldn't ever be mad at Marie long. She looked at her friend with amusement.

She hesitated. "It was a good week."

"C'mon. You have to do better than that. Should I be expecting any phone calls?"

"I apologized—"

"Don't be defensive. I'm honestly curious, considering that you're the mack-mommy and all."

"Who's the mack-mommy?" Mai finally joined them.

Both Kennedy and Marie stared at her, not sure what to say. Although she was dressed, something wasn't quite right. Both Mai and Calvin liked to look good all the time, and although she didn't look bad, Mai just didn't look as together as she normally did. She looked just ordinary, and Mai Mott never did anything ordinary.

Kennedy looked at her friend from head to toe, trying to take it all in before Mai sat down. Where was her one trademark thing? Mai always wore that one thing that stood out from the rest of her outfit, a fabulous bag, great shoes, a Hermes scarf. Of the three of them, she had the best sense of style. Normally. Where was that item today? Not only did nothing stand out, nothing seemed to go together either. This was very strange for the friend that always redressed them or added the finishing touch to their outfits before they went somewhere. Being friends with Mai was like having their own personal *What Not to Wear* consultant only a phone call away. Today she looked like a *Wanted* billboard for the fashion police.

Marie stared at Mai, too, her eyebrows slightly raised. While the two of them obviously had gotten dressed for a night out on the town, Mai wore wrinkled-looking khakis that even Banana Republic would reject with flat suede shoes and a button-down denim shirt. Who wore denim on top? Her hair wasn't even done, much less perfect, and her makeup was almost nonexistent. Her eyes were puffy, too. What happened to that two-hundred-dollar-an-ounce under-eye-circle preventative she'd been touting? From the looks of things, she was taking her husband's misfortune very hard.

Mai made her rounds, air-kissing first Marie, then Kennedy. "Did you guys order me one?"

Surprised, Kennedy covered her nose and mouth with her hand, then quickly removed it. Had Mai brushed her teeth today? She gave Marie a questioning glance. It was apparent from the look on her face that she'd noticed too.

"The waitress will be back in a minute. She saw you sit down." Kennedy raised her eyebrows then lowered them while looking at Marie. She was more than concerned for her friend. This was going to be a very interesting evening, indeed. "Marie was just telling me about her escapades this week."

Marie hesitated, still baffled by Mai's transformation. Where in the world had their friend gone? "Like I said, it was a good week, hectic, but good."

Mai slid into her chair. "Girl, c'mon. You know what she wants to know. Did you meet anyone? You know that's what you were doing. Out hoeing as usual."

"Harsh." Marie sipped her drink. "I wouldn't exactly call it that. Where in the hell is the waitress? We need to get this woman a drink. I enjoy meeting new people."

Mai leaned in. "Okay. I like to meet people, too. But tell me how you move from meeting them to whatever you say doesn't happen afterwards?" She winked at Kennedy conspiratorially.

Kennedy quickly recovered from her surprise. She was the one who usually jumped on Marie. Was this Mai's way of deflecting any questions they might have? Make someone else the center of attention and cut them off before they'd had a chance to even think about asking. "Yeah, girl, you need to give me a few pointers," she muttered hastily. It was better to make light of the situation and try to defuse some of the tension before things got nasty. She made a "play along" face at Marie. "Tell me how it goes."

Marie took the hint and leaned in conspiratorially. She mimed dialing on a phone on the bistro table. "Hey, It's Marie. Thanks for keeping me company on the flight. Uh-huh. It was nice meeting you too. I have to admit, I don't talk to strangers while I'm traveling, but buying me a drink on the plane, that was smooth." She laughed and threw her head back.

Kennedy opened her mouth to speak, but Marie held up her finger to stop her. Her own thumb was still pressed against her ear and her pinky was still near her mouth, as if she were holding a phone headset. "Yeah, so what are you getting into tonight?" She let out a fake laugh again, running her index finger around the rim of her martini glass. "Me? You'd better be careful with those jokes or HBO is gonna come calling. Hmmm. It's kinda late, but I suppose I could meet you for a drink."

They both stared at her, wide-eyed.

"What?" She looked from one to the other. "You told me to show you how. Well, that's how." Marie sat back in her chair just as the appetizers arrived. Her little demonstration had shocked her friends.

Mai laughed, then smoothed her hair. She was more comfortable now. "I told you, you were hoeing." She sipped the drink the waitress placed in front of her and grimaced. "Just flirting my ass."

"Whatever." Marie shrugged dismissively and put a few of the appetizers onto her plate.

"Okay, hold up. I agree with Mai. That doesn't sound like just flirting. I'm not trying to start anything, but whatever happened to being true to your love and monogamy and all that?"

Marie laughed in mid-chew and almost choked. She took a sip of water. "I never said I believed in monogamy."

Both Kennedy and Mai stopped breathing for a second, staring at their friend unbelievingly. Kennedy recovered first. "What? Of course you do. We all do. That's why we get married, right? Louis was your be all and end all, remember?"

Marie crossed her arms in front of her. She really was going to have to break it down for them. "Sweeties, marriage ain't got a thing to do with this. I suppose you think that love and sex are the same thing, too?" She paused. "Puh-lease. So many women get that confused. I married my husband because we had similar goals. We planned to make a life together, and we have. Sure, it hasn't turned out exactly as I would have liked, but it's good."

"So why jeopardize all that?" Mai's voice had a critical tone to it.

"Who said I am? Louis gets it. I can't deny that I am married to the absolute best man for me, I've said that before. But I don't get it twisted. I travel, I meet people, and sometimes an occasional thing happens, but I keep them to one time only." She looked over at Kennedy. "That's why I never give them my phone number. Sex is just that. Sex. It doesn't make a relationship. Love and respect is something else."

Kennedy was totally bewildered by her friend's words. "That's not what I call respect. How would you feel if Louis was having an affair and you didn't know? You wouldn't feel too respected, would you?"

"I never said I was having an affair. Ladies, you're just too idealistic about things. Let's be real. Sex is not an affair either. I told you, it's just sex. That's that whole tree falling in the woods argument. If I'm not there to hear it, who the hell cares?"

"Wait, wait." Kennedy couldn't believe what she was hearing. "So, you're saying that you don't care if your husband sleeps with another woman."

"I never said that. What I said was if it happens, so be it. He just better take care of his business and not bring home no diseases or bastard children, and we're all good."

"If you say so. I thought you said nothing happened."

"We're talking hypotheticals here."

Mai didn't know what to say. She couldn't really argue with what Marie was saying, especially if both she and Louis believed it. And she was so matter-of-fact with her answer that she was almost convinced that her friend really believed in what she was saying, too.

"It seems like you have it all together then. No diseases, no kids, no outside relationships, but the occasional sexual encounter, that's all good, huh?" Kennedy gave an anxious little cough. "Interesting, huh, Mai?" Kennedy raised her arm to flag down the waitress. "I think we need more drinks. What about you? What's going on in your world? Do you have it all together?"

Mai fidgeted in her chair, then shrugged. She spoke while looking down at the table. "It's the way it always is, you know. I have ten thousand too many things to do. The kids have sports. Calvin works too hard." She looked up and put her hand on Marie's arm. "Thanks for picking up the slack for me. I've been a little overwhelmed lately. Seems like I am okay for months at a time and then I wake up one day and I'm just tired. Anyway," she waved her hand in the air as if to dismiss everything she'd just said, "you know how it is."

"Hmm. I just don't know how you do it. You were always so good at juggling." Marie was glad to have the attention off of her for a change.

"It's nothing. I think it's how I'm made or something. Although I do think I've been falling down on the job lately."

Was Mai about to actually *share?* Kennedy wondered. "Really, how so?"

Mai seemed hesitant. "Well, Lishelle has been terrible. We got called to school for her last week. I was mortified. I thought I was going to die." Both women looked at Mai expectantly, waiting for her to spill more details.

"I'm not going to tell you what she did, so don't ask." Mai blushed and her face darkened.

"She *was* a little rude and withdrawn when I had her at the soccer game," Marie added.

"What? Why didn't you tell me? If we let it get out of hand now, she'll be impossible by the time she's sixteen."

"She didn't mention anything to you? I called her on her behavior. There were things at the game that she seemed to be very upset about." Marie stared at Kennedy.

Was she baiting Mai? Kennedy's eyebrows lifted in anticipation. It might be a little cruel, but she wanted to hear the details and help if she could, but she knew that Mai was not the type to ask for help.

"She was fine when she got home." She hesitated. "At least I think she was. She went straight to her room to talk to her friends on the Internet. Like I said, she's been really withdrawn. I don't remember this happening to me when I was her age."

Alarm bells went off in Kennedy's head. "I remember it happening to me. And you should watch her. There's no telling what she could be getting into." Was Mai aware of all the sickos that were out there lurking in cyberspace? Did she even watch the news? "What did Calvin say about her behavior?"

Mai shrugged. "What he always says. He tells me to handle it. That man is too busy working to pay too much attention to the kids. Or me for that matter."

Kennedy and Marie exchanged a knowing glance. It was different to hear that Mai's life wasn't all peaches and cream. It was unlike Mai to complain about her relationship. "Do I sense trouble in paradise?"

"No trouble, just annoyance. Hell, we met at the school to talk about Lishelle, and he went right back to work afterwards and left me to take care of things. I get tired of doing it *all* sometimes."

Marie's heavy lashes flew up. "When did you go to the school?"

Mai sat back, both hands on the table. "Friday, why?"

"*This* Friday?" Marie and Kennedy spoke at the same time, then were silent.

"What? Why do you ask?" Mai tensed her jaw, betraying her frustrations as Kennedy contemplated what she should say next. A woman only wanted to hear so much about her man from her friends, she knew that. Say the wrong thing, and their fifteen-year friendship could be dashed on the rocks.

She spoke slowly. "I thought he lost his job."

The air around the table was so still it was as if the three women were sitting in a vacuum.

"What? That's crazy. Where did you hear that?" Mai searched the faces of her friends expectantly.

"I heard two men in the bathroom at the park talking about it." Marie's voice was hushed, almost as if it hurt to say the words. "At the soccer game. That's what upset Lishelle so much. We heard them through a vent in the wall, and there are only so many *Mais* in this town."

Mai smiled in exasperation. "Don't you think if my husband was unemployed I'd know?"

You would think so. Kennedy's expression grew still and serious. "Mai, it was in the paper. I saw it myself."

Mai's face flickered then it was calm again, similar to a television screen with a poor signal. Kennedy watched her intently as she first sipped her drink, carefully placed her glass back on the table, then used the white napkin that had been on her lap to carefully dab at her lips. She cleared her throat then finally looked back up at her friends.

She took a deep breath and adjusted her smile. "Ladies, don't you know that the news is all hearsay? They have been known to be wrong, too. If something like that had happened, Calvin would tell me." She paused. "Now. Can we please discuss something else? It's been a little rough lately, but we've just had a few minor bumps in the road of life. I got this."

A momentary look of embarrassment crossed Kennedy's face. She felt bad for Mai. She was trying so hard to keep it together. Wouldn't it be easier to just talk it out among friends? She sighed. Every one of them was different, but it was all good. They all dealt with things in their own way. Mai was her friend, and if this was her way, then so be it. "You know what," she said. "I hate to break up a party, but I have to go and check on my father." She pushed her chair out from the table.

Marie cleared her throat, pushing her chair out too. "I need to go anyway. I told Louis I would be home early so we could spend some time together. I've been gone all week and he needs a break."

"I hope you two aren't leaving because of me." Mai's eyes widened.

They both shook their heads, speaking at the same time. "Of course not." Kennedy noticed that Mai seemed much more her old self now, almost as if hearing bad news had strengthened her. It was amazing to her how Mai always seemed to blossom in the face of adversity. She needed to learn that herself one day. When things got tough, she crumpled.

Mai didn't make eye contact with either of her friends. She pushed her chair in hurriedly and placed a few bills on the table. "I'll talk to you guys tomorrow." She turned and waved at them over her shoulder, foregoing the usual good-bye hugs. Her exit was so abrupt that it barely had time to register with either Marie or Kennedy.

They stared at each other wide-eyed, both frozen in place. Kennedy took some cash from her bag and placed that on the table. "That ought to cover it." She and Marie started ambling toward the door. "You think she believed us?"

"Absolutely," Marie said. "Mai's got one helluva game face. You know she likes things to look perfect. Think we should warn Cal?"

Kennedy tugged on her friend's arm. "Are you nuts? I think we should mind our business. Mai is only going to tolerate so much of our meddling. I think we should go home and then check on our girl tomorrow. She needs to handle her stuff in her own way."

Marie agreed. Sometimes you just had to go away and process to make sense of a bad situation. "However she decides to handle her business, I'll be there for her."

Kennedy smiled. "That's what we do." She waved at the waitress again. "You know, you may be mean, evil, and have a strange thing going on with your husband, but you are certainly a loyal friend."

The Truth Shall Set You Free

Cal sat with his head down. He clenched his teeth together, listening to the annoying drumming sound that Maxfield was making on the restaurant table. "Could you stop that?" His voice was gruff.

"Hey, I'm not the one in trouble. You asked me for help, remember?"

"You're right. I can't think with you doing that." Everything was a distraction. He couldn't keep a train of thought going in his head.

Louis returned from the bathroom. "I don't see what's to think about. You tell your wife and you solve the problem together."

Calvin whipped his head up. Was he nuts? "You obviously don't live with my wife." He shook his head in disbelief. "She would be devastated. Mai would be crushed. I just can't do that to her."

Maxfield's mouth twitched with amusement.

"I see nothing funny. Are you going to help or what?"

"Damn. I'm sorry," Maxfield said. "It's just that if this child that you haven't met does exist, she's gonna know sooner or later. And then what? You can't keep this a secret forever, you know what I'm saying?"

"I don't see either of you spilling your guts to your significant others. What about you Louis? Why are you hiding from Marie?" He didn't wait for an answer. "The way I see it, I can order one of those home paternity tests. They have to let me see the girl, especially if I tell them that I'm willing to pay the money." Calvin's voice shook as he spoke, as if he wasn't sure of his plan himself.

"What?" Louis looked at his friend in surprise. "How in the hell are you going to do that? If I know Mai, she knows where every penny is. Man, do you even have a checkbook?"

Calvin closed his eyes, squeezing them shut. Louis was right. Mai paid all the bills. The best he had was an ATM card, and moving that kind of money in dribs in drabs would take forever, and he didn't have forever. At best, he had a few weeks, considering that Davon was supposed to catch up with him in a few days. Maybe Maxfield was right. Perhaps he should bite the bullet and go talk to Mai. Maybe she would understand. Or maybe she would have a nervous breakdown. Or worse yet, kick his narrow ass all the way up and down their street and burn up all his shit in some *Waiting to Exhale* fit. He hadn't even told her about his suspension yet. He couldn't risk that.

Maxfield took a swig of his beer, then cleared his throat. "Look, I wouldn't worry too much. She can take it. Our women are strong. Lots of women are married to men with kids somewhere else. This ain't new. It happens all the time."

"It's new in my family. If Mai found out, she would leave me. After she broke me in two. This is some fucked-up shit. You're the lawyer, Max. Tell me what to do." Cal's mind reeled with confusion.

"I think you should tell her. Matter of fact, I see no way around it."

Louis huffed. "Man, since when did you become so honest? What happened to the man who was telling me I should find me a little thing on the side while Marie was gone?"

"Hey, I'm just being real. That home paternity test thing won't work for two reasons. First, you have to have access to the child. You have to be able to take a sample from her mouth. *With a cotton swab.* What teenager you know is going to let some man she has never seen before stick a cotton swab in her mouth? She might not even talk to you. If she thinks you're her father, she's bound to be pissed that you're just showing up now, after thirteen years. Even if they let you see her, they won't let you see her alone. Second, if you do a home test, it won't be admissible in court. For that to happen, you gonna have to man up and go to a collection center to have the DNA done. And then you're back at square one. No kid."

Cal mulled over Maxfield's words, stirring uneasily in his chair. He wasn't particularly interested in court admissibility. "I just gotta know, that's all. I'm not really interested in pursuing this legally. It might come out worse than it is."

"And then you're back to square one," Louis said. "They want money. Which you don't have. And if things go the way they are going, you won't have any means to get any more either, not without telling Mai. And do you really think she is going to let you spend your nest egg on some child she's never met nor heard of when you have others at home to take care of? She'll fight that tooth and nail. You're fucked either way. I'm starting to agree with Max. She's a strong woman. Tell her."

Maxfield nodded. "That's right. That way they'll have to make it a legal battle. If you're going to be fucked, you might as well fuck yourself than let someone else do it."

Lishelle stared into the rain as the car entered her school's circular driveway. Her mother hummed along with the radio in the front seat and Lishelle tried to ignore her, concentrating instead on the raindrops as they slid down her window. The car slowed down and she grabbed her backpack.

Several faculty members stood by the curb in the rain, holding huge umbrellas emblazoned with the school logo. The yellow letters seemed too bright on the dismal day. The greeters snatched open car doors, escorting the younger children to their classrooms and directing others. As soon as it slid to a stop, Lishelle opened the car door and hopped out, ignoring her younger sister and her mother's words of encouragement. Sarai left the car more slowly, calling after Lishelle as she walked away from her. Lishelle barely looked over her shoulder, knowing that one of the faculty members would make sure that Sarai would get where she was supposed to be. She waved over her shoulder at Sarai and her mother, then pulled her windbreaker closer around her body.

Lishelle was glad to be free of the madness in her house, even if it was just for a few hours. Was it written somewhere that when you become a parent you become corny as hell? Was it even necessary to remind her to do a good job in school? It wasn't like she was a baby or even a bad student that needed a daily reminder. Why in the hell couldn't she go to a normal school, where she could wear jeans instead of a skirt and stupid knee-hi socks that did nothing to keep her warm? A few raindrops found their way to the unprotected skin on the back of her neck and she shivered, walking faster away from the carpool line and into the building.

As soon as she walked through the door, Lishelle felt herself relax; some of the tension that had built up in her shoulders melted away. Everything at home was so tense lately, she almost hated to go there. At school it was different. Sure, there were the usual pain-in-the-butt classes and a few people that got on her last nerve, but otherwise, she could be whoever she wanted to be. The first bell had not yet rung, and the hallway was abuzz with laughter. She paused just inside the door to shake off some of the water, then made her way toward her locker, inhaling the damp smell that permeated the hallway and reminded her of a wet dog. No, a bunch of wet dogs.

As soon as she rounded the corner, she spotted her friends huddled around the locker area they shared. Sk8tr had Kool-Aid dyed her hair overnight; her bright blond was streaked with red. A grin spread across Lishelle's face. It looked good. She wished that she had the courage to do something like that, not that a Kool-Aid dye would work on her own chestnut-brown fuzz.

"Good Girl Mott." Sk8tr called her by the nickname that had now seemed to take the place of the sister-girl name she'd grown to hate.

Lishelle nodded at the group of kids.

"Can you puh-lease fix those socks?" They all looked down at Lishelle's thin legs with disdain.

Her stomach quivered. She hated that they checked her out so hard. There was nothing wrong with her socks. They had a few splashes of water on them, but otherwise they were stark white and perfectly in place just below her knee. Her mother would have had it no other way. The only thing wrong with them was that they were where they were supposed to be. "My mom dropped me off." She blushed, then bent down and pushed the socks downward anyway.

They nodded in approval, then carried on their conversation. Lishelle tried to act nonchalant, but she listened intently to the chatter her friends made. They were meeting for lunch, maybe to try and go off campus somewhere. Lishelle's breath caught in her throat. "We aren't supposed to leave the grounds. Only seniors can do that."

Sk8tr sneered at her. "Whatever. You're so busy worrying about what we're *supposed* to do. It's no wonder you don't have any fun.

Lishelle looked down at the floor, biting her lip. "I'm just saying, Sophia."

The girl bristled at the sound of her given name. She opened her mouth to speak, but was interrupted by a teacher stepping outside her door, just a few feet from where they were standing. "Shouldn't you girls be on your way to homeroom?" The woman stood with her hands behind her back and one eyebrow raised. The girls glared at each other but didn't speak; instead they moved faster, a few throwing books into their lockers while others hurried away.

Lishelle closed her locker and headed to her homeroom. What would happen if I wasn't such a good girl, she wondered. Would they find something else to call her? What if she were sick and tired of doing what she was told? The bell sounded, interrupting her thoughts. She picked up the pace, hurrying to make it to her room before the second bell. If she were tardy, her mother would be on her case even more. One thing she'd learned from her parents. The difference between being upstanding citizens, rather than a junkie and a womanizer, was that the upstanding citizens kept all their shit undercover. Likewise, the difference between a good girl and a bad girl was that a good girl didn't get caught. A neat smirk appeared on her face just as Lishelle broke into a trot. And that made it easier to get away with everything.

Herbal tea, yoga, meditation. None of it worked. Mai flung a pot-holder across her kitchen. All of the so-called remedies, things to calm your nerves and relieve stress, all of them, were a crock of shit. Her hands were shaking like a junkie in withdrawal. *I'm no goddamned junkie*, she thought, *just a woman with a case of nerves and a family life that's a stone-cold mess.*

She grabbed a glass and pressed it to the ice dispenser in the refrigerator door, holding her breath as the cubes dropped. Her hand trembled and she struggled to steady it as it filled with water. This would pass and she would feel better with time. After hours of searching, she still hadn't found a place on the Internet where she could order Valium. She leaned back on the counter and sipped her water, emptying the glass in one long gulp. It froze her chest, hurting as it went down. Mai welcomed the chill. She'd been sweating all morning and it was almost unbearable. If she were older she would think she was going through menopause, but she knew that she wasn't old enough to be experiencing personal summers.

The day had started out fine. She'd even felt good this morning when she'd dropped the kids off. And then it went downhill from there. Every little thing annoyed her and made her want to cry. She'd sweated on and off, took two showers and searched the Internet endlessly. Nothing that needed doing had gotten done. All that and it was only one o'clock in the afternoon. Mai was dog-tired.

She poured herself more water. Mai was a smart woman and it was obvious that she had become just a little too dependent on Valium. She sipped her water, sloshing some of it out of the glass and onto her hand. She had to get it together before the kids got home.

The alarm system sounded, announcing the opening of the garage door. She jumped, spilling water down the front of her blouse. Mai swore under her breath and grabbed the front of it, pulling it away from her chest.

"Oh, hey." Cal looked surprised to see her. He walked past her and opened the refrigerator door.

Mai froze. As casually as she could manage, she asked, "What are you doing here?" She stood where she was, holding her shirt to keep the ice-cold water away from her. Her body was tense as she waited for his answer. She wanted him to tell her the truth, but part of her didn't want to find out that she was the last to know what everyone else did. She didn't want to know that the man she had trusted and sacrificed for was lying to her. He hadn't lied directly, of course, but a lie by omission was a lie just the same.

"I live here." He closed the door and kissed his wife on the forehead. "You okay? You look like you're having a rough day."

"I'm fine." Mai's voice was strained. "I mean what are you doing here now? It's the middle of the day."

Cal paused and looked his wife in the eyes. Mai got the sense that he wanted to tell her something, that he was holding back. "I thought I'd work from home. No crime in that, right?"

Mai sensed an odd twinge of disappointment. She wanted to believe Cal, but something was just not right.

A Hot Mess

Mai looked a hot mess. Again. Marie didn't say a word about it though, as they drove to the mall. She didn't care what Kennedy said, she had to go and see about her friend, and from what she could tell, it was good thing she had. The woman obviously needed some kind of diversion to help her relax. Her hair was in disarray and her clothes weren't typical, again. Everyone was entitled to a bad day, but so many in a row was definitely out of character for Mrs. Mott. And she was chattering endlessly, as if she was restless and unable to concentrate on just one thing, so it was almost impossible to get a word in edgewise.

Marie rubbed her forehead to help remove the creases that had settled there. No use in worrying herself into a few new wrinkles. She pulled her car up to valet parking in front of Neiman's. A Monday off was certainly a luxury and Marie had planned to enjoy the day shopping and relaxing with her friend at one of San Antonio's newest luxury shopping spots. She didn't need anything in particular, but the sweeping landscape of the mall with its extensive foliage and running water was sure to be a soother for both of them. And from what she could tell, Mai needed soothing a helluva lot more than she did.

She flipped her visor down and reapplied her lipstick just as the valet attendant reached her door, then winked at Mai. They grabbed their bags and left the car. Marie didn't even care if Mai didn't want to discuss any of her drama. She could keep it all to herself if she wanted to. Sometimes the mere presence of a friendly person would help, and being there was the least she could do. Mai would tell what she wanted to in her own time. Or she wouldn't. Whatever the case, they were friends and Marie was certain that Mai would do the same for her. But in the meantime, there was a sale going on.

As soon as they stepped into the mall, both Marie and Mai started to relax. Marie watched her friend's face and noticed a visible difference. She immediately seemed less tense. Most of the mall was outdoors, so it was good thing that the weather was mild. There was just no telling what South Texas would offer up sometimes.

A jewel in the Hill Country, the mall was paved with limestones and the elaborate landscaping was labeled so that you would know exactly what grew outside Tiffany's if you cared to. A stream meandered through the length of it, complete with small waterfalls. La Cantera was more an oasis or botanical garden than an institutional shopping area.

"You ready to get your shop on?" Marie quipped. "Do we need to get some coffee first?"

"I think I might need some. To calm my nerves." Mai's voice

was hushed. She fumbled with the opening of her bag as they walked toward Starbucks.

Marie pursed her lips. Marie loved fine things, but she loved fine things on sale even better. Two weeks ago, Mai wouldn't have dared to stop for coffee. She would not have wanted to waste a minute of her shopping time, leaving Marie racing to catch up with her as she dove into Neiman's head on. Marie couldn't take it anymore. "Where is my friend Mai and what have you done with her?" Although she was joking, her voice held a certain sense of urgency. Over the years, Mai had been the rock that held them all together, so she couldn't be the one that crumbled to pieces.

The two women stopped near a bench, and Mai sank into it. The tenseness of her jaw betrayed her frustrations and her eyes filled up with tears. She covered her mouth with her hand.

"I was just joking. I didn't mean anything by that." Marie was stunned. Not only had the shopping diva disappeared, but so had the woman who was always strong for her friends. Mai seemed to be crumbling inside her own private hell. "You need to talk about anything?"

Mai shook her head, obviously fighting back tears.

Marie sat down next to her. She was at a loss. What, exactly, do you do when you friend is perched moments from tears in a public place? "Can I do something to help at least? You don't have to tell me anything." In all the time she had known Mai, Marie had never seen her this distraught. She would have never thought that Calvin's losing his job would be a cause for all this. If anything, it was more in Mai's character to rally and find a way that they would come out looking better than ever when all was said and done.

Mai sniffed. "Well, you might be able to help."

Marie couldn't read her face, but she certainly wanted to help her friend. Mai had been there for her time and time again. "Okay—"

"You can get me some Valium."

Marie looked into Mai's stone face. What in the hell was she talking about?

"I'm out. No refills."

"I didn't even know you took Valium. That's easy to solve. Make an appointment to see your doctor. You can get more if you need it."

Mai shook her head. "They won't give me any more."

The gravity of what she was saying hit Marie. She was out and couldn't get any more because she'd used up everything before she was supposed to. How long had this been going on? "Mai, I don't take Valium. Even if I did, I couldn't give it to you."

Mai rolled her eyes. "I know that." Mai knew the answer before she'd even asked. Desperation had her grabbing at straws. "But don't you have any supplies or something? Maybe you have some Xanax or something else like it. Isn't that what you do, give the doctors samples?"

Marie's shock yielded to anger. "What you are asking me to do could jeopardize my job. I'm a pharmaceutical sales rep, not a drug pusher. And I don't have any access to controlled substances anyway." Her nose flared. "I can't even believe you are asking me this. You were a pharmacist! Unbelievable." Marie stood up and walked into Starbucks, leaving Mai sitting on the bench.

She stood in line and fought back her own tears. Mai had

turned into a nut. First she was needy and looking all disheveled, and then she was an insensitive asshole. In all the time she'd worked in the pharmaceutical industry, none of her friends had asked her for so much as a bottle of lotion. Now Mai was asking her to risk her job by supplying her with narcotics. What had she missed?

She ordered her coffee and stepped back to wait. The magic of the shopping trip had certainly been spoiled. So much for therapeutic hunting and gathering. Marie wasn't sure she felt like it any longer. Obviously Mai knew she was wrong or she would've followed her into the Starbucks. And if she had, Marie would be talking to Cal about drug rehab for her as soon as she could.

The sound of the coffee machines drowned out the conversations around her, so Marie almost missed the person calling her name. She stiffened, at first thinking it was Mai. She certainly had no intention of talking to her now. They needed time to cool down, away from each other. She could meet her back at the car later.

"Marie." The voice called again, closer this time.

Marie whipped around, intending to tell Mai that she just needed a minute or two. Her words caught in her throat. Josie smiled at her from across the Starbucks.

"Hey," she said. "I thought that was you, but I wasn't sure. Especially when I called you from the door and you didn't respond. I thought that I was mistaken, but no, look at you." She paused, smiling. "I'm so surprised to see you here." Josie was dressed for shopping in a form-fitting velour sweat suit and Nike sneakers. Her hair was swept into a neat ponytail, highlighting her eyes.

"I'm surprised to see you too. You shop way over here?" What did Louis know? Obviously Josie was more "her type of people" than he'd imagined.

"Doesn't everyone? This place has the best sales. Are you here alone? Maybe we can have lunch. I know it's a little late—"

"I couldn't." Marie stammered, remembering Mai. "I'm here with a friend. Besides, I only have a little while. We both have to pick up the kids. You know."

"So how are the kids? They're so sweet. It was so kind of you to invite me in the other day. You didn't have to do that."

"They're fine."

Josie kept nodding while she spoke. "I see. Maybe some other time. I'd like to get together. Drinks or something, you know. I want to return the favor, seeing as how you fed me and all."

Marie blushed. "No worries. It was no big deal at all." Her coffee was ready. She picked it up from the counter where the barista placed it and took a sip. "It was nice seeing you. I think I should check on my friend. She wasn't doing too well when I left her. You take care."

"Okay. You take care, too. I'll give you a call about getting together." Josie stepped out of the way for Marie to get by.

"You too. Are you ordering coffee?"

"I will in a minute. I always have to take a minute to figure out what I really want. The menu is so complicated." Josie stared up at the menu behind the counter.

Marie left the store, feeling as if she were being stared at the whole way. Running into Josie was certainly an odd coincidence, she thought. Once outside, she glanced back inside the Starbucks. Josie still hadn't ordered anything, and she seemed to have been staring at Marie, glancing away when Marie turned around. How strange. If she didn't know better, it felt as if Josie had been sneering at her as she'd walked out. She shook the feeling off and looked around for Mai, who'd wandered a few stores away by now. She looked lost. Things were worse than she thought.

Louis slung his gym bag over his shoulder and headed to the parking lot. He'd finished his workout just as the after-work crowd began to trickle in. Maxfield walked beside him, and for once since they'd hit the gym, he'd stopped talking. Louis would have been grateful for the reprieve from his endless yammering, but instead he found that he was uneasy. Silence from Max was not always a good thing.

They were parked across the lot from one another, and instead of going to his car, Maxfield stopped with Louis, waiting as he opened his trunk and dropped his bag in.

"So, I'll see you later, then?" There was a question in Louis's voice. He could tell that there was obviously something that Max wanted to say.

"So. Josie is the one you wanted out of the building, right?"

Louis nodded. "And?"

"You sure about that? I saw the woman, and she is fine as hell. I still say you should—"

"Don't even go there. She ain't the type to keep things quiet. I told you that she was already at my house. It felt like she was casing the joint or something, seeing for herself who her competition is, you know?"

"That sounds dangerous." Max looked alarmed. Louis was

glad that even though Max was a little off sometimes, he wasn't totally nuts.

"So, you see my point. If I were inclined to step out on my wife, it wouldn't be with her. Doesn't matter how fine she is or how willing. That one doesn't want to share a man, she wants to take over. My life is complicated enough and I have to think about my kids." He paused and closed the back of the car. "But it's okay. I'm not worried anymore."

"Really?"

"Yup. I've decided to hire a super. For the building. That way I won't have to deal with her. I'm going to put myself out of a job."

The men laughed and the mood was lighter for a second.

"What does your wife say about that?"

"Haven't told her." He paused. "It's time I got another job anyway. Been thinking about getting back into the corporate world."

"It's not all it's cracked up to be."

"Or do something else. I've got skills. I used to be good at sales. That's how I met Marie." Louis smiled at the thought. Marie was good at what she did and he'd admired that. They had dinner once and were married less than a year later.

"But I thought you wanted to be around for your kids and all that. You mean you are going to give up being a kept man? All the guys envy you. I can't believe it."

Louis bristled but otherwise ignored Maxfield's obnoxious comment. He couldn't expect him to be normal too long. It just wasn't his nature. He felt as if he had a handle on things for the first time in days and he wasn't about to let this idiot spoil his good feelings. "I can find a job where I don't travel."

Max shrugged. "Hey, if you think that'll work." He rubbed his chin and stared past Louis, looking pensive again.

Louis waited a second, but couldn't stand it anymore. "I know you have something else to say—"

"It's nothing." He spoke tentatively. 'It's just that from everything you tell me about Josie, I just don't think that she will go away that easily." He shrugged. "But you know how to handle your business. I gotta go. I'll see you later."

Louis tilted his chin upwards in a half greeting as Maxfield got into his car and drove away. He was in a trance, thinking, as he got into his. Their conversation was disturbing. He didn't start the car, instead he sat in the parking lot. Maxfield annoyed him beyond words sometimes. Sure, it was great that he was always there for legal advice, even if he didn't practice law anymore. He was a big help and not a bad workout partner, once you got beyond the incessant chattering and the shit-talking about women. The thing that annoyed Louis the most, even frightened him, was Maxfield's damned insight into people.

Ignorance Is Bliss

The office was bustling with activity. Kennedy watched all the action in slow motion as she approached her office. Normally, there wouldn't be this many people working until almost nine o'clock. Not a good sign. She shivered and looked around. She hated it when she was the last to know something, and from the concerned looks on everyone's faces, there was obviously something she'd missed.

She checked her watch, thinking that perhaps she'd gotten the time wrong. Stranger things had happened, but not this time. She'd arrived when she normally did; everyone else was just unusually early, like they'd all responded to some secret wake-up call, one that only she hadn't received. What in the world was going on? Usually perky and attentive, the admin didn't even look up when she grabbed her mail, answer her good morning, or even seem to notice the intern that flew by with her arms full of papers. Unusual, considering that she was the type to always be in everyone else's business.

Kennedy paused to greet her anyway. "Good morning," she said, then cleared her throat.

Instead of responding, she barely lifted her eyes, nodded almost unperceptively, then looked back down at her desk, making Kennedy's greeting seem more of an intrusion than a pleasantry. Surprised, Kennedy wanted to ask her what all the commotion was about, but thought better of it.

Administrative types always held the key to everything, but they never really knew all the details. Instead of prying her for details, Kennedy stuck her head into the office a few doors from her. "What's going on?" she mouthed. The man in it had his ear glued to the phone. He barely acknowledged her and instead of answering, he turned his back and waved her away. Another bad omen. People didn't typically wave her away. She was an account supervisor for goodness sakes. Folks paid attention when she was around, sucked up even. Kennedy walked slowly down the busy corridor, peeking into a few more offices on the way.

Absolutely everyone was wide awake and on the phone, even the people who managed to look like slackers even when they were working. And they all seemed frantic, and not in a good way. Kennedy threw her light jacket across the back of her chair, then picked up her phone to dial her own secretary. If there was anything out of the ordinary, she would know. It was her job to keep abreast of anything.

The phone rang in her ear and she jumped as the sound reverberated through her head. *Now I'm not only out of the loop, I'm deaf, too.*

The vice president of the department didn't wait for her to

answer. "Be ready for a meeting in the conference room in ten minutes."

"What are we meeting ab—" Kennedy didn't get to finish. He'd hung up the phone. All she heard was the annoying buzzing of an internal dial tone. Kennedy looked at the handset in disbelief. Not only was she in the dark, but she had to go into a meeting blind.

Her stomach clenched tight as she grabbed her portfolio and a pen. Her office wall was glass and through it, Kennedy watched her co-workers hurrying by. She couldn't hear the sounds from the hallway, but from the looks of things, all hell had certainly broken loose. Hers was a generally fast-paced office, but today was unusual, people walked more quickly than they normally would, and a few had even broken into a run in the general direction of the conference room. It would've been nice to at least have a cup of coffee to ease into her day, but from the looks of things, coffee was going to have to wait.

The conference room was one of the largest rooms on the floor. More of a hallway that had been partitioned than a separate room, one wall was completely glass, like many of the offices. Kennedy paused at the door. More than half the department was already waiting. From outside the room, Kennedy noticed that no one was really talking. Instead they were all seated quietly around the large rectangular table that dominated the room, more than a few with worried looks on their faces. She slipped in the rear door, dropping her portfolio as she held it open for the man behind her.

It hit the floor with a clang and several of the people in the room jumped as if they'd heard a gunshot instead of a book hitting the floor. *What in the world?* Kennedy slowly picked up her things and gave the man across from her a puzzled look. He shrugged and averted his eyes. A sense of dread came over her. If she at least knew why everyone was so on edge, she would feel a lot better.

She stood up to meet the eyes of her boss, who was watching her from the other end of the table, along with everyone else in the room. The room was unusually silent. Kennedy slid back into her chair, silently refusing to apologize.

He cleared his throat. "As most of you have heard by now, we have a major problem. One of our largest clients, Star State Oil, is threatening to leave us."

The room was suddenly abuzz with activity as a swarm of whispers circulated the room. Kennedy's face blanched. Star State was her client. Why was this the first she was hearing of any problems? If anything major was wrong, they should have contacted her first, but she was clueless. She opened her mouth to speak and then noticed that her boss was looking straight at her with venom in his eyes. He held up his hand and the room quieted.

"Allow me to read to you from the memo they sent over." He donned his reading glasses and looked down at a paper he picked up from the conference table. "This campaign has been full of disappointment for us. Our numbers are down. The account supervisor assigned to our account appears to have had her judgment compromised by personal issues and may be inappropriately involved with a member of the marketing team." He paused and removed his glasses, then looked directly at Kennedy. "Are they accusing someone on our team of dipping their pen in the company inkwell?"

The room was as silent as death.

"Kennedy?" he asked. "Is there something you need to disclose?"

Kennedy colored fiercely. *What in the hell—?* "Not as far as I know. I'm not aware of any inappropriate relationships on my team." It was strictly against company policy for anyone to have a relationship with a client. *Dipping a pen* was how they referred to dating a client. In the advertising world, doing so was up there with sexual harassment on the no-no list and certainly considered a career-limiting move, especially for a woman. People took a long time to forget it and it bred resentment all around.

His eyes narrowed. "You're not aware? Are you sure of that?" He turned to the other people in the room. "James, you are now heading up this team—"

"What? I assure you that I can handle this—"

His angry gaze swung over her. James, her major competition, gave her a mocking, self-satisfied look.

The boss continued. "I want you and the rest of the team to get on this right away. You have four hours to contact the client and make them happy." There were a few rustles in the room as accusing glances and smirks were thrown at Kennedy.

"Go. Now." He roared. "Kennedy, not you."

Still clueless, Kennedy's thoughts raced as her co-workers filed out of the room. She shuffled her papers to try and look busy. What had just happened that could justify public humiliation? She usually enjoyed the open atmosphere in the office, but right now, the place felt awful. Kennedy felt naked, stripped of any shred of dignity she might have had.

He waited until the last person had left the conference room, and then came over to where Kennedy was sitting. He leaned back on the table and folded his arms across his chest.

"I would have expected this from some of the younger members of the department, but not you. You've been in the business long enough to know how this works."

A lead weight hung in her stomach. She looked at him, bewildered. "I assure you—"

He held up his hand and Kennedy immediately stopped talking. "So, you have a new boyfriend, huh?"

"I do. But I don't see what that has to do with the Star State account?" she stammered, searching her brain for an answer. Troy had never mentioned any association with her client.

He gave her an unbelieving glare. "He's on the marketing team."

Kennedy couldn't believe her ears. Troy hadn't mentioned anything like that to her. She shook her head. "He's a geologist. He never said—"

"He's on the marketing team."

This was serious. She tried her best to remember any reference that Troy might have made. They never talked about what he did much at all. "I swear I didn't know." Her voice became almost a hushed whisper.

"You sure?"

"We haven't met very many people from their marketing team at all. I know they take stuff back to be reviewed in their offices—"

"—and they draw from an interdisciplinary team, across

the company. Your friend serves on the team in an advisory capacity."

The lack of coffee combined with the excitement left Kennedy's head pounding. Her shock was subsiding, leaving behind anger. How could Troy have done this? She could lose her job. "I really had no idea." She paused. "I can fix this."

"It's too late for that. Someone else is going to handle this account."

Kennedy wanted to scream, but held her temper. How could she have missed something so important? The office grapevine would love this. People loved it when stars fell from the sky. How many of the people in the office begrudged her success? She'd seen them congratulate her and then whisper later. Not to mention that she would forfeit any bonus that might come from working with the account. "I'm so sorry. If you let me—"

"No, Kennedy." He spoke with unwelcome frankness. "Sometimes you have to know when to fold 'em. I want to believe you didn't know. Hopefully we haven't lost the account. But if we have, I'm going to have to take some action." He paused. "I'm sorry."

Finally alone in the conference room, Kennedy was frozen in place, glued to her chair. The level of activity in the office was still high. Everyone was scurrying around trying to fix what she'd messed up, what Troy had messed up for her. While her boss had been in the room, passers-by had at least averted their eyes, afraid that if they looked, some of his wrath might come down on them. They were no longer afraid now and a few stared boldly into the room, probably expecting her to crack and break down into tears or something. Each piercing glance stabbed at her like a poke in the gut, and she cringed.

Kennedy kept a stone face, but didn't move. She felt crushed. What could she say? How could Troy not tell her that he was working on the marketing campaign that they were handling? In all her years in advertising, she'd never made a mistake like this, but she planned to do everything in her power to keep it from being a career-ending mistake. As for her relationship, that was a different story.

The day was unusually warm and the sun shone brightly. David Johnson turned his face up to the sky and enjoyed its warmth. He loved days like these, they brought back memories of when he'd been a young man. They would stay outside all hours of the day and night. These were also the days when he missed his wife the most. She'd loved the outdoors too; gardening had been a favorite pastime of hers, and sometimes they would sit outside on their porch and just watch people together. Although he'd tried to describe the feeling to his daughter, Kennedy would never understand. She always thought he was making things up or remembering incorrectly. Sure, his memory failed him sometimes, but he wasn't an imbecile. At least not yet. She patronized him and treated him like he was a child or something. Hell, he was damn near seventy years old, far from being a kid.

Suddenly, the idea of a walk was really appealing. It would be great to go for a stroll. He felt better than he had in weeks and full of life, so why not? The opportunity might not present itself again, or he might not be able to handle it at all next week.

David stood up, went inside, and grabbed his coat. A walk around the block never hurt anyone. It was early in the day and still several hours before Kennedy would get back. He couldn't think of a better way to spend his afternoon.

He stopped by the door. *Maybe I should let Kennedy know that I'm going out for a walk.* As soon as he thought it, he dismissed the idea. Kennedy would tell him that he shouldn't go and talk to him in that damn voice she used, the one he hated. Since when did a father report to his daughter? He was a grown man and if he wanted to take a walk, he should be able to do so, no questions asked. He'd always been a free spirit anyway. His wife had known that and it was okay with her. Kennedy knew that. David glanced around the room one last time. He closed the door and stepped out and into the sunshine, humming to himself.

The Calm Before the Storm

"*I*'m coming through." Davon's words didn't register at first. What in the hell did he mean, coming through? Cal couldn't think of anything to say.

"Okay."

He repeated himself. "You hear me? I'm coming through. Today. Can you meet me?"

"Where? Here?" Cal rubbed his forehead.

"You're not a smart man, are you? Yes, San Antonio. Can you meet me or something?"

What in the hell would the "or something" be? Cal's stomach turned a flip. He'd thought he had more time.

"Uh—"

"Don't *uh* me, nigga."

The *n* word. Cal hated it. But what did he expect from the likes of Davon? "How?"

"Don't you worry about how. I'm coming through. I got a load that I have to take down to Mexico, to a plant down there and

I am going to be in your area *today*. I want an update. Face to
face." He paused. "Meet me at the Pilot truck stop in about two
hours. I'll call you and tell you where my rig is."

Cal jumped as the phone clicked in his ear. Davon was a truck
driver. He hadn't mentioned that before. That meant he was
highly mobile. He cursed under his breath. There goes the idea
of just ignoring him until he goes away. He was the real deal,
and not only was he not going away, he was going to keep coming to him until he got what he wanted.

He sighed and then stood up and stretched, shaking off the
groggy feeling that he hadn't been able to get rid of all morning. He'd been curled up in the hotel room chair too long.
Homewood Suites wasn't the best, but it was cheap and relatively clean. Cal had rented a room for the remainder of the
week. He had yet to tell his wife about being suspended, so he'd
just told her that he was out of town. It was better that way; she
wouldn't have a chance to get suspicious and he would have
some time to think things through. Besides, he didn't want to
be home when he got his HIV test results. If the answer were
something he didn't want to hear, he wouldn't be able to conceal it from his family. At a hotel, no one would see him break
down. Cal thought he was a strong man, but in a case like this,
he might break down before he could even think of getting up.

His small black toiletry bag was on the dresser. Cal grabbed
it and headed into the bathroom to brush his teeth. He was still
immaculately groomed. Other than the shirt that he'd taken
off to avoid wrinkles, he was dressed just as he would be on a
normal workday. He washed his face, brushed his teeth, and
then picked up his white shirt. He examined it, then shook it

out before putting it on. In a truck stop, he was sure to stick out like a sore thumb. He sighed. There was a bright side to all of it. He would be able to ask Davon about a paternity test again.

He'd passed the truck stop ten thousand times, but had never actually been to it. It was one of those large ones, with at least ten trucks lined up. Cal pulled his car into the back of it, parking so he wouldn't be visible from the highway, then laughed at himself. There were at least several thousand other cars in the city that looked like his, so what exactly was he hiding from? Everyone that knew him thought he was out of town on business; at least everyone that mattered did.

He killed his engine, then flipped open his cell phone and hit redial. Davon answered on the third ring. Cal cringed and pulled the phone away from his ear as music blared through his earpiece.

"Are you here? I'm at the truck stop."

Davon turned his music down. "I'm in front. My rig is the third one in from the highway. Come on over."

Cal felt a heavy sense of dread. He didn't want to leave his car. Davon could be a psycho. How many people disappeared at truck stops every day? There had been several cases in the news of truckers being found dead in their rigs, right in the middle of town. He didn't want to be one of them.

"Well? I ain't gonna bite. Damn."

Cal truly wanted to believe that Davon wasn't a bad person, but he knew that it wasn't true. A good person wouldn't try to extort money. "I'll be right there." He stammered as he spoke.

He left his car and locked it, then looked over his shoulder. Cal slipped his phone in his pocket, then pulled his suit jacket tight around him, trying to gauge how far away Davon and his truck really were. He started to walk around the building but then thought better of it. It was probably smarter to walk through the convenience store. That way, if anything happened, he'd at least be on some surveillance camera somewhere. He didn't really know anything about Davon except that he was from Atlanta, a truck driver, and he was a thug.

The glass door swung open easily. Cal paused by the door. He cleared his throat and looked around. There were several other people in the place, truckers and people passing by. He made eye contact with the clerk behind the counter and nodded. An extra precaution. Never could be too careful. He took his time strolling through. Picked up the paper, read the headlines, and put it back. Just as he reached the door that led out to the other side where the trucks were parked, his phone vibrated. He took it out and looked at the caller ID.

Cal sighed heavily. Mai. He glanced at his watch. She would be on her way to get the kids. He stepped to the side and flipped open his phone, turning so he could make eye contact with the clerk. "Hey, babe."

It was her check-in call. She wanted to know how it was going. He half-listened, half-looked through the door out in the parking lot, craning his neck to see if he could pick out Davon's truck. He counted the rigs to pinpoint it.

He swallowed hard. The trucks were bigger than he thought. Huge. Ugly fronts, like monsters about to swallow you up. Mai called his name.

"I'm sorry. I can't hear you too well." He was letting his imagination get away from him. "I'm on the way to a meeting." At least he was sort of telling the truth. "I love you, too." Now she wouldn't worry.

Cal nodded at the clerk, then pushed the door open. No use in prolonging the inevitable.

They stuck out in the McDonald's like a sore thumb. Their navy and white uniforms announced to the world that they were a bunch of school girls hanging out where they weren't supposed to be. Lishelle's eyes sparkled. Getting off campus had been a lot easier than she'd thought. They'd all been so busy laughing, none of them had eaten much, except Sophia. While Lishelle's fries had already turned cold and hard, Sophia scarfed down everything she'd bought and then a few of Lishelle's nuggets, too.

"So." Sophia spoke in between chewing, showcasing the contents of her mouth. "I'm surprised you found some guts to come with us. What's got into you?" She winked at Star, and they both burst into a fit of laughter.

Lishelle blushed and then shrugged. She had to admit, the freedom was good. She didn't believe that she'd done it herself.

"Did you see? I thought she was going to shit her pants when the security van rolled by." Star laughed in between her words as they were caught up in an adolescent fit of giggles. "Dang, I'ma change your name from *skater* to *skank* if you don't start chewing with your mouth closed. Don't none of us want to see all that."

Sophia stopped laughing, her mouth suddenly a straight line. She put the french fry she was holding back down on the table. "Why you gotta hate? Shit." She parodied chewing with her

mouth closed, moving her lips like a horse. "See? Is that better?" Sophia rolled her eyes, feigning her disgust, then turned
back to Lishelle. "I knew you had it in you. I knew you could be
down. But hey—" She leaned in and lowered her voice. "You got
to come to The Pilot Stop with us, for real. It's slamming over
there." She nodded her head, her thin blond hair bobbing in the
wind.

Lishelle's stomach churned. Sometimes she couldn't remember why she was still friends with these two. They teased
her endlessly sometimes, but other times they made her feel as
if she belonged somewhere. Just because they had known each
other since they were two, it didn't mean they had anything in
common anymore. Matter of fact, she was almost certain that
they didn't. She sighed as they stared at her.

"Well?" Star said. Sophia sat back in the booth and folded
her arms across her chest.

In slow motion, Lishelle put a fry in her mouth. They were
testing her. They did have a certain appeal. Why was it that
everyone seemed to have more fun than she did?

Sophia rolled her eyes. She tapped Star heavily on her shoulder. "You see, I told you. Baby girl is scared." She chuckled. "It's
all good though. Someone's gotta be a good girl."

Lishelle ignored them, acting as if she were sipping her shake.
Her friend's voices seemed far away. She wasn't oblivious to their
teasing, she was used to it. They'd been teasing her as long as she
could remember. Her mother used to tell her it was because they
were jealous. But her mother hadn't had one of those talks with
her in a long time. Not like she could. Her hands were damn full.
She had no time for her and her siblings, it seemed.

But Star's and Sophia's parents, they always gave them mad love, always bragging on how well they were doing and what great people they were, and the two of them never followed the fucking rules. Her parents didn't notice shit. Unless she was bad. *Unless she was bad.*

"I'm in."

Both Star and Sophia jumped. "Shhh," Sophia said. Their eyes were wide. "For real?"

It was Lishelle's turn to sit back in the booth. "Sure. You just tell me what to do."

They exchanged glances, then shrugged. "All right then." A wide grin spread across Sophia's face. "We'll tell you exactly what to do. Even what bus to take." She paused. "Right after we figure out how to sneak back into school."

Mai hummed along with the radio as she waited in the carpool line. She felt more relaxed than she had in days, thanks to the little Internet hookup she'd found. Cyberspace was an amazing place, you could find anything or anyone anywhere. Life was good.

Her phone buzzed in her ear and she pressed the button to connect. She cringed, not expecting to hear from Marie so soon.

"You okay?" Marie's voice sounded as tentative as Mai felt. She was so embarrassed. How could she have jeopardized their friendship by asking her for Valium? Not to mention she was letting her know more than she needed to. Marie was a smart woman.

She took a deep breath and tried to sound as chipper as possible. "I'm fine. Much better."

Marie paused a long time. "You sure? I didn't want to leave it like it was. You know what I mean."

"You know what? No worries. I was the one who was wrong. I shouldn't have put you in a spot like that." Mai swallowed. Her mouth was dry. "It's just been so stressful for me lately. Nothing a good night's sleep couldn't cure. Much better."

"Really?" Marie sounded unconvinced. "I mean, I'm glad. You had me worried. I thought that maybe we were going to have to go to Narcotics Anonymous meetings or something with you." Marie chuckled, and Mai laughed along with her.

Had she really looked that bad? Sure, she needed a little calming every now and then, but it wasn't like she was a crack head. She'd always been a fine, upstanding member of the community. Things had just gotten a little out of hand.

"Promise, I'm fine. Listen, I'm in the line to pick up the kids—"

"Okay. I'm glad you're better. Does that mean we can still expect you for dinner later this week?"

"Absolutely. Just me though. Cal is traveling."

Marie didn't answer immediately. "Is he?"

"*Yes*, he is." Mai was more brusque than she intended. She could tell that Marie was wondering about her husband's job, but it really wasn't her business. Everyone was misinformed sometimes and they'd been wrong about Calvin. He'd gone to work as usual. The one thing they had going for them was trust and if there was a problem, Cal would have told her.

"Okay. I wish him well."

That was the most cryptic response that Mai had heard in a while, but she shrugged it off. The truth always came to light and she had no doubt that it would this time too. In the meantime, she planned to carry on life as usual.

Her kids were standing by the curb, waiting, but she was still several cars back from reaching them. She could tell from their body language that Lishelle was also in a good mood today. She appeared to be actually standing right next to her sister, even talking to her. *God is good sometimes.* Maybe they could actually have a relaxed and normal evening at home for a change.

They hopped in the car, the younger of the two immediately started chattering away. Mai smiled. Her kids always had a way of warming her heart. Sarai was still at that innocent age, still filling her mother in on everything. It felt good when the kids still believed in their parents and their family. Mai loved that she still wanted to share with her all the politics of second grade. Lishelle used to be like that too. Although she seemed to be in a lighter mood than she had been lately, she still gave one-word answers and stared out the window. She leaned up against the glass, barely mumbling an answer to her mother's questions, and then only if she asked twice. Still, you had to take every blessing, even if it was a little one. This was a lot more than what she had been getting in the past few weeks. Lishelle sometimes wouldn't answer at all. There'd been a few times where Mai had been tempted to hold a mirror under her nose to make sure that she was still breathing.

Her eyes caught Lishelle's in the mirror.

"You look good today, Mom." Lishelle crossed her arms in front of her.

"I do?"

"Yup, fresh. Doesn't she, Sarai?"

Sarai nodded and Lishelle gave her mother something she hadn't spotted in a while, a wide smile.

Mai blushed, suddenly feeling guilty for being so harsh on her earlier in the week. Perhaps whatever phase it was that her daughter had been going through was over and they would have a good afternoon after all.

Here Kitty, Kitty

*L*ouis sat perched on the edge of his seat in the quiet office. Other than the receptionist across from him, he was alone. She stared at her computer screen, intermittently hitting keys. Every third one or so she would take a peek his way. If they made eye contact, Louis made it a point to smile politely.

"Is it cool outside?"

"A little," Louis said. "But you know how the weather goes around here. There's no telling what the day will end up like." He made it a point to speak clearly and in an even tone. She could be testing him or something, trying to figure out if he were nervous. He'd read somewhere once that you should be very careful what you do in waiting rooms when you were looking for a job, that some companies observed the candidates while they were waiting. Louis had no idea if he was what they were looking for, but he had all the qualifications of the job and he didn't want to screw it up. His stomach was full of nerves. Although he used to be very good at what he did, he hadn't held a full-time job, other than managing their building, in over five years. He'd been a stay-at-home dad since his company had let him go. Although he felt he was making the right decision, he had to admit that he was a little uncomfortable. Things changed quickly in so many industries. Five years could be construed as a long time.

Louis sat perfectly straight and his back was already aching. He wanted to let himself slide back and lean into the comfortable-looking shape of the very modern leather chair, but resisted. He was ready to take the next step in his life, and that meant making the best impression possible, even if it meant he would be slightly uncomfortable for a while. He could handle it.

There were several business magazines on the table and he stared at the titles and tried to keep his mind occupied. In between, he thought about his wife. He wasn't sure how she would react to his decision to get a job. For the first time in a while, Louis hadn't discussed his choice with her. He would eventually, though, and knew that she might disagree at first but once she knew everything Marie would have to agree that it was best for their family. Aside from their psycho tenant Josie being a little nuts, he was no longer happy just managing the building. And if she didn't agree, the least she could do was support him and his choice, right? After all, he'd certainly supported her over the years.

A door to the side of the room opened and a well-dressed man stepped though. He looked down through his glasses, stared at the papers in his hand, and then adjusted them loudly in the quiet room. "Louis?" He spoke without looking up and closed the manila folder in his hand. He scanned the room as if it were full of people.

The phone in his pocket vibrated and a surprised Louis jumped to his feet. He smoothed his jacket and ignored it, instead walking forward with his hand extended and a smile on his face. It was probably Josie again and this was certainly not the time. Louis shook the interviewer's hand eagerly as they exchanged pleasantries.

He stood a good four inches taller than the man. Confidence flooded his body. A while had passed since he'd interviewed like this, but his height left him feeling empowered. Louis followed him down the hallway and into an office. He could handle this.

The interview took a full half hour. He wasn't sure if he'd done well enough to get the job, but Louis felt good when he left, confident that he could go back into the corporate world. He still knew a lot about the high-tech industry, and had spun his management of the apartment building as having been a program manager extraordinaire. As far as he could tell, he'd been received warmly, too. He might not get the job, but one thing was for sure, if nothing else, the interview had been reassuring.

Louis thanked the receptionist on the way out and made a mental note to follow up on his interview with not only a note for the hiring manager, but a small token for her too. The company was small, and it wouldn't hurt to have multiple folks that could put in a good word for you.

There were twelve messages on his phone. Three text messages. He scrolled through his missed calls. All but two of them were from Josie. From the looks of things, Maxfield had been right, she was not going to go away that easily. Louis shook his head. As fine as she was, odds were that Josie wouldn't have been interested in him if he had been a single man. He guessed that part of the attraction was that he was somewhat unattainable. That was okay though, he was high from good feelings about his interview and he wasn't about to let that psycho put a damper on things. Hopefully, if he didn't call or see her, she would eventually get the message and go away. Or so he hoped. But he couldn't worry about that now. It was time for him to pick up his kids.

Louis spotted Junior from his car. He was on the playground with the other kids and appeared to be happy. Louis smiled, but then felt a pang of guilt. Staying after school was a new thing for them. They were used to Louis picking them up as soon as they were dismissed. Although Junior appeared to be adjusting fine, Walani was another story. When he'd told them that they could stay late, she'd been the one who was unhappy. She'd done that crying thing that she did and crumpled onto the floor, devastated. Louis marveled over how she was just a little thing and already knew what to do to pull at her father's heartstrings. She'd sat on the floor whimpering until Louis had picked her up and he felt terrible, but how in the world do you explain life to a little kid? And she would probably be the one whose reaction would alarm Marie most.

Walani was inside drawing. As Louis got closer, it was obvious that she was sulking, too. He crept up beside her and kissed her on the top of her head. She barely turned her head to acknowledge him, instead continuing to move the green crayon she was using back and forth on her paper. Why was it that kids always knew how to push the right buttons?

"Nice picture," he said. It was a lame attempt to make peace, but it was the best he could do. "Let's go. Where's your sweater?"

She didn't answer. Walani put her crayon down on the table with a thud, then sighed and stood slowly.

Louis wanted to laugh but held it back. How was it that someone so young seemed so old? Walani was already looking like her mother. He helped her get her things, and then signed her out. Together, they tracked down Junior. He was still running around the playground like a madman and was covered with dirt from head to toe. It looked more like he'd been out there for days, rather than just an hour and a half. At least one of them was having a good time.

He buckled them into their respective seats. "What do you guys think you want for dinner?"

Walani shrugged, and Junior shouted what he always did. "Pizza!"

Louis laughed. He should have known. Tonight would be a good day for pizza, too. They were never really hard to cook for but he was more tired than he thought. The interview and preparing for it had been mentally taxing. He felt drained, but pleasantly so. "We'll see."

"Am I invited?"

Louis froze. He knew that voice anywhere. Josie. She'd managed to catch him off guard. He slammed his car door and stood up so quickly that he saw floaters in his eyes. He pressed his eyes tightly shut, then opened them and blinked. "What are you doing here?" He looked around quickly. There was no telling who might be standing back, watching, even taking notes. The grapevine could be vicious.

A smile spread across Josie's face. "I knew when I couldn't reach you that I'd find you eventually." She bent down to the car window and waved at the kids. Junior waved back, but Walani just blinked. "You know I'm the type to get what I want." Josie's smile was deceptively friendly. "Your kids are so adorable."

A twinge of anger hit Louis. He didn't even want her to so much as breathe near his children. Showing up at his house was one thing but being at the school qualified as stalking. The woman was obviously a bigger weirdo than he'd thought. He stepped between the car and Josie, blocking her view. He leaned back onto it, his forehead now creased with stress and worry. "What is it? I have to get them home." He didn't try to mask the annoyance in his voice.

Josie's eyebrows flew up, but she quickly recovered. "I won't keep you. I've been trying to reach you. I just wanted to see you, Louis." She lowered her voice when she said his name, as if she were purring like a cat. "But you didn't even come to take a look at my sink. It—" She seemed less sure of herself now and flustered by Louis's anger.

"I don't do that anymore." He cut her off. "Take care of the building, I mean. We've hired a super. A professional." Louis took a card from his shirt pocket and scribbled the number on it. If there was ever any uncertainty about having hired a super, it was gone now. He was sure, beyond a shadow of a doubt, that he'd done the best thing he could possibly do. "He's the one you should call when you have a problem from now on." He held it out in Josie's direction. "He'll take care of everything you might need."

Josie took a step closer. She smelled as good as ever. Why did he even notice these things? She seemed to be enjoying his struggle to remain composed. The woman either had amazing confidence or she was a total nut. Louis didn't understand how some people seemed to have to do what they wanted, no matter what it might do to other people.

"You think? Not *everything?*" Her smile had a sinister edge to it. "I met him. That man doesn't have half the talent you have."

Louis looked around. There could be any number of parents watching them and reporting back to Marie that he'd lingered too long with a strange woman, someone they hadn't seen before. There was a code among married women, or at least those that his wife knew, and Josie didn't seem to care that she'd violated it. The rules were simple, things like you don't visit another woman's house when she isn't home, for any reason. And if you should and the husband answers the door, it was common courtesy to decline an offer to go inside. This little conversation with Josie was surely violating one of these rules too. He let out a tired sigh. "Look, Josie, I don't know what you're playing at, but I'm not interested. Whatever it is that you are looking for, I can assure you that you won't find it here." He gave her a hard stare, and for the first time, he could see her wavering. His message couldn't get any plainer than that.

Her body language changed and she softened, then she returned Louis's cold stare. She looked down at the card in her hand, waving it back and forth. "Mario is his name?"

Louis nodded.

Her eyebrows jumped up as she spoke. "You take care of your babies," she said, then turned and left.

Even pissed off, Josie still had a certain swagger to her walk. Louis took a deep inhale and stood there watching for a minute. Part of him felt relief, but part of him was even more wary than he had been. The fact that Josie had come to his children's school in the first place left a bad taste in his mouth. It was one thing to mess with him, but now this game that Josie was playing seemed to be on a whole other level with rules he didn't quite understand. He had to admit, when it first occurred to him that she'd been interested in him, he'd felt a little flattered, even good about the fact that someone found him attractive the way his wife used to, but things had turned a little bizarre. Josie seemed obsessed with him, even hell bent on seeing how far she could go. He had no choice. This had become something he must discuss with Marie.

All Jammed Up

Kennedy was torn between giving Troy a piece of her mind and totally ignoring him or just blowing him off, but right now, neither side was winning. At first she was so angry about what he'd done, she just didn't call him. After she'd cooled down a little, her plan had been clear and simple in her mind. He was supposed to keep calling her until she got bored with ignoring him, then she would take his call or agree to meet him and tell him where the hell he could go. Thing was, he obviously wasn't aware of her plan. In fact, he'd totally foiled it by not calling her at all since their date in the park. He hadn't sent flowers like the first time, nothing. After a few days, she couldn't take it anymore. She'd broken down and called him. She'd just finishing dialing his number for about the thirteenth time since, and she was as frustrated as ever. She hadn't been able to reach him on any phone and now there was a nagging feeling in the pit of her stomach. If she didn't know better, she might mistake it for actually missing Troy or something. And that was bad, because she also had a feeling that Troy was avoiding her. Sure, they'd had a great time and the date had been incredibly romantic, but the missing him thing was something that was totally alien to her. And try as she might to hold onto it, her anger was dissipating.

The phone was glued to her ear, as if he would somehow miraculously answer if she pressed so hard that she created suction between the phone and her ear. Kennedy's whole body was tense. She sat at her desk with her legs crossed at the knee, nervously bouncing her foot and chewing the skin off her bottom lip. She would regret this later, she knew, but she couldn't help herself. How could she get any satisfaction if she couldn't even get the object of her ire (or whatever) on the damned telephone?

It was already not a good day; in fact, there hadn't been any good days since she'd been kicked off her project. People who'd been sucking up to her before seemed to be ignoring her now, and management had a long memory about things like this. Kennedy was sure that the only thing that had saved her so far was her otherwise stellar record. They'd given her what amounted to nothing more than busy work and every decision she made was double-checked by someone else. This wasn't the first time she'd seen something like this and knew that this would last until they figured out whether she was forgiven or not. She sighed and hung the phone up again. Unfortunately, they probably wouldn't decide that until it was clear if the account was staying or going. And for her sake, she hoped that it would stay. She really loved her job and the best thing to do was to be on her best behavior until things returned to normal.

She grabbed the phone to try and call Troy again but stopped herself. She was obsessing over saying her two cents to the man. It was all her fault anyway. If she'd only listened to her gut in the first place, this would have never happened. It would have been a few good turns in the hay, and then it would have been over and she wouldn't have become so damned side-tracked. The problem was that she'd trusted him further than she should have, and now she was the one acting like the Klingon person. All those years of watching "Star Trek" with her father, she should know better. She should have trusted her instincts. Instead she was sitting at her desk on the bad side of management, mad at a man that she wanted to tell off but didn't really want to do without.

She leaned back in her chair. For the life of her, Kennedy couldn't figure out why she cared so much in the first place. He hadn't called her and she'd been unable to reach him. The sensible thing to do would be to let it go and just move on. Could it be that she needed to hear an explanation from him? That she actually wanted to believe that he had no idea that his withholding information had jeopardized her job? Blood trickled to the surface of her newly skinned lip. Or could it be that Troy had somehow gotten under her skin? Kennedy gave in to the urge and reached for the phone. At least there was one good thing about being Klingon. Klingons didn't win the things they wanted, they conquered them.

David felt better than he had in weeks. Kennedy seemed to linger too long at the house this morning, asking him all kinds of questions about taking his medication. She was glad that this new stuff seemed to be working for him, or at least it appeared to be from where she was standing. Truth was, the dang medication had nothing at all to do with his mood and he knew it. He'd tried to tell her, but she'd brushed him off, as usual, talking to him like he didn't have good sense or something. She'd always been a little pig-headed, but he couldn't blame her for that one. David chuckled to himself. He'd been known to be a little stubborn himself, so the child had come by that trait honestly.

"Dad, you aren't a doctor, really. Just be grateful," she'd said. She'd been so happy, he didn't want to burst her bubble. He stopped taking those nasty pills the day he went out for that first walk. It was an easy thing to do, too. He held them under his tongue just like they do on television, then he'd spit them out as soon as his daughter left. Damned doctors didn't know everything. No one knew his body better than he did and he knew that he was getting better, plain and simple. A walk in the fresh air was his elixir and he'd taken one every day since then.

Most days, he didn't stray too far away from the neighborhood, but the last few, he found that he walked further and further each time. Physically, he was really in great shape, although he did make sure to take a few Aleve every night just so he wouldn't be too sore the next day. He found that he enjoyed the feeling of the wind rushing past him and the smells of the city, even when they weren't too fresh.

Today, he must have left the house not ten minutes after Kennedy. He couldn't wait to get out; the walls of his room had seemed to be closing in on him lately. Now, it was well past noon, and he was still walking. A dog barked right near him and he jumped, but he really wasn't afraid. Even if the animal bit him, David felt freer than he had in many months. If this kept up, he would talk to Kennedy about moving out and getting a place of his own again. She would fight, he knew that, but having some space of his own would be worth it. She didn't get that. As long as he was under a roof that she was paying for, he'd feel like he was a guest, a moocher, and he didn't want to be either. Maybe he would move to one of those senior apartments or something.

He crossed the street and picked up the pace just a little. David exhaled heavily, a little out of breath. He probably should be getting back soon, he thought, and waved at a young woman in a yard he was passing. The wave she gave back was tentative at best, but it was better than nothing. He frowned. He'd just waved, for goodness sakes. Folks these days needed to learn to be friendlier to each other. In the old days, it would have been unheard of not to speak to someone who spoke to you, especially if they were as well dressed as he knew he was. He'd taken extra care in putting himself together this morning. He wanted to look good. He'd found a lot of things on his walks. One of them was a small, old-fashioned diner that he'd stopped at every day since and he'd even met a few people there. Emara crossed his mind. She was something else; around his age, but looked a good fifteen years younger. They'd been having coffee together for several days. She'd even invited him to dinner, and he planned to take her up on that, too. Good thing for her that he wasn't twenty years younger. He sighed. Good thing for him, too. She reminded him of his wife.

A car came too close. David froze and suddenly realized that he was in the middle of an intersection. He looked around, confused. When had he crossed the street? Another car came speeding up to him as he looked around. His eyes widened in terror.

"Watch it, old man!" They yelled at him from the car. Young folks, so disrespectful, he thought. He started to shoot them the bird, but then remembered that he wasn't young anymore. He couldn't fight. He couldn't even run. David tried to move, but he stood riveted to the spot as car after car barreled toward him and swerved around. Terror gripped his body. Finally, the light changed and he sighed and was able to walk to the other side of the street.

The woman he'd spoken to earlier came up to him. She put her hand on his arm. "You okay, sir? I was watching you. In the traffic."

David blinked. Her words didn't make sense to him. She looked familiar, but he couldn't place her. He looked around. He couldn't place any of it. Where was he? David didn't know where he was or how he'd gotten there.

She touched him again, then turned and yelled over her shoulder to the man back on the other side of the street. "He's trembling."

"He crazy. Leave that man alone and come on." He yelled back.

"You see. You evil." She pointed at him while she spoke, then turned back to David. "Are you lost?" She searched his face. "Do you know where you are?"

Tears streamed down David's face. The girl's eyes were kind. The answers to her questions were right on the tip of his tongue, he just couldn't seem to put them into words. "My wife—"

"You want me to call your wife?"

He didn't answer. He couldn't. A confused look clouded his face.

The girl looked at him with pity in her eyes. "Pop was like this. I would bet someone's looking for him." She spoke to the man who now stood by her side.

"You don't know that. He could just be some drunk."

"Look at him, dummy. He ain't no drunk. How many drunks you know wear Stacey Adams all shined up like that?"

"Vintage Stacey Adams. Them shoes as old as dirt."

"That was the gayest thing you said yet."

"I'm not gay, I'm just enlightened."

She narrowed her eyes at the man. "Let's take him to the hospital or something. Maybe he got ID on him." She paused. "He ain't no drunk."

The man sucked his teeth. "Shee-it. You always gotta be a good Samaritan. Damn." He crossed his arms in front of him.

"Somebody's gotta be."

"I guess this means we ain't going to the game, huh?" She glared, then started to lead David in the direction he'd come from, toward her house.

"Kennedy?" David's voice trembled.

The woman smiled. "You can talk." She smiled. "I ain't her, but maybe we can find her for you."

He frowned. "Your skirt is too short, young lady."

Her friend laughed. "Oh shit. He ain't Pop, but he sure sounds like 'im."

"Just shut up and come on."

A Rock and a Hard Place

No physical ailment could make Calvin feel as bad as he did now. His head hurt, his stomach churned, and he hadn't slept a wink in days. His facade of control was crumbling and the stress of his predicament was getting to him. Today was a day of phone calls and he hoped the next one was better than the last had been. He looked at the phone he was still holding in his hand, and was suddenly filled with anger. What the fuck? He flung it across his hotel room and it landed with a crash. The paint chipped where it hit and a strange curio shelf that had been hanging on the wall fell down on one side. An ugly faux marble statuette crashed to the floor. No doubt the hotel would charge him for that and he would have to explain it to Mai when she read the bill. He was going to have to explain eventually anyway, since he probably wasn't going to be able to use his corporate card for the hotel charge. Instead of making things better, he was just digging himself into a deeper hole, one that he couldn't seem to see his way out of. The location of the hotel would scream from the page and there was no way in hell he'd be able to hide that he'd been across town, not across the country like he was supposed to be. He sighed. She'd probably think that he'd been holed up in some love nest or something. Calvin pursed his lips. Mai'd hate that. Another thing to cause him grief. She was going to be pissed.

As if he needed more shit from anyone. Calvin felt like he just couldn't get a break. He'd just gotten off the phone with the human resources department at his company. What a fucking pain in the ass. They weren't able to help him at all. Had no idea when they would reach a decision and tried to act like they had no idea what he'd been talking about, like he was some kind of nut. He knew the runaround routine well. He was in marketing; runaround was his business. Someone had to tell him something soon, or he was going to have to take money from his retirement account to keep his family going. Shit. They needed to either fire him or let him come back to work. As it was, he was in a state of perpetual limbo, a purgatory for a crime he wasn't even sure he'd committed.

It was eleven o'clock. Less than two hours. He walked across the room and retrieved the phone from the pieces of the statue. Davon was coming back through on his return trip this afternoon and they were supposed to meet again today. His time was up. Either he had to start coming up with some cash, or call Davon's bluff. Cal paused. He still had no idea how the man would react if he refused to give him money. He didn't know enough about him, and that didn't seem right. Everywhere he'd looked, he came to a dead end. He'd been so busy trying to fix it alone that he hadn't asked any of his friends for help. He'd been afraid to. Now he had no choice. He'd gotten to that place where it was necessary to pull out all the stops and do whatever he had to do to get the job done.

Calvin called Maxfield. He hated to do it, but he had no other choice. His head throbbed as he listened to the phone ringing in his ear. Maxfield wasn't exactly his kind of people, but they'd somehow stayed friends over the years. He was crass, and they had very little in common. Max was the one that always said embarrassing things when they were all together, the one they were perpetually making excuses for. He hadn't gone to the right schools, and he hung out with all the wrong people in places the rest of their married friends wouldn't be caught dead in. He certainly talked more shit than anyone that Calvin knew, but whether he wanted to admit it or not, Max had skills of a certain type. Not to mention that whenever you needed help, he was always there to give it. You just had to be able to live with the gloating.

"Maxfield." Calvin swallowed hard. Max cleared his throat. " 'Sup? You get that paternity test yet?"

"Paternity test ain't going to happen."

"Shit. Then no money should be happening either."

"They won't consent. Something ain't right."

"Is that so?" He paused for what seemed like a long while and Calvin imagined Maxfield rubbing his chin between his thumb and forefinger, the way he did when he was thinking. "How much time you got?"

Calvin's head throbbed. He hated to tell Maxfield this much, but he knew that if there was a way, legal or otherwise, Max would find it. "None."

The silence on the other side was just a little too long for Calvin's taste. "I wish you'd come to me earlier. It might cost a grip."

"Less expensive than the alternative, I hope."

"How old you say the kid is? Thirteen? Probably."

"I don't have a choice."

"All right then. I'll see what I can uncover. Tell me what you know."

"I don't think I can stall him for long. You know the last thing I need is for some stranger to go marching up to my wife and tell her some story about a love child or some bullshit like that."

Maxfield chuckled. "That would be bad. But I told you what to do about that."

Calvin thought about Mai hitting the roof, possibly asking him to leave. He wasn't willing to go that route. "Not an option."

"Okay then, I'll see what I can do."

The hotel hallways were crowded with women, all talking at once. Mai sat behind a table, banging at the computer next to her. Her cash box was open and the people standing around were giving her angry stares, as if she were the one having technical difficulties, not the computer. She wished she could blue screen too and just blink out of the middle of this mess. "Can you please give me a minute?" She felt so annoyed that she was seeing spots. It wasn't her fault that the computer system wasn't working. She looked around at the bunch of women in front of her, searching for hotel staff. "Will someone track down a person who can help me make this damn machine work right?"

The woman next to her cleared her throat. "It's not their fault, either. There is no need to be vulgar."

She was right of course. Mai glared. She wanted to tell her to go to hell too. Let her try to straighten out this ticket mess with all these folks yelling at her. Today was the day that all of her club members were picking up their tickets for their fund-raiser next week, the biggest one they ever had. And she was the chair of the committee. What had she been thinking when she'd signed up for this duty? To be sure, she hadn't counted on all the extra stress she'd have with Calvin out of town and having to watch Lishelle like a hawk. Not to mention that something was obviously wrong with the prescription she'd procured over the Internet. Although they'd said the strength was the same, it obviously was not. Mai felt as anxious as ever and she'd been snapping at everyone who even looked at her funny.

She looked across the room where several of her sister members stood, glaring at her and occasionally talking through pressed lips. She couldn't tell if it was from concern for her health or if they were gossiping about her. Two other ladies stood off to the side, obviously throwing her unmasked looks of disapproval. Mai glared back. Who in the hell did they think they were anyway? If they disapproved of the way she was trying to get the job done, let them do it better. It wasn't happening. No one dared take her on. "Those bitches don't think I see them over there talking about me."

The woman next to her put her hand on Mai's arm and she jumped. "Are you okay, Sister Mai?"

She nodded and found herself blinking back tears. Mai sighed heavily; the frustration was weighing down on her. "You know, I think I'm not feeling well. I think I need a break."

"I'll take over. Why don't you go home for the rest of the

afternoon. You've done your best up until now. I think we can handle it."

She was being let off the hook. Mai nodded, grateful, then stood up too quickly. The chair she'd been sitting on over- turned behind her, making a loud clanking sound on the mar- ble. The din in the room quieted and it seemed as if the room closed in around her as everyone stared in her direction.

Mai blushed. She fiddled with her skirt, smoothing it unnec- essarily. The nubbly feeling of the fabric beneath the palms of her hands was somehow soothing. She gave a weak smile, then walked around the table as steadily as she could. She held her head up and made her way toward the elevator. The sound level in the hall began to rise slowly again. With each step, her compo- sure slowly slipped away. A few were kind enough to at least act like they weren't staring, but she could feel their eyes burning holes in her back as she left. Some people could be so hateful. As if they never had a bad day. It would feel good to get back to the safety and comfort of her house. With all the extra stuff she had going on, she really wasn't up to all this social stuff today. There was no way in hell she needed the stress these biddies were giv- ing her, not today. She had a few hours before the kids would be home, a few more hours to try to recharge her batteries.

The overly full bus shook from side to side. Lishelle and Sophia were wedged in the back, between a fat lady and a very thin man. Lishelle's face blanched with disgust. She couldn't remem- ber ever having taken the city bus anywhere, ever. Her mother always drove her wherever she needed to be. Sophia, on the other hand, seemed to be a pro at it, not minding that she could probably smell the fat woman's deodorant. She chattered nonstop, not realizing that Lishelle was paralyzed from fear. She hated the bus. She hated the smell of the man behind her, who, unfortunately for her, seemed to have skipped deodorant altogether in favor of too much cologne. More than that, she hated the realization that a part of the man was poking her in the back. She felt sick to her stomach.

"How much longer, Sophia?" She hissed at her friend, cutting her off in mid-sentence. "You sure you know where you're going?"

"Uh, stop tripping. And I told you before that ain't my name."

"Whatever. Sk8tr. It's all the same." Lishelle elbowed the man in his stomach, then glowered at him over her shoulder. She rolled her eyes and tried to stick her plastic bracelets under her sleeve again. What was the big deal with the names anyway? "I can't take this much longer." She was glad that her friends had the foresight to tell her to stuff some jeans in her backpack, otherwise, the weirdo would be rubbing up against her in her skirt. That would certainly be too close for comfort.

"Just hold your horses. Next stop."

"Thank goodness. I'm tired of folks getting their jollies off me because of this damn bus swaying. I think I'm going to be bus sick."

Sophia chuckled. "Girl, you better take it where you can get it. You and I both know that no male has ever been that close to you." She looked over her friend's shoulder and stared at the man, hard. He didn't seem to care. "The world is full of weirdos."

Lishelle tried to pull away from the man behind her, but he followed her every move. The bus slid to a stop and relief flooded her body. She was disgusted and she elbowed him in the stomach one last time for effect. He grunted in pain this time and stepped back just as the door opened. The two girls made their way out of the rear door of the bus and Lishelle turned to find that he was grinning a sick-looking grin at her through the window. She'd certainly made his day.

"You shoulda charged him. McNasty got his jollies for free."

"You're stupid," she said, but it was true she felt used. Sure, no boy had been that close to her, but she would bet that that nasty old man hadn't been that close to any teen ass in a long, long time.

Lishelle looked around. "This isn't a truck stop."

"Duh. It's an Exxon. The truck stop is over there."

Lishelle looked in the direction her friend was pointing. "How the hell are we going to get over there?" The truck stop was across the highway, on the other side of about four lanes of high-speed traffic and a grassy median. Cars whizzed by at top speed and there was no overpass anywhere in sight.

"Carefully." She paused. "You scared? You can still go back. But unless you cross the highway to take the bus in the other direction, it'll take you a while to get back. You'll have to ride the bus almost all the way to the end before you can get one that will take you in the other direction."

"Where's Star?"

"There already. Her older sister dropped her off. I'm surprised she hasn't called me." Sophia stared at her cell phone, then shook it.

Lishelle knew better than to ask how they called each other on their Firefly phones, cell phones that were only supposed to allow them to call their parents and an emergency number. Sophia and Star had hacked that long ago. Last semester they'd made a killing out of reprogramming almost everyone's phone in the school, or at least anyone and everyone who'd had a few bucks to pay for the service.

Star had it down to a science. Lishelle followed her as she dodged traffic to make it across the highway. She held her breath and prayed the entire way, feeling perhaps that she wasn't really cut out to be a bad girl, that perhaps the name Good Girl Mott suited her just fine. She vacillated between feeling high from the excitement and wondering if she was going to be killed on the highway, but they finally made it. By the time they did, her tee shirt was almost soaked through with sweat. Overheated, she pulled off the hoodie she was wearing and tied it around her waist.

The truck stop was divided into two sides, one for trucks and one for cars. They paused by the sign that directed cars to the left and Lishelle stared at the huge white-brick building. It was still daylight, so the red and yellow awning didn't appear to be lit. They had to run through what seemed like acres of trucks to make it to the building, and from where they were, she could see that it was a reasonably busy place. The truck stop was divided into several sections. A Pizza Hut. A convenience store. And to the left, a place whose dilapidated sign announced itself as Lone Star Café.

"What's so special about this dump?" Sophia pointed toward the white star outside the end of the truck stop where Lone Star Café stood. There were several cars parked off to the side by themselves there. "That place. A lot of kids come here."

They walked toward the building. Lishelle laughed, almost breaking into a skip. "A greasy spoon café? We came all this way for heartburn? We could've stayed at school for that."

"There's Star."

Star was holding court in the far corner of the eatery, kicked back in a booth. She was surrounded by four men and had just thrown her head back in an exaggerated laugh. Lishelle barely recognized her and she certainly didn't recognize any of the people with her. Star was heavily made up, and those were men, not kids.

Star waved to them from across the room and Sk8tr waved back. Butterflies bumped against Lishelle's insides and the hairs of the back of her neck prickled her. She wanted to leave, to flee, but if she did, her friends would never forgive her, maybe never talk to her again. She swallowed and managed a weak smile. She was here now, so she might as well make the best of things.

The sound of the men's laughter filled the room and mixed with the tinny music playing in the diner. "Your friend looks scared. You can tell her that we don't bite."

"Not unless we want you to." Star seemed older than her fourteen years as she laughed along with the men. "She'll be okay. This is her first time hanging out with us, right Lish?"

This was a new nickname, not a teasing one. She licked her lips and nodded, afraid to speak. The men moved away from the booth to make room for the two girls to slide in. Lishelle hesitated, then watched as Star used her eyes to plead with her. Reluctantly, she moved in and sat next to Sophia, but wished she'd had the foresight to go in first. The four men immediately closed in around them.

They didn't smell like the man on the bus, but they didn't exactly smell good either. Three of the men were dressed similarly, jeans and tee shirts, boots or sneakers. The fourth had on jeans, too, but his had been pressed hard, maybe even dry-cleaned, and he wore nice-looking shoes that looked as if they had recently been shined. They all wore baseball caps and Lishelle guessed that two of them were covering up balding heads. They looked to be around her father's age or at least close to it. The thought made her sick to her stomach. They immediately started talking again, asking questions.

One of them sat across from her. He stared at her hard, as if he was trying to look through her skin and into her soul. Lishelle's skin crawled. She tried to be pleasant, but his eyes froze her in place as if she was staring into the face of Medusa. Not that he was bad looking or anything like that. The only black man among the four, he even had a pleasant face and she might not have minded so much had he been younger. A lot younger. When he spoke he had a southern accent and his face was clean-shaven. He did look younger than the other three, but not young enough. Around fourteen was more her taste. Her hands were folded on the table and he reached out and ran his finger across the top of her hand. She jumped.

"You scared?" The other men continued to talk to her two friends as he mouthed his words at her.

Lishelle's face was tight as she shook her head. She didn't want to talk to any of them. What was it Auntie Ree told her? Act like you belong and people will think you do? She could hear her voice telling her to hold up her head and put her game face on, but she couldn't seem to hide the fear that she felt right now.

"I have to go to the bathroom. Can I get out?"

They all turned to look at her.

"Now?" Sophia said. "We just got here."

She pursed her lips hard and her nose flared. "Yes, we did, and it was a long bus ride. I need to use the bathroom and I need you to go with me."

The men moved aside and Lishelle slid out from the booth. She moved defiantly and stood, waiting for her friend to follow.

"Women always gotta go in packs. Go on with your friend. We'll keep Star company 'til you get back."

The bathrooms were down a narrow hallway. The sign that pointed the way hung from the ceiling by one chain, floating back and forth in the stream of air coming from the air conditioning vent overhead. Lishelle waited until they were out of sight of the table to talk. They slipped into the hallway, and Lishelle immediately pushed Sophia against the wall, not caring if the old-fashioned white paneling hurt as her back slammed against it.

"Damn," Sophia said. She rubbed the back of her arms.

Lishelle was so angry she was breathing hard. She pushed back on Sophia's shoulders with her palm, keeping her from moving. "You told me we'd be hanging out, but you didn't tell me we would be hanging out with men our fathers' age. This ain't fun to me."

"Can you ease up? We just got here."

Lishelle released her grip.

"You'll have fun and you don't have to do anything you don't want to." She paused and straightened her shirt. "These are nice guys. Star comes here a lot, sometimes with her sister. She

keeps in touch with one of them. They call her when they have a
load through—"

"What do you mean, a load?"

"Truck stop. Truckers." She paused. "Duh. These guys have
more money than any boys our age and they spread it around.
They can buy us drinks and shit. If you act nice, they may even
give you smoke—"

"I don't smoke."

Sophia rolled her eyes. "Okay. Whatever. The point is if you
loosen up, you can have yourself a good time. On their dime."

Lishelle didn't speak. *On their dime.* So, that's why Star always
seemed to have the best clothes in her closet, even though they
wore uniforms to school. She'd always thought that she and Sophia were hustling other kids out of their money, but there was
more to it than that. A chill ran through her. She leaned against
the wall. She could leave whenever she wanted to, right?

"If you're afraid, Mott, it's all good. You can go."

"I'm not afraid." If things got out of hand, she *could* always
leave. She held up her chin, trying to look unfazed, trying to
convince herself. Her eyes narrowed. "What do they want in
exchange?"

Sophia laughed. "Nothing you can't handle. I told you, these
are nice guys."

Sophia didn't say *nothing*, she'd said *nothing she couldn't handle*. The two were not the same. She was hearing her mother's
voice again. Damn. Only this time she was no longer telling her
to hold up her head. This time she was telling her that everything in this world costs something. The question was, what
was she willing to pay?

A Rose by Any Other Name

There was a plus side to not checking bags. You never had to worry about your luggage getting lost. Marie wheeled her bag past the baggage service office where there was a line of people that had been on her flight. Apparently, the weather delay had been bad for luggage. She waved at a man that made eye contact with her, recognizing him from the plane. He looked familiar, and she thought that she remembered sitting next to him during her layover in Houston.

The international sign for the ladies room was in front of her and Marie planned to duck into it before she found herself a taxi to head home.

"Marie!"

She cringed. After such a long flight, she wasn't really in the talking mood. She contemplated ignoring whomever was calling her, but from the way the person sounded, he was already on his way in her direction. Marie sighed, then turned around slowly. It wouldn't be the first time she'd run into a neighbor or someone she knew in the airport, but this time it was neither. She paused, trying to quickly place the man she'd just smiled at near the baggage service office. He had a broad smile plastered across his face, one that looked almost like a sneer.

She couldn't figure out where they'd met, not at first. He did look familiar, though. He stopped in front of her, still grinning from ear to ear and she noticed how huge he was. He towered above her.

"I can't believe I'm running into you like this. Can you believe the coincidence?"

Marie smiled, searching her memory. She met so many people, it was sometimes hard to remember where she'd met them before. She was surprised that she'd forgotten him though. He had an interesting face, for sure. Sometimes the faces all just meshed together, especially when she was tired. "Yes, quite a coincidence."

"We have a conference down at the River Walk." He stood there a minute, hands crossed modestly in front of him, still smiling.

Marie smiled and nodded, too. If he didn't get to the point fast, she was going to break into the bathroom dance.

"I thought I never was going to hear from you again. I tried to call you a couple of times but I could never get you."

Marie tensed. This wasn't good. And she thought she could sense a little hardness in his face. "I'm sorry. I don't—"

"We met in Chicago a couple of months ago. You gave me your number, remember?"

She looked around. "I gotta go—"

His smile vanished. "I'm not going to keep you. I just wanted to let you know that it's cool, but we're all adults here. If you didn't want to talk to me, you could have just said so. Common courtesy, especially since I was nothing but respectful when we met."

Marie was speechless. She did remember him. He been very nice and they'd had a few drinks together in the airport bar. He'd asked for her information, and she couldn't say no. Instead, she'd transposed numbers and given him a number she'd made up. It'd been easier that way. No confrontation possible. It was obvious from the look on his face that he was pissed. She felt terrible. It was always easier than saying no, that was really what it was about for her. What had she been afraid of then? What was she afraid of any other time?

Finally, she managed to stammer an apology.

"No apology needed. Just remember that next time. If the shoe had been on the other foot, you women would've been quick to call a man a dog." He leaned in. "Just think about that. What does that make you?"

Marie gasped. What the hell? If she didn't know better, she'd think she'd just been called a bitch. Or worse. She didn't have time to reply. He gave her a disgusted look, then turned and walked back toward the baggage claim office. She'd been dismissed.

She didn't know whether to be angry with him for what he said or not. The truth was, he was right. Kennedy was right. She deserved whatever he'd said. What he'd held back. She deserved it all. She rolled her bag into the restroom, feeling as if a deep hole was inside of her. Marie was clueless as to why she did what she did. She only knew that something was missing that she couldn't quite seem to find.

The playground for the smaller children was separated from the one that most of the kids used. They needed to be separated; sometimes the older children were just too rough. A group of teachers stood in the middle, talking to one another while keeping a watchful eye on the kids and the clock.

The sandbox was to the rear of the playground, almost off to itself. It formed a private hideaway that the children loved to use for their secret theater. Walani played happily there with another little girl, just as she did every day. They'd only been there ten minutes and they were already covered with sand from head to toe.

The warning bell rang, and the teachers started to line up the students. Most came forward to find their class, but Walani was lost in her own dream world. She and her friend stayed put, pouring mounds of sand on imaginary people. Knowing where they would be, a young teacher volunteered to go round them up. Those two loved the sand box and usually spent most of their recess playing there. She walked around the corner to find them. She could hear their voices as she approached, but she couldn't yet see them.

She smiled at the sound of the young girls, chattering away with each other. Imaginative play was encouraged at the Hill Country Episcopal School, especially for very young ages. As she got closer, she thought she heard another voice, an older-sounding one. She slowed down to listen.

"And then you can come live with me. Would you like that?"

The teacher was alarmed. The sandbox was right next to the fence that separated the playground from the surrounding neighborhood. She quickly stepped around the corner to the sandbox. She gasped. Walani appeared to be talking to someone on the other side of the fence. "Walani! You two come on. Recess is over." Her voice was stern.

The woman flashed a smile, then walked away quickly. The teacher grabbed Walani and the other little girl by the hand. "Who was that, Walani?"

She shrugged. "That was the lady from before."

"From before when?"

"You're hurting my hand," Walani whined.

The teacher loosened her grip. "From before when? Did you know her?"

Walani nodded, then rubbed her nose. "My mommy knows her."

The teacher pursed her lips. Why had she left so quickly? "Well, you know about stranger danger, right?" She tried to make her voice sound more normal. There was no need to alarm the kids now.

Both girls nodded. "Are we in trouble?" Walani's eyes were wide.

"No, sweetheart. You're not in trouble. But I think we are going to have to relocate that sandbox or something. It's too close to the fence." She scanned the street for a sign of the woman, but she'd disappeared into the neighborhood. This was certainly something for Dr. Greeley to hear about.

Kicked to the Curb and
Bit in the Booty

Kennedy turned off her desk light, glad that the day was finally ending. She never did get to talk to Troy, and it was still nagging at her. She'd lost her anger somewhere after the gym hour, and now she just felt sorry for herself. The damned dating cycle and all its rules had long since flown out the window, and she was feeling terrible. Ever since Damon, she'd practiced never getting too attached and it had worked well. She'd been the queen of the social scene. Normally, she felt like she ate men like air, but all she felt now was that she'd had the air shit-kicked out of her. And being kicked to the curb still felt as bad as ever. Unfortunately, it was a feeling she remembered all too well. How many times had Damon stood her up or not returned her calls?

Kennedy grabbed her handbag from her desk drawer, then paused. She realized that she hadn't thought about Damon in quite some time. Hadn't had that crazy recurring dream either, where she relived the last time he'd stood her up, in a major way. Back then, she'd given up almost everything and it backfired. His betrayal had been as inevitable as the surprise thunderstorm on a sweltering mid-summer day and she hadn't seen it coming. It'd haunted her for ages, until she met Troy. Then she'd been too preoccupied with not getting involved, then getting involved with him to spend her time on regrets of things past. And where had that gotten her? Right back to the goddamned start. Wouldn't it be a funny thing if he was married, too?

The clicking sounds her heels made on the lobby tile seemed too loud. Kennedy tried to walk lighter so as not to disturb the evening calm that enveloped the office. Her admin was already gone. Almost everyone was. She wasn't surprised considering that the better half of her day had been spent redoing a presentation. No surprises there, either. Redoing had become part of her penance. It wasn't really about her work, it was about her paying for her mistake. She got it. Just seems like she'd made several mistakes lately.

She glanced at the clock in the lobby and another mistake occurred to her. She hadn't checked in with her father the way she usually did. She'd gotten into the habit of checking in with him before she left the office, just in case she needed to stop and get him something on the way home. Kennedy leaned her bag and other papers she was carrying on the receptionist's desk and rummaged in her bag for her phone. It was late, and if anything, she should have called to make sure her father had eaten, but he'd been so clear the past few days she didn't want to annoy him. She was happy that he seemed to be doing okay right now. Some days were better than others and she'd learned to take whatever it was she got. There was no answer. Kennedy frowned and dropped her phone back in her bag. She could try him again once she got into her car.

He never did answer the phone. Kennedy turned the corner onto her street and vowed that she would allow herself some time to destress before she stormed in on her father. When he ignored her requests like he was doing, it made her crazy. The doctor had told her time and time again that it wasn't really his fault, especially when he was doing as well as he had been. He couldn't understand why she was being so overprotective, why it bothered her so much when he wasn't in touch with her, but how many times had she heard horror stories of something happening to people because no one was looking out for them or checking on them the way she checked on her father? She was probably overreacting, so she was going to take a few minutes to just step back and relax. Her father was stubborn as an ox and he was probably holed up in his room, watching old movies again, ignoring the phone. She simmered with anger, but she was also exhausted from her day.

Someone was sitting on her front porch. She turned into her driveway and pressed the button on her driveway remote and then stopped her car. If she didn't know better, it looked like Troy. Her heart skipped a beat. He stood up and strode toward her. It *was* Troy. Anger came flooding back, but not just because of losing her client. Kennedy was mad for a myriad of reasons. Not only had he humiliated her at her workplace, but then he hadn't thought to call her after their date or return any of her calls for several days.

The reaction surprised her. She'd almost convinced herself to put the whole thing behind her and move on, and here she was paralyzed in her driveway when she should be thinking about running his grinning ass over with her car. What in the hell was wrong with her?

Troy came around to the driver's side of the car, smiling as if nothing had happened. Kennedy had so many questions for him, things she wanted to say, but she knew she would get none of them out. He waited for her to open the window and she just sat there, unable to move. She didn't know what was going on at first. It had been quite a while since she had let herself experience this much emotion. Quite a while since she'd let someone get close enough to hurt this much.

It all seemed to hit her at once and a tear rolled down her face. Troy's grin changed to a look of concern and he knocked lightly on the window and called her name.

She hesitated, then pressed the button to open her window.

"I thought you'd be happy to see me," he said. Although she wanted to, Kennedy refrained from telling him all the kinds of asshole she thought he was. She wiped away a tear with her index finger. After everything that happened, he was going to be a smart ass, too? She could play his game. "Why in the world would you think something like that?"

Troy paused, and a wounded look flitted across his face.

"Why didn't you return my calls?" Her voice had a steel edge to it.

He looked confused for a second. "I was out of town—"

"Bullshit. They didn't have phones where you were?"

"I'm missing something here obviously. I don't have international service on my mobile. I got your messages as soon as I landed, so I came on over, to surprise you."

Kennedy looked at him skeptically. Did he really think she would buy that story? "You didn't mention that you were going out of town."

"Actually, I did. I invited you, remember? After our first date? You said you didn't want to go, so I didn't bring it up again." He paused.

Cancun. The memory came barreling back. Troy had invited her to Cancun with his friends and she'd said no. That was why he hadn't answered his phones anywhere. Troy hadn't been in his office or at home. She felt just a little stupid for leaving all those messages, probably somewhere around twenty or so, but that didn't excuse the little problem they had about work.

"So, are you going to go in your garage or what? We can continue this discussion inside, although I'm sure all your neighbors are certainly enjoying the show. You can tell me what was so urgent."

Kennedy peered into her rear-view mirror, in the direction of her neighbor's house. Sure enough, the woman across the street was being nosy. Her curtains could barely hide her, halfway behind them, checking out what was going on in Kennedy's front yard. It was a miracle she hadn't called the police as Troy sat on her porch.

"How long have you been waiting?" she asked.

"Long enough. Can we go inside?" She nodded, then eased her car forward and into her garage, out of the way of her neighbors' prying eyes.

Kennedy remained reticent once they got inside. She dropped her things near her garage door and kicked off her shoes. Mexico was to Texas what Caribbean travel was to people on the East Coast. It was convenient and often inexpensive, but since they'd never discussed it again, the thought hadn't occurred to her that perhaps that was where Troy had been, but there was still the question of work. Why hadn't Troy mentioned that he was on the marketing team?

He didn't appear to even realize that anything was wrong. He followed her to the kitchen, standing behind her as she pulled down a pair of glasses. Kennedy was truly embarrassed and ashamed at her messages now.

"I'm sorry I didn't bring up Cancun again. You were so adamant about it, I thought you truly didn't want to go."

"No big deal. That's not a problem, really." Kennedy was still struggling with her feelings. After her last relationship fiasco she'd made a vow to herself never to be caught in this position again. If she felt this bad, she was already too attached.

"So, can we move on? You and I can go to Mexico together if you like."

"Move on? The only one who might be moving on is me, considering that I may lose my job. There aren't too many advertising firms around here. I may have to move to another city. Uproot myself and my father. Move away from my best friends."

"Because I went to Mexico for a weekend with friends? That seems a bit drastic, doesn't it?"

Kennedy left the corkscrew in the top of the bottle she was trying to open and whirled around. Her head throbbed from anger. "How in the hell could you do that to me and then stand here and make glib remarks? My job is really important to me." It was a good thing she'd already started opening the bottle of wine. As angry as she was, if she still had the corkscrew in her hand, she might use it as a weapon.

Troy held his hands up like a shield, totally confused. "I'm really lost."

"I can't believe you're acting so clueless. Tell me what I did to you? Why didn't you tell me that you were on the marketing team for Star State Oil?"

"I didn't think it was relevant for me to tell you about. I'm just an advisory member. It's like being an outside board member—"

"I know what it is. That little detail almost cost me my job. Still might. The job that I have worked many years to be respected in."

"That's ridiculous."

Kennedy saw red. She swept both wine glasses off the counter and onto the floor. They crashed to the stone and splintered.

Troy jumped back, confused.

"I fucking agree. I agree that it is ridiculous that my boss called me out about the new man I was sleeping with, in a conference room full of my colleagues. It's ridiculous that he took my largest account away from me and gave it to a man several years my junior. One who is now walking around my office gloating. And it's ridiculous that they are treating me like a damned intern. All because my choice of boyfriend violated a company policy I didn't even know I was violating." She paused. "We're not supposed to date clients, Troy. You being on that advisory council or whatever makes you a client."

"I truly had no idea. But you don't have that account anymore, right? So we're cool." He stepped toward her.

Kennedy stepped back. She was overcome with anger. Tears would be next, but she didn't want to cry, not now. "That's not the point. I let you in and you failed me."

"I didn't fail you. Don't you think you're overreacting?"

"No, actually, I don't." Kennedy spoke lower now, but there was still venom in her words. "People depend on me and my job. If I don't have it, I can't take care of my father. I can't take care of me. Did that ever occur to you?"

"Kennedy, I'm sorry. I didn't know about the policy. We don't have that; it's internal to your agency, I swear. I was planning to leave the committee anyway since it's so awkward now. I only agreed to do it as a favor to the woman I used to date. She heads the whole thing up for the company. How was I supposed to know? I would never intentionally do anything to hurt you. We weren't talking about our jobs since it was an obvious sore spot with you. You were the one who didn't even want me to know what you did, remember?"

His words knocked the wind out of her as the pieces came together. Her own actions coming back to haunt her. She didn't tell him what she did originally, so they never discussed it again. The woman he used to date. After her father's display in the kitchen that time, they never discussed who they used to date.

"How did they find out? It's not like I—"

"She wrote a letter. She went around me and wrote a letter to the president of my agency." Kennedy wanted to sink through the floor.

"I'm so sorry." Troy reached out to Kennedy again, only this time, she didn't move. "I'll fix it. I'm resigning from the team anyway, she's made it too uncomfortable. And I'll write a written apology myself."

Kennedy whispered an apology. "It's my fault, too. The way we started—"

He didn't let her finish. Troy pulled her close and covered her mouth with his. He kissed her tenderly, and Kennedy welcomed his kiss.

Tears streamed down her face as relief washed over her. Kennedy was relieved that there was an explanation she could believe, relieved that the one person she'd picked to trust after so long hadn't been as uncaring and callous as the people in her past. He kissed away all of the tension that had been building up over the past few days.

Troy had missed Kennedy, too. A few days away had given him time to think, and all he'd been able to think about was her. The fact that he'd hurt her so badly without even knowing it bothered him. She had some baggage from her past and a temper, but that didn't deter him from wanting to spend more time with her.

They sat on her sofa talking and he drew her close, enjoying the scent of her hair and the sound of her voice. She was a special woman, even if she tried to keep it all bottled inside and not share any of that specialness. Whatever'd happened before, she deserved better, and he wanted to give it to her. He wanted to know all about her life and what he'd missed while he was gone.

"How's your father been? You haven't mentioned him."

"I was supposed to be relaxing a minute before I went over there. He's been a lot better though, much clearer. But he refused to answer the phone today and I needed to lay into him about that. I call to check on him a few times a day."

He smiled. "That's a sexy thing you do. The way you take care of him like that. How do you keep from being exhausted?"

Kennedy shrugged. She wasn't sure how. All she knew was that up to now, God had been good to them, for sure. Other than his memory, her father hadn't progressed to the point where he was having any of the other health problems that were some-times associated with Alzheimer's. At least not yet. "Part of the reason I work so hard is for him. His care could get very expensive."

Troy nodded. He did know. "It was for both my parents in the end. Just don't tax yourself too much. The emotional toll can be the biggest one."

Kennedy didn't know what to say. "You didn't tell me your parents—"

"I guess there's a lot we have to learn about each other." He smiled. "Both of mine are gone."

His words made Kennedy feel guilty for the few times she'd been angry about the state her father was in. At least she still had him.

The phone interrupted their stillness. Kennedy looked at her watch and sighed. It was about time for her to go check on her father anyway. She reached over and grabbed the handset. She didn't check the caller ID. She half expected it to be either Mai or Marie and hoped it wasn't one of Marie's men friends calling again. She promised that she'd put her shenanigans behind her, at least where Kennedy was concerned and Ken-nedy hoped she would stick to that promise.

"Yes?"

It was a woman. "Hello? May I speak with David Johnson, please?"

"Excuse me?" The name didn't register at first. It had been quite a while since her father had gotten any phone calls. Kennedy didn't think he kept in touch with any friends at all.

"Is this Kennedy?"

"It is, who's speaking?"

"I'm sorry, honey. You don't know me, but your father talks about you a lot."

Kennedy's eyes opened wider. This woman was talking in the present tense. Maybe this woman had Alzheimer's, too. Maybe she got time mixed up, the way her father did. As far as she knew, he didn't mention talking to anyone about her at all, not recently.

"My name is Emara and I'm a friend of your father's. I was just calling to check on David." She let out a deep-throated chuckle. "We were supposed to meet for coffee this afternoon, and he never showed up. Is he okay?"

All kinds of thoughts ran through Kennedy's head. The roles were suddenly reversed and Kennedy was the one that wanted to scold her father about the people he was keeping company with. Who was this strange woman calling the house and what did he really know about her? She searched her memory for a time when they'd met some woman named Emara but she drew a blank. "Coffee? That doesn't make sense."

"Sure it does. We meet almost every day, at the diner, and he didn't show up and didn't tell me he wasn't coming so I was concerned. When you are old like we are, anything can happen—"

Kennedy didn't wait for her to finish. She dropped the handset and raced toward the guesthouse. As far as she knew, her father was in his room where he always was. He never went further than the front porch.

Troy picked up the phone and raced after her. "Kennedy, what's—"

She threw open the door from the main house, and sprinted across the breezeway, then stumbled into the small bedroom that was her guesthouse. There was no television or radio playing as she expected, and the shades were wide open for a change, with light streaming in through the windows. "Dad?" She called her father, but didn't expect an answer. It was obvious he wasn't there.

Timber!

"So, you never wanted to be with her?" Marie paced the floor, shocked at her husband's admission. And to think that the two-faced hussy had sat down at her kitchen table and Marie had served her pancakes as if she were a friend. The whole time she'd been plotting and scheming a way to get to her husband.

"I'm not telling you this because I want you to go crazy, Marie. I'm telling you because I want you to be safe, that's all." Louis hung his head into his hands. He knew that telling his wife about Josie would be hard, but he felt as if he were being accused of a crime he hadn't yet committed. Whoever said that honesty is the best policy had obviously never been between this particular rock and hard place.

"You didn't answer my question." Marie's eyes were like daggers. They were in the kitchen and she leaned up against the counter, her arms folded across her chest.

Louis stepped in close to his wife. He was no fool. There were some things she just didn't need to know, at least not if he wanted to keep peace in his household. "I'll admit she's attractive." He rubbed his hands up and down her arms. "But I love my family. I love you. That's all there is to it."

The kids came running through. Marie lowered her voice. "And I can't believe you hired someone without my input. And interviews, too? Is there anything else I need to know because you know how I feel about surprises." She glared. "I've got to go over to Kennedy's, but we will certainly talk about this when I return. I need to know all of the details."

Louis could take the tenseness in the kitchen. After his last encounter with Josie, he was sure it was for the best. They stopped talking just as Junior cut in front of them, headed for the refrigerator. "Mom, I'm thirsty."

Marie didn't take her eyes off her husband. "Help yourself." She paused. "Where's your sister?"

He motioned toward the doorway. Walani stood in the doorway, watching wide-eyed. Her bottom lip was slightly poked out.

Marie forced herself to smile. Adult problems shouldn't be kid problems. Neither one of them had asked to come into the middle of adult drama. "You thirsty, too?"

She shook her head.

"I have to go over to Auntie Kennedy's house for a while. She needs some help with her daddy. Will you guys be okay until I get back?"

Junior closed the refrigerator door just as Walani's eyes welled up with tears.

"What's wrong, sweetie?" Marie scooped Walani up and hugged her tight. "I won't be gone long."

"Will you come back?"

Marie's breath caught in her throat. Why was it that kids always knew what to say to tug on your heartstrings? "Of course I will, sweetheart." She kissed her daughter on her forehead.

" 'Cause that lady said she was going to be our new mommy, but I don't want a new mommy. I still want you."

Time stood still in the kitchen. Her daughter's words assaulted her. Louis had obviously let things get way out of control. Marie leaned back on the counter to keep herself from falling. What in the hell had been going on while she was gone? She exhaled heavily to stop herself from saying all the things she wanted to say to her husband. If any of them left her lips the kids would surely be scarred for life and their opinion of their mother changed forever. It was one thing for Josie to be making moves on her husband, but her kids were another story. She'd been the strange woman the school called about. *What had she told her babies?*

"Honey, we talked about this and you said you were going to be calm, remember? It won't do any good for you to be doing any crazy stuff."

Marie gently put Walani down. There was no way in hell she was leaving her kids at home now. "Go get some coloring books and your sweater." She waited until the kids were out of earshot, then turned to her husband and smiled. "Don't worry, Louis. I'm not some hoodrat who can't control herself." She yelled back to the kids. "Junior, you bring something to entertain yourself. You guys are coming with me."

"Why? They're just going to get in the way. Kennedy must be really distraught."

Marie's eyes were hard as steel. "My children are never too much trouble. I don't feel safe leaving them here with that psycho woman around. They are going to be right by my side. With their mother." She spat the words like they were leaving a bad taste in her mouth. "You call your bitch and tell her to stay the hell away from my family. She's crossed the line, Louis." Marie paced the floor, fighting back tears. "I can't believe this shit. How could you let her get so close to our children?"

"I didn't let her do anything. You were the one that invited her in." Louis knew he'd made a mistake as soon as his words were out. He was trying to avert a fight, not cause one.

"What? You were the one who invited her into our life when the little voice in your head didn't make it clear that you weren't interested in the first place. Thanks to your fucking hormones, we might have our very own fatal attraction on our hands."

"Isn't it the same chance you take every time you have that little extra drink with a stranger or get too friendly with someone you meet on the road?"

Marie gasped.

Louis folded his arms in front of him. It was hard not to be smug. "Oh, I always knew. Marie, I know who you are and have from day one, so don't look so surprised."

"Nothing happens. Louis, I'm—"

Louis had never given her any indication that he had any idea what she did while she was on the road. Marie felt lower than low.

"Nothing has happened *yet*. At least nothing you're willing to admit. But how long do you think it will keep being that way?

How long before someone takes things a step further than you're willing to let it go, or maybe you'll find someone who you *do* want to be with. You know how hard it is for you to say *no* sometimes. Marie always wants to please people, isn't that the truth? Tell the truth Marie, part of you is still looking for The One. You think that maybe, somewhere out there, there is someone who might be better for you. Someone who might be a better provider so that you can be a lady of leisure like your friend Mai?"

Marie swallowed hard. "That's not true and you know it."

Louis raised his eyebrows. "You sure?"

"I'm sorry, Louis. I didn't mean—"

"There is no need to apologize. But don't point fingers because no one is perfect here. All I'll say is, I'm committed to us, but are you?" He cleared his throat. "We need to focus on the immediate problem right now. I think you're overreacting by taking the kids."

Louis's words surprised her. This was the first time he'd ever said a word about her behavior. She didn't think he really noticed her at all sometimes and Marie was left was a large lump in her chest, a slow ache that hurt to the bone. "But what if I'm not?" She sniffed. "You can stay here if you want to, but I don't think it's safe." She grabbed her handbag and her car keys.

Marie's tears tore at Louis and he immediately softened. "Well, maybe you should wait until you calm down a little—"

"I'm fine. Besides, Kennedy needs me. Haven't been able to contact Mai. She's been having a rough time lately so I'm all Kennedy has right now."

Louis groaned. He knew he was going to answer a helluva lot of questions over the next few days. They had a lot to talk through. "Okay. I guess I'm coming, too." He might as well start on the short ride over to Kennedy's house, and if they didn't talk, at least he would be with his family.

Close Calls and
Guardian Angels

She couldn't sleep. Mai was dog-tired, but she couldn't make her body shut down no matter what she did. She'd kicked off her shoes as soon as she hit the house and by now had taken way too many pills. She knew this without even counting, but for some reason, she was still restless. She called her husband several times. They'd spoken briefly once, but he'd rushed her off the phone on the way to some so-called meeting. She wasn't stupid. He hadn't told her anything yet, but after she didn't get an answer this last time, she called the office and found out the truth.

Why couldn't he have just told her what was going on? She reviewed the receptionist's words over and over again in her head. "Calvin has been suspended pending investigation. He didn't tell you?" His little secret made her look like a fool. That woman was probably still cackling with the rest of the people in the office over that one.

But it got worse. If he wasn't at work, then he wasn't on a

business trip. Where in the hell was he? She sank into a chair and groaned. Kennedy and Marie had told her the truth, and she'd blown them off. Once again, she was his fool. "Don't you miss him when he travels so much?" Kennedy'd asked.

"No, girl," she'd said. "If he stays home too long, I get antsy. This is the way we operate. You'll see. No girl needs a husband seven days a week." That was the joke. Only this time, the joke was on her.

Wine would be good about now. Mai walked to the small wine steward in the kitchen and selected a bottle of red. She looked at the bottle and changed her mind, returning it to its shelf. She chose a bottle of Cakebread instead. The wine Calvin had been saving for a special occasion or visitor. Who was more special than she was? If Calvin didn't know it, she damn sure did.

He got to the truck stop early and sat in his car. Things were just as busy as they had been last time. This truck stop was a major one on the interstate, even though it was in the middle of the city. He watched the people coming and going for a few minutes. He'd had no idea that this many people that weren't truckers came to truck stops. There were teenagers just hanging out, neighborhood people coming into the convenience store to pick up forgotten items like milk or newspapers rather than going to the supermarket up the road. And of course there were people like him who were meeting some guy who was basically trying to extort money.

It'd been a rough week or so. Two months ago his life was totally different. He'd gone from being a well-respected corporate executive with a promising career and a wonderful home life, a great wife and respectful children, to an unshaven man, damn near unemployed, not sure how he was going to make his next mortgage payment, with belligerent children and a wife who was sleepy all the time and quickly becoming a recluse. How the hell had this happened to him? Sure things done in the dark come back to haunt you, but after more than a decade? He wasn't even sure of anything yet and his life was a shambles.

Fear and anger knotted inside him. In one way or the other, it was all his fault too. Calvin gripped his phone in one hand, tapping it on his steering wheel. Waiting had almost killed him, but it was time to solve part of the mystery. He could get his HIV result today. And at least if he knew, he could deal with it better, keep himself from getting an ulcer. At least not a huge one.

He pulled the slip of paper he'd taken from the clinic from his wallet. The number to call and his ID number were on it. This number would tell him his future. Calvin knew the statistics. Chances are, after this long, he probably didn't have HIV, but he needed to be sure. If it ever came down to discussing it with Mai, this was sure to come out and he needed to able to say for sure that he knew his status.

He had to dial three times before he got it right. The machine answered and Calvin gasped slightly. A shiver of panic ran through him. He half-listened to the recording, which told him to press *two* to transfer to a nurse counselor if he needed to discuss his results. He plugged in his number mechanically, then waited. How could a few minutes of fun that he couldn't even remember have led to so much anguish? It felt like he'd been living a soap opera, but Calvin knew that he was for sure when he burst into tears. His phone slipped from his hand and he sobbed, letting all the tension leave his body. Calvin Mott III cried huge tears of relief and was not ashamed of it either.

A new determination took over him as he slid into the cab of the truck for the second time. He rubbed his chin with the back of his hand, several days of growth scratched at his skin. He felt grungy, but relieved. Half of his problem was solved.

Davon came from the back, wiping his hands on paper towels. He nodded, then slid into the driver's seat. "Right on time."

Calvin was filled with disgust at the sight of him. He sneered, barely nodding back. From the way that Davon was dressed, you would never peg him as a truck driver, or at least Calvin wouldn't. He was dressed comfortably, but his clothes were stylish. And his shoes were still as shiny as they were the first day they met.

"Why do you wear those?"

Davon looked himself over, perplexed. "What?"

"The shoes, man." Calvin pointed at Davon's feet. "I don't even wear shoes like those. They're a little extravagant, especially for someone in your profession."

Davon sucked at his teeth, as if he were trying to remove the last bits of his lunch from the back of his mouth. "Well, I guess you don't have the taste I have. The one nice thing I do for myself." His face darkened. "And I may not be living high on the damned hog like you, but I do all right for myself, so don't worry yourself about my shoe budget, Mr. Big Willie."

Calvin stared out the window, suddenly getting a glimpse of blue in the side-view mirror. He craned his neck to see. "I think there's someone behind your truck walking around."

Davon shook his head. "Don't worry about that. It's nothing. A visitor just left."

"You got other friends in this area?" Calvin couldn't help his curiosity. Davon had made it his business to know so much about him, yet he still knew very little about him. Calvin was hungry for a little clue about his life too. He seemed to be a complex person and was certainly good at not revealing any meaningful details about his life. So much so, that Calvin was left with very little to work with.

Davon snorted. "I wouldn't call them friends. Lot lizards, you know."

It took a moment for what he was saying to register. His face gave away his confusion.

"Women. Ho's." Davon broke into a grin. "*You know.*"

Calvin's skin crawled with disgust. "No, I don't know. That ain't me, and after all the shit we're talking about and your sister dying the way she did, I'm surprised it's you."

"You're right, you don't know me." His face hardened. "Me and my sister are two different people. And I know you ain't judging me. Don't think 'cause you got more money that makes you better, 'cause it don't. It just makes your pockets fatter and that's about it. Don't get the shit twisted." Davon sighed, then reverted back to his sinister smile. "So, my man, as I was saying, your time is up. This is what I decided—"

"I don't know how you could decide anything. If I'm paying for a daughter, I think I should at least be able to see her. Something. And there is that issue of paternity."

"I wouldn't dream of you not being able to see your child. But the fact of the matter is, we can't afford no test or no lawyer." He paused. "With that being said, we think you ought to start paying us soon. Then we can get a test done."

"And if I refuse?"

"I go to the missus. We been over this, fool."

Calvin's face blanched. "So, how much did you *think*?" He racked his brain. He had enough for three mortgage payments, tops. Something was going to have to give. He was just going to have to come up with something to tell Mai.

"A few thousand ought to do it."

"And just how do you define a few?" Calvin's voice cracked. "You know I got suspended from my job, right?"

"That doesn't sound like it's my problem." Hatred blazed in his eyes. "Six is a few in my book."

Calvin choked. "What's so special about six? Most people would say three is a few."

"I ain't most people." He shrugged. "I just like the number. Not enough? Think I should ask for more? He grinned. "I didn't think so. Six. And don't even think about writing me a check. Your credit ain't no good here."

"It's not like anybody walks around carrying six grand. Whaddaya think I am? It's not like I have First National Bank stamped on my forehead."

Davon raised his eyebrows. "I see it clear as day. Listen, just because I got an accent doesn't mean I'm slow. Why're you trying me? Seems like I got all the good cards here, Mr. Mott."

Calvin held up his hands. "Okay. What then?"

Davon stretched in his seat, taking his time answering. "I think I like San Antonio. I'm going to take in some sights tonight, maybe check out your famous River Walk. Who knows, maybe even find me a real woman, that last one was too young for my taste. I don't like my women all timid and shit." He shrugged, licking his lips. "And then I'll meet you here tomorrow afternoon, that is, after you've gone to the bank and gotten me a cashier's check." He paused again. "I wouldn't want to carry that much cash around, na'mean? Could be dangerous."

Calvin nodded. He didn't have much choice. Six thousand was a break really. That would buy him some time.

Davon reached down and into a folder by his foot. "Here's who to make the check out to." His cold eyes glinted in the moonlight. "Don't be late."

Lishelle didn't know what to do. She was in over her head and was two minutes from hyperventilation. She took a deep breath in an attempt to calm down. Both of her friends were fine, they didn't seem to have a problem with any of this, but hanging out with these old men, for any reason, was creeping her out.

"So, where are we going?" She could barely conceal her anxiety.

"Chill. We are just going out to their rigs with them, that's all. Remember that you don't have to do anything you don't want to. Just play it by ear."

"Rigs?"

"Their trucks, Lishelle. Their trucks. I'm going to go with him," she pointed in one guy's direction and he winked at her. "You're going with him. He seems nice."

"I'm not sure I want to do that." She gulped.

"Get it together. It's okay. You will probably just talk and then when you are done, he'll hook you up."

"Hook me up?"

Star laughed. "Will you stop repeating me? Yes, and don't

take anything less than fifty bucks. We're not some two-bit prostitutes."

Lishelle thought that her friends were just talking shit about what they did, but apparently they weren't. And this was much worse than anything she heard them talk about. This was for real. No, they weren't prostitutes, but wasn't this the same thing?

Star read her mind. "Get it together. This is no different than what our parents do. Mom acts right, dad buys jewelry, get it?"

She shook her head quickly. She didn't get it. She was so terrified, she could hardly breathe.

Sophia and the men came from inside the diner. This time Sophia was in the center, laughing along as if this was an everyday occurrence for her. She didn't look at all concerned. "You ready?" She raised her eyebrows in a mischievous look, then reapplied her lipgloss without a mirror as the others looked on. They hung on her every movement. She smacked her lips together, then grinned. Lishelle was shocked as she looked on. Her friend had become so provocative.

"Perfect."

She giggled in response and slipped her hand through the arm of her friend.

Lishelle leaned back against the building for support. What was going to get her out of there? If only she'd listened to her mother and just stayed at the school. What in the hell had she been thinking? All she wanted was to have a little fun, but this was something else. She shuddered as images of prostitutes on television flashed in her mind. They all looked nothing like her, all dirty and skanky. She didn't need money or things bad enough to make this worth her time. She swallowed. It wasn't worth her dignity either.

"You sure you're okay?" The one with the nice eyes spoke to her softly. He hung back with Lishelle.

Lishelle stuck her hands in the pocket of her hoodie and didn't answer. She felt woozy and her head throbbed. She couldn't just say that she was scared shitless. Her friends would tease her to no end. They would probably just stop talking to her, and then what? Spread it all over school that she'd killed their good time.

He put his arm on her shoulder. "C'mon. Let's go talk over here." He tried to guide her further away from the groups, but Lishelle didn't get very far. She fainted dead away.

She didn't recognize where she was when she woke up. She was lying down, but she wasn't on the ground. She was in what looked like a bunk bed and there were two gray cabinets on the side. She looked up at the ceiling. The top bunk was folded back against the wall. The blue coverlet she was laying on scratched the side of her face. She moved a little to rub her face and then moaned.

She noticed the face then. It was the trucker with the southern accent and nice eyes. He was sitting in front of a brown, vinyl curtain that appeared to open in the middle. His grin chilled her and the memories came rushing back. Lishelle panicked, and he shushed her.

"You're okay and I'm not going to hurt you. Have a drink of water." He pushed a glass toward her and she shook her head. He sat it in a drink holder inside the cabinet near her head.

"My friends?"

"They're around. I told them I'd take care of you. Make sure you were okay. Them some silly bitches you were hanging out with."

So much for sticking together. It was obvious that neither Star nor Sophia gave two shits about her. They'd left her with some strange man who'd done heaven knows what with her. "I need to go."

"You should. You don't belong with those girls. They didn't even make sure you were okay. Is there someone you can call? Do you have a phone?"

Lishelle thought for a minute, then sat up. Her head swam and she pressed her lids together to try and steady the small space they were in. She couldn't call her mother. And she didn't have time to sneak back into school. "Where am I?"

"In my cab. I carried you here when you fainted."

Lishelle blushed. She'd obviously gotten the better end of the deal. "I don't know what happened."

"Really? I do. You were scared shitless. But I don't know why. According to these," he snapped one of her bracelets, "you ought to at least be down to give me a blow job before you go."

Lishelle's face blanched. "These are just bracelets. I don't—" Lishelle burst into tears, her stomach sickening. "Please."

He was silent for a minute. "I ain't going to hurt you. I like my tricks a little more seasoned." He paused. "You can use my phone if you don't have one, but you gotta leave. I got a meeting in a few and I'm not sure how it's going to turn out. Can you walk? I won't touch you again if you think it'll make you faint."

Lishelle managed a weak smile. "I have a phone."

"I can say I ain't never had that kind of effect on a girl before." He opened the door for her. "You really should have thought this through, been more careful in your choice of friends. You seem like a really nice girl." He looked away. "It's a good thing you remind me of someone. Get out."

Lishelle nodded, then slipped out of the door. Someone was surely looking out for her today. Her Auntie Ree would have said that God watches out for fools and small children. There was no doubt in her mind that she'd been a fool today. Just as she hopped down from the truck, she heard a door slam. Her body shook as she hurried toward the convenience store and slipped inside. Neither one of her friends were anywhere to be found. That figured. Not that it mattered; as far as they knew, she couldn't hang. She'd been Good Girl Mott forever, and from where she was standing, that didn't seem like such a bad problem to have.

There wasn't much in her bag, so her phone was easy to find. It was a Firefly, just like the other girls had. Four choices. That was all she had.

The clerk eyed her as she leaned against the wall to hold herself up. Her legs were so weak, she doubted they would be able to carry her any further. Her chest was heaving as the full impact of what might have happened hit her. She could have been raped or worse. And no one knew where she was. Any way she put it, she was in deep shit, but it didn't matter. Right now, she just wanted to go home. *Breathe.* Her hands trembled as she pressed the button to call the least of the evils. She held it long enough for the phone to make a loud screeching sound. *Breathe.* It was going to be all right.

"Hello?" Marie's voice was music to Lishelle's ears.

Lishelle was so overwhelmed that she couldn't speak. The words caught in her throat.

"Hello," she said again.

"It's me," she said. "Lishelle." That was all she could get out before she burst into tears.

Marie left the engine running, jumped out, and ran into the convenience store, leaving Louis and the kids in the car. She spotted Lishelle immediately. She was standing by the door, still sobbing. There was a clerk near her trying to comfort her. Marie hurried over, trying not to panic. The girl had obviously called her because she needed her to be strong.

"What in the world? What are you doing here?"

Lishelle cried harder and threw her arms around Marie. Tears ran down her face and into her mouth. "I'm so sorry."

Marie turned to the clerk. "What happened?"

"I don't know. She came in and stood here and then she just broke down. I asked her if she wanted me to call the police or something but she said no."

"Are you hurt?" She looked her over quickly. "Shhh. Let's go. I'll take you home." Lishelle was in bad shape. She gave new meaning to the word hysterical. They would have to talk later, after she found a way to calm down.

Marie took a tissue from the counter and dabbed at Lishelle's face as she led her to the car. She had lots of questions, like how does a thirteen-year-old end up in a truck stop way across town in the middle of the school day? They would have to wait though. She could only wonder what she'd gotten into. Whatever it was, it was bad enough that she'd called her first. That could only mean one thing, that whatever the chain of events were that led her to the truck stop, they were bizarre enough that she was afraid to call either one of her parents.

Lishelle fell asleep in the car. Louis didn't speak, but he and Marie exchanged lots of questioning glances on the way to her house. They planned to drop her off and then head over to Kennedy's.

Marie tried to reach both Mai and Calvin several times, but she couldn't get either one. That in itself was unusual. It had been quite a tiring day already and all the trauma was making Marie even more tired. She snuck a peek at Lishelle as they pulled into the driveway of her house. She hoped that she and Louis were the kind of parents whose kids felt they could talk to them about anything, and if not, she hoped that her kids would feel as comfortable with her friends as Lishelle did with her. She prayed they always felt they had someone to call, someone that she and Louis trusted to do the right thing.

"You want me to go in?" Louis's voice was gentle.

Marie shook her head. "No, I'll walk her in and make sure that Mai doesn't kill her. She's been so bizarre lately." This drama with Lishelle only put their struggles in perspective. Louis was a good man and he tried to do the right thing. "I'm sorry, Louis. I didn't mean all those things I said earlier."

His look was full of tenderness. Louis leaned over and kissed his wife gently on the lips.

Marie slipped from the car, opened the rear door, and gently shook Lishelle awake. They walked to the house together.

"Your mother didn't answer when I called, so hopefully she's here."

"I think she is. I know she had some meeting today."

"And is your dad still out of town?"

Lishelle's face darkened and she shrugged. "They don't tell me anything anymore."

Mai didn't comment. She knocked on the door, then waited. The house sounded very silent. "You have your key? If no one is here I'll feel more comfortable if you came with us over to Kennedy's. Is that okay?"

Lishelle dug in her pocket for the key. She nodded and handed it over. She had no intention of staying alone, not now. After what she had been through, she would do anything her mother or Marie told her to.

The door swung open easily. "It wasn't locked." She smiled and stepped aside to let Lishelle go in first "Your mother must be here. She probably didn't hear us. She never leaves the door unlocked like this." She followed Lishelle inside. "Mai? Where are you?"

Lishelle dropped her small handbag by the door and Marie walked toward the kitchen. She didn't have a good feeling about today, but could it possibly get any worse?

"You want something to drink, Lishelle? Some water?" She walked around the island to the refrigerator. "You look like you feel a lot better than you did earlier—" Marie choked on her words. She was right, Mai was home. Mai Mott was lying on the floor in front of her, legs and arms akimbo, passed out.

Doctor, Doctor

Kennedy cringed and paced the floor. She felt terrible. If anything had happened to her father, she would never forgive herself. *Lord, please give me patience.* Emara sat in front of her, taking her time explaining her story. She was a very put-together woman. Mai would certainly approve of her fashion sense. She was dressed head to toe in a column of cream and smelled of expensive perfume. Her salt-and-pepper hair was immaculate. Dad still had good taste, and Emara seemed genuinely concerned. She'd come right over as soon as Kennedy asked her to.

"You have to excuse me. My father never mentioned you at all. In fact, I had no idea that he left the house at all without me."

"Well, he left a lot. We have been having tea for almost two weeks." She giggled like a schoolgirl. "I have to admit it's been a while since I've had a beau."

"A beau?" Kennedy couldn't help but smile. "It's been a while since I heard anyone say the word *beau*."

"Yes. That's what Davy is." She patted Kennedy's knee. "Don't worry honey. I'm sure he's okay. He probably needed to go somewhere and forgot to call me. You know we don't always like to report to our kids. He probably forgot to call you too. That happens at our age."

She had to get past this nickname, one her father never liked. Kennedy hoped she was right, but just in case, she was going to call all the neighbors and see what they knew. She'd already called the police. Troy was in the other room making calls. "Did you know that he had Alzheimer's?" Kennedy asked Emara.

"Not Davy. He was as clear as a bell."

Kennedy pressed her finger to the spot between her eyes, pressing them tightly shut. It took everything she had not to break down. "That may be, but he was on medication. He gets disoriented sometimes, so anything you can tell us will really help. You said he went on walks. Maybe you can take me where you think he went."

Troy burst in from the kitchen. The phone was still plastered to his ear. "Marie's on the phone for you."

Kennedy glared at him. They had agreed that he would quietly call the neighbors while she tried to get any details she could from Emara.

"You need to talk to her."

She took the phone from him. "I thought you were coming over here. I'm really worried about my father and I need you here. I can't find Mai. I need at least one of you—"

"Mai is here. With me." Marie paused. "Kennedy, you need to get here. Your father's here, too." She paused. "We're at the hospital."

Kennedy's head spun. "What? Is he all right? How did you get there?" She gave Troy a stressed look.

"They won't tell me anything since we're not related. I'll tell you everything when you come. We're at Methodist."

The waiting room at Methodist Hospital looked more like a family reunion than a trauma center. Marie, Louis, and their children sat waiting with Lishelle, trying to comfort her as tears streamed down her face. She'd almost fainted when the paramedics took her mother in the ambulance. Calvin stormed in and Marie's mouth dropped open in surprise. Lishelle cried harder when she spotted her father with her little sister and brother trailing behind.

"What in the hell is going on?' he demanded. He sat down and immediately tried to hug Lishelle. She surprised him by pulling away.

"How'd you get here? We couldn't get hold of you. I thought you were out of town." The words tumbled out of Marie's mouth.

"Louis tracked me down."

Louis looked away and cleared his throat. There was a heavy silence in the room for a minute as Marie glared at her husband again. "More secrets, Louis?"

He shook his head. "I called Maxfield. I knew if anyone could track him down, Max would be able to. He's on his way over, too."

"Where is she?" Calvin looked around expectantly. Worry creased his brow. He'd aged five years in the past few weeks.

Marie motioned with her head. "In trauma. We found her

passed out in the kitchen. Apparently too much mixing of her Valium with alcohol."

Calvin glared at Marie. "What the hell are you talking about? She doesn't take Valium." His words were full of anger.

"Don't shoot the messenger." She left Lishelle and pulled him into the corner by his shirt sleeve. "Keep your voice down. The kids don't need to know all the details."

Marie paused. "Seems as if you two have been a little out of touch, lately, huh? She does take Valium. Has a regular prescription for it."

"Where's the doctor?" A range of emotions surged through him. He'd obviously put Mai under too much stress. "Did she try to kill herself?"

"The doctor doesn't think so. He said it was probably an accident. But they did find way too much Valium in her system."

"I had no idea." The gravity of the situation began to sink in.

"You didn't talk much in the past few weeks."

He opened his mouth to speak, but decided to let it go. She was accusing him, but it didn't matter. What Marie or anyone else thought wasn't important right now. The only thing that mattered was his family, and he was pretty sure that some of his own stupidity was responsible for the state they were in. "And Lishelle, how did you end up with her?"

Lishelle had finally stopped crying and now leaned back in her chair, her head against the wall. Her eyes were closed and she looked tired and defeated. "I think you two need to talk about that. She called me on her emergency phone and I picked her up." She lowered her voice. "She was at a truck stop. We didn't have time to talk about it, but she was pretty distressed."

He looked at his daughter incredulously. "She was supposed to be in school." A memory played in his head in slow motion. The color of the hoodie she wore. The shadow in the rear-view mirror. Could it be that he'd seen his own daughter leaving Davon's truck? He couldn't imagine how the two would be connected, but he was going to find out.

Kennedy almost fainted with relief. Not only was her father fine, he was his normal, belligerent self. The hospital staff couldn't tell her anything about the young woman that had brought him in, the only thing she could get was that she was very young looking, and her skirt was too short. Emara stood behind her pouting, but she sensed that the two of them would work it out.

She fingered the card the nurse had given her. It was the business card she had dropped into her father's pocket. He had no real identification on him since Kennedy had taken his driver's license a while ago.

"That was the only thing we found on him. He also had a few dollars in his wallet. You can claim all his things when he is discharged." The nurse smiled warmly. "We're going to need you to fill out the rest of the forms before you go. I tried to call the number on the card but I didn't get an answer. Was going to try again tomorrow. He's too mean to stay a John Doe for long."

Kennedy laughed. "He can be tough sometimes."

"Davy was always sweet to me. But I guess there was a side to him I didn't know. I can't imagine him hanging out with a young hussy, whoever she was."

"Emara, she did bring him to the hospital, so it worked out."

She ignored Kennedy and huffed away. Troy rubbed Kennedy's back as the nurse handed her a ton of paperwork.

"Is he home alone a lot?" she asked.

"I work. He lives with me." Kennedy tensed. She didn't want to explain herself to a stranger.

"That's tough. I went through the same thing with both of my parents. I discovered that letting them go to an assisted living facility was the best thing I could have done for all of us."

She drew in her breath. "I don't want him in a home."

"I'm not suggesting that. But I can have the social worker fill you in on some of your options."

"Thanks," she said tersely.

Troy was quiet as he watched Kennedy scribbling away on the paperwork. She would be busy for a while. "I'm glad we found him. I didn't think you were going to make it." He paused. He'd been genuinely worried about her. "You know, I can go check out some of the places with you. I wouldn't mind."

"No."

"At least consider it. I'm pretty sure if your father realized what was happening, he wouldn't want you to be this stressed about his care. It's your turn to live your life, and he might appreciate being able to continue to live in his own space with people his own age. You see how fast that Emara glommed onto him. He might like being with a bunch of old ladies. They would probably think he's still a hottie."

Kennedy fought back tears and a smile at the same time. "You're just saying that because you don't want him kicking you out of my room again."

He chuckled. "Maybe. No, definitely. I'm not going to lie, but promise me you'll think about it."

She poked him with her elbow. "We'll see."

"Seriously, it's not about me, or even you. You have to think about what the best situation is going to be for him and his quality of life. They're not all bad. In fact some of the senior communities are very nice."

She swallowed hard. He was right. The thought of putting her father in some kind of home was not a pleasant one, but the past few weeks with him had been rough, and the only thing she knew for sure is that maybe living alone wasn't such an appealing idea after all. Having someone to grow old with was looking better all the time, especially if he was going to chase her around the streets when she was old and crazy so her kids didn't have to. Both of her friends had someone who was there for them. Their situations might not be ideal, but at least they were all in it together.

Done in the Dark. . . .

Calvin and Maxfield stood quietly in a corner of the hospital waiting room. Louis flipped through the papers that Maxfield produced, weighing the evidence. How in the world had he gotten himself mixed up with all this? One day, his life was normal, the next, everything was all shot to hell.

"How'd you get this stuff again?" he asked. He couldn't believe the information that Maxfield had gotten hold of and didn't really want to know how he did it. Fortunately, most of it looked like it would be very helpful.

"The birth and death certificates were easy. The Internet is a wonderful thing." Maxfield grinned a slow, sly smile. "Turns out tons of people want to research their ancestry. The rest, well, I can't tell you that. Just know I have my ways. Friends with access to hospital records. Everyone went to law school with someone in the right place. You just have to ask."

"I underestimated you."

"Happens a lot. Sometimes it's to my benefit."

Calvin's mind whirred. All the times Max acted crazy or tried hard to act like he didn't matter were obviously hiding skills and talents that none of his friends knew about. Skills that could help when you needed, and none of the men doubted that not all of the skills were legal.

Part of Davon's story was true. The rest, Calvin couldn't figure. "Well, his sister did indeed have a child, and from the timing, it could have been mine." He rustled the papers and studied them harder.

"But look at these dates." Max pointed over his shoulder. "According to this, the child only lived about two weeks. So you're off the hook."

"Maybe." A child's death was a sad thing, no matter what the situation.

"And the mother did die, but the cause of death listed isn't HIV or HIV-related."

"We can't tell that from this. We don't know whether she was HIV positive or not."

"But we do know that she overdosed on something."

Calvin paced the floor, still pensive. All of the stress he and his family had been through was caused by a bunch of bullshit. If he'd had the courage to talk to his wife in the first place, they might have found all this out a while ago and saved himself a few gray hairs, not to mention the humiliation of that free clinic.

"You should be overjoyed. You're off the hook. Davon is a con man and he picked you as an easy target. For all we know, he might be doing this kind of thing to anyone and everyone who was ever associated with his sister in any way."

"So you say. But I have another concern." He looked into the next room at his daughter. She was still distraught and sat flanked by Kennedy and Marie.

"What? I would be more worried if she wasn't upset. She found her mother passed out on the floor."

"That's not it." Calvin lowered his voice. "I'm certain I saw her at the truck stop. She was coming out of his cab—"

"Whose?"

"Davon's. She was with him." He punched his hand with his fist. The magnitude of the implication almost knocked him over. "She's only a child. If he messed with my baby—"

Louis had been listening quietly to this point. "Calm down. You gotta get yourself together."

"I'm still going to meet with him. If he even touched one single hair on her head—"

"Wasn't one brush with the law enough? You want to jeopardize your family any more than you already have by keeping this stuff from Mai? You know better than that, Calvin." Confusion and anger riddled Louis's face.

Calvin looked from Maxfield's face to Louis's. Louis was right. Jail was not an experience he wanted to revisit anytime soon. He'd been strip-searched and thrown in a cell with all sorts of people. He shuddered to think of even walking past a jail again. "What am I supposed to do?"

Maxfield cleared his throat. "I'll tell you what. I'll make sure it's taken care of, but you can't ever speak of this again, not even to ask me any questions. People like Davon deserve a special kind of justice."

"I'm not sure I approve of vigilante justice—" Louis shook his head.

"If it were your daughter, what would you do?" Maxfield paused, searching Louis's face. "You're not the one who has to approve." He extended his hand toward Calvin, who didn't take it immediately.

He cocked his head to the side, contemplating the offer being made to him. Max's seedy side ran deeper than he thought, but people did what they had to in order to survive. He shuddered to think of the kinds of people he obviously knew, but Max had come through every time he'd needed him to. "Can I—?"

Max shook his head and stared his friend straight in the eye.

Calvin waited a second, then slowly took Max's still-outstretched hand. His family was worth it.

And Now for the Light

Mai watched as Lishelle arranged fresh flowers in a vase on the kitchen counter. She smiled. She'd taken her punishment to heart and without complaint. Whatever had happened when she cut school had scared her straight.

Lishelle looked and returned her mother's smile. "You feeling okay, Mom?" she asked.

Mai nodded. Ever since she'd come home from the hospital, they'd all been on pins and needles, like they expected her to pass out any minute. Truth was, she hadn't so much as had an aspirin since she'd been home.

"I'm going to my room to do my homework."

Since she was grounded, her room was about the only place that she could go. And there was little fun to be had there since her computer had been moved down to the family room. Lishelle had lost the privilege of being able to talk to her friends online. As a matter of fact, Louis and Mai had a talk with the headmaster and her friends' parents. Lishelle was not allowed to speak to Star or Sophia, much less hang out with either of them, in school or out.

She and her father hadn't quite made peace with each other. He walked into the kitchen and turned on the television on the counter. Lishelle rolled her eyes and left her parents standing silent in the room.

The awkwardness hung heavy between them as the early evening news blared in the background. Mai'd been attending outpatient drug counseling diligently and she'd had a major breakthrough today, one that involved her husband. She was sure that somehow he was at the center of everything she felt about her life and herself. She waited until Lishelle was out of earshot to speak.

"Calvin, I think you need to move out."

He swallowed hard. "You want a divorce?"

"I'm not saying that yet. I need space to just be with myself. All I've done over the past few years is be your wife, I can't even remember what Mai was like." She looked away.

"Just like that?" It wasn't like he hadn't known it was coming. They'd been skillfully avoiding the issue for a while.

Mai nodded and fought back the tears. It was hard, but she knew she had to stay strong.

A Woman's Worth

Mai raised her drink for a toast. Both Marie and Kennedy raised their eyebrows at her.

"I know you heifers ain't tripping over a glass of wine. I'm not an alcoholic, for goodness sakes." She looked from one to the other. "I can have a glass of wine. It's actually a better choice than a bottle of pills. I just got carried away with the prescription, that's all."

"Yeah, carried away and dropped on your natural ass." Kennedy sipped hers discreetly.

"Whatever. It happens to people all the time." Mai waved their concerns away. "I got this. It's been months and I'm fine."

"You scared the hell out of us. You scared the hell out of Lishelle, too. She was a wreck in that car with me and Louis."

"I know. I feel so bad about that. I truly had no idea that I would be knocked out like I was. But I'm still going to therapy to help handle my stress. And I've taken up yoga with all those skinny, pretzel-bodied, little women that can throw their legs over their shoulders and stuff."

Marie was happy to see her friend in such good spirits. "A little therapy never hurt anyone."

"Lishelle is going too."

Kennedy cleared her throat at the obvious admission. "So, what about Calvin. Is he going?"

"I knew you would bring him up, being that you have your newfound faith in relationships and all. I'm happy for you, Kennedy." There was a touch of sadness in Mai's voice.

"Why don't you let him come back home?" Marie said.

"I'm not ready. He lied to me, big time. Louis lied to you too. They all lied together."

"Louis didn't lie, he omitted."

"That's different?" Mai rolled her eyes.

"I wasn't exactly honest with him either. We had to take a good long look at our relationship. It was a good thing for us, actually. I realized that I didn't want to travel so much—"

"No, what you realized was all that talk about trees falling in the woods was a load of crap. It was all good when you were the one out there, but when you realized that Louis might be cutting some branches of his own, you couldn't take it. I told you that was a bunch of mess." Kennedy sat back in her chair and folded her arms. She still believed that Marie had been wrong all along.

"And you can stop interrupting me, missy. Don't get all high and mighty because someone has your nose wide open for the first time in years." She paused. "For your information, I missed my kids. And he needed to go to a regular office—"

"To get away from that crazy woman," Mai said. "I don't know what I would have done if someone like that was trying to get all up in my family. I don't see how you didn't just roll up on her and do something to her, like that astronaut in Texas or that other woman who ran over her cheating husband. Remember that one?"

"Then I would be no better than she was." A mischievous smile played about her mouth. "Louis was already mine, ladies. There was no need to fight over him. Did I tell you she moved out of the building?"

Both Mai and Kennedy gasped. "Really?"

Marie nodded. "Seems she could no longer stand her living conditions."

Kennedy narrowed her eyes. "You did something."

Marie tried her best to look innocent. "I didn't. Just because the super wouldn't fix anything in her apartment and that awful odor that somehow developed. Who would have thought that the super couldn't keep up with the repairs in her place? He was so competent in other areas."

"I see." Kennedy said. "He kept up with everyone else's repairs, right? Just not hers?"

Marie didn't answer. She just winked and took a sip of her wine.

"Makes perfect sense to me too," Mai agreed. There were nods all around the table on that one.

"I suppose you're going to tell me that you know nothing about that trucker found at the truck stop. The one dead in his cab, barefoot?"

"I'm a lot of things, but not a murderer," Mai said. A chill ran down her spine. "We don't even know if it's the same guy."

A phone trilled.

"It's mine." Mai flipped her phone open while Kennedy and Marie waited patiently. Her face looked a little tense as she said a few words, then flipped it shut.

"Sorry. That was Calvin. His turn with the kids this weekend. He needed to know about sitters."

Marie blushed. "Aren't you being a little hard on him? There was no love child, that's a good thing, right?"

Mai shrugged. "I wasn't even mad about the kid thing. I was mad because he didn't tell me. Then he was going to try and pay that thug without including me. That's a problem." She sighed. "He needs to get to know me again. See what he's missing."

"Don't take too long." Kennedy sipped her drink. "You don't want some young thang to turn his head."

"He's not going anywhere. We're just taking our time to re-align our family objectives."

Kennedy laughed. "You sound like it's a business."

Mai nodded her head. "It is. And I'm handling mine." She stood up to leave. "We're finding new ways to make each other remember to appreciate what the other does, all of the time." She winked. "And if you'll excuse me, I gotta go get ready for my date."

Marie looked crushed. "A date? How could you? You're technically still married to Calvin."

There was a mischievous look in her eye. "I am. But that doesn't mean I can't date him. Take a lesson, ladies, take a lesson."

A+

AUTHOR
INSIGHTS,
EXTRAS, &
MORE...

FROM
**NINA
FOXX**
AND
AVON A

Acknowledgments

$\mathcal{A}$ long time ago, in a conversation with a very close friend, we were discussing the merits of a commuter marriage. She's been married almost forty years to the same man (of course she's a lot older than I am), and her husband works in a different city for most of the week and has been doing so for ten years. I asked her how she was able to stand the separation. She looked me straight in the eye and said quite plainly, "Honey, no girl needs a husband seven days a week."

Later, another friend, married to a man who travels regularly, told me if he stayed home too long, it was tense. She loved when he was home and she loved when he left. They'd developed a routine. Last summer there was an article in the Chicago *Times* about how African-American women didn't seem to be getting married as much or are getting married much later. I looked closely, and it seemed that this was true across the board. So many women are not defined by the *Mrs.* in front of their names anymore. Relationships are coming in all different shapes and sizes and flavors, and I tried to think up a few, throw some drama in the pot, and hence this book was born.

That being said, none of the characters are real, although we all know someone who fits the general type of each couple. We all know a Mai and Calvin or a Kennedy who thinks she doesn't believe in the fairy tale anymore. Although you may think I wrote your life, I really didn't. The characters wrote themselves, of course with some help from my friends who have no idea how comical they are to me in that funny world inside my head. Thank you to all the characters in my life that do things that get me saying "What if . . . ?"

And of course, many of the places are real and I've taken some liberties with others. Things in the news caught my interest and got thrown in. Down here in Texas we had several truckers that were found dead in their cabs at the same truck stop, and of course those multi-colored bracelets were in the headlines and have indeed been banned from several schools.

And then there's the scary bunch who said things I'd already written, leaving me feeling as if I was in the middle of a Stephen King novel. If I write it, they will come. Can anyone say "Twilight Zone"?

Deepest gratitude to my writer friends, who always at least acted like they were listening when I'd hit a wall. Carmen Green, Lori Bryant Woolridge, Reshonda Tate Billingsly, and to my other writer friend who helped me see things from a male perspective, Eric Jerome Dickey. Thanks to other soccer moms who used to be ad execs for the insight into the advertising world, specifically Cindy Ferrell-Moore, Gina Harris for the drug advice, and to Jihan El-Rady for drawing the inside of a tractor-trailer cab for me. My editors at Avon, Carrie Feron and Esi Sogah. My agent, Elaine Koster. So many girlfriends breathed life into my women—Pam Walker Williams, RosCet Varner, and Tonya Terry at WSFA in Montgomery, and of course thanks to my family and closest friends for being patient and reading and re-reading without too much griping: Lynda Scott, Brandie Scott, Barry Jennings, Sydney, Kai, and Major. The rest of my family who will read and support without question: Dina, Stephanie, Brian, Charlenne, Gloria, Vincent, and Pring and the rest of the Foxx, Greer, Horton, Hamilton, and Gilliam Clans, my sorors of Alpha Kappa Alpha Sorority, Inc., my Link Sisters the world over, and my sisters in Jack & Jill. Last but not least, thanks to the readers. Go readers! It's your birthday! Go readers!

From Nina's Journal

November 2006

I got an interesting email the other day. It was from someone at ABC. They read my blog and wanted to know if I would consider being on "Wife Swap." We have watched the show many times. It's the one where the woman either comes home looking like she is a stone-cold weirdo or she is a saint and ends up being more appreciated by the ungrateful slug she left at home. Question is, which woman would I be? Hmmm. I mighta done it. I could use a break. It would be a vacation.

Then they told me I couldn't pick the family I swapped with. Just who would I give to my family, and who would I pick for myself?

I discussed it with my family. My oldest daughter begged me and begged me to try it. "Mom, the new mom would probably let me write on the wall. Or I wouldn't have a bedtime."

She might, but she might also only dress you at Wal-Mart

(forget that Juicy sweatshirt you want) and allow only one pair of shoes. The ones you wear with your school uniform. I assure you the shoes would not be pink or purple as you requested. Or she might not cook at all, and believe me you would get tired of macaroni and cheese if that was all you had to eat five out of seven nights a week. You bet your iPod Shuffle you would be scrounging for vegetables.

The youngest one went along with the flow because it looked like fun. Her bigger sister was hanging on around my neck, swinging back and forth like a wayward necktie in a 1970's disco as she begged me to give it serious consideration. That one would change her tune the minute the new mom told her to get over it when her sister picked on her, instead of commiserating just to make her feel better. And custom-shaped pancakes for everyone on Sunday morning? Forgetaboutit. God forbid you would have to eat a round pancake instead of one shaped like a gingerbread woman. Worse yet, she might make you one shaped like a gingerbread man! Not to mention that her little heart would be broken when the new mom informed her that her bacon doesn't come from an animal that goes "gobble-gobble" and milk comes from the Chik-fil-A billboard cow rather than miraculously produced from a bean with a multitude of uses.

The babysitter—she didn't say no, she said, "Hell no." She was worried that they would get some weirdo who didn't clean (not that I do, don't get it twisted), or worse yet, the new mom would make her leave. The new mom always makes babysitters, nannies, help, and grandparents leave. Time off. She claims she would come back to watch because it was sure to be hilarious. She wasn't going anywhere, she assured me, she belongs here. Babysitter gets a raise.

Now, we get to my spouse. He said, "Of course you told them no." He wouldn't participate. Period. Wouldn't want America to see the inside of his life. Who would really? For him it would take a lot more than what they are offering. He's the pensive kind, prone to few words. I'm sure many of my friends think he doesn't talk at all, or at least he only talks to me. They'd probably swap me with a wife who talked *all* the time (instead of one who writes all the time), and he would end up locking himself in the TV room so he could catch a break.

Truth is, I can't imagine who my opposite would be or where they would send me. I've lived everywhere but in a trailer, so that is certainly where I'd go. To a trailer park in West Virginia (no offense to West Virginia trailer park inhabitants), where they have never seen a black person much less a dreadlock, in a city where the only anchor store in the almost nonexistent mall would be JC Penney and not Neiman Marcus (my favorite), and there is no satellite TV or Starbucks. I would have to do without "Nip/Tuck" (which I officially gave up when they made the doctor's wife sleep with the midget), and eat red meat and pork three times a day for the entire time. And shoes, forget it, I would be relegated to Wal-Mart brand work boots.

The new husband would spit his tobacco on the floor and balk when he found out the truth—yes, they would get custom breakfast on Sunday, but those work shirts, they gotta go to the cleaners because I don't iron. I have an iron, normally reserved for guests, but how, exactly, do I make it work? And vacuum? Uh-uh. I gave that up about ten years ago when I broke my toe on one while I was vacuuming trying to get ready for a holiday party. Good thing I realized the toe was broken before it had time to swell up,

I bandaged my foot with the Giuseppe Zanottis I planned to

wear to the party and hobbled through it, while I medicated with the holiday punch. Don't let it ever been said I'm not a trouper. It hurt like hell but it sure looked damn good.

What, trailers don't have dishwashers? Well, how do the dishes get clean? I rub them with what? A rag? You're shitting me, right?

And the house, it has to be clean, so Merry Maids would gain a new client.

I think I would make it through the week. The new mom would be happy when she returned. Her husband would take her to dinner at least once a month, to a place with actual waiters, and her kids would be respectful or locked in the closet and she wouldn't have to home school them anymore. My kids, they would learn about actual *chores*. Not the piddly ones they have, like feeding the cat and dog and clearing the table. Or the hardest one the big girl has, pushing the *start* button on the dishwasher. They would learn about real chores like chopping their own fireplace wood. I mean, why buy it? We have a backyard full of trees. Or they might discover that *doing your laundry* means actually washing the clothes as opposed to just throwing them down the laundry chute, and no, the cat doesn't belong in there at all.

I have just one question—do those work boots come in pink?

July 2006

Warning: The following contains graphic language and is an absolutely true story. It is not for the faint of heart and children are advised to leave the room.

Moving is a muthaf—.

I couldn't sit still and let the packers pack my stuff, I had to walk through and see if there was something I could do. Of course, there is always stuff behind stuff, especially in a kid's room. Behind my daughter's kitchen playset, a discarded nightgown was lurking. I decided to pick it up and put it where it belonged when—ouch, no sh—(*&^^%%), I heard a snapping sound and felt sharp pain on my fingers.

Ohmigod!

I threw my phone and the nightgown and grabbed my finger, crunking again. I was getting good at this. My kids screamed, "What's wrong, Mom?!"

Something had bitten me. Immediately, I thought the worst. I grabbed my finger and tried to hold the poison I knew to be coursing through my veins down in the digit. Maybe I had been stung by a brown recluse? I thought better of holding the finger and reached over to the bathroom sink and ran water on it.

Wait, I needed to remove my ring because I liked that ring, and if my finger started to swell (it was doing that already), they might have to cut my ring off. Couldn't have that. I was calm and rational in the face of adversity.

I told the babysitter. "Something bit me."

"What?" They all stepped back.

"Something bit me. It was in that nightgown."

I watched every eye in the room widen.

"Carefully pick up that nightgown. Let's see what it is."

I needed to know if I was going to lose a finger or if I was just suffering some more after-effects of my oil-bred mosquito incident on Monday.

She didn't see anything at first.

"I'm not crazy. Something bit me."

She turned the nightgown around and around. My nine-year-old screamed and sprinted across the room. "I see it, Mom. It was a scorpion. Oh, no! Not you, Mom!" She said that like it was *curtains* for me.

"Stay calm. Is it pink or black?" I was holding my finger again and letting the water run over it.

"I see it! I see it!"

My four-year-old screamed. That *emer-efer* was just sitting there, happy, curled up on my baby's nightgown. I tried to hold back the anger I was feeling. That thing that happens when a mother feels her child has been endangered.

"Let me kill it," the sitter said.

"No, we can't do that. We might need it."

They looked at me like I was a little loopy. And I was feeling a little loopy. Light-headed. Was my tongue swelling?

Oh, Lord.

I tried to remain calm. "I'm not sure what to do."

My four-year-old was the voice of reason. "Mommy, you are going to have to get a shot!"

"Poison control?" the nanny suggested.

We settled on dialing 911. They would tell us if it was an emergency. I was sweating as she dialed, wondering if my switch to Vonage would prove to be a mistake. It wasn't.

But they listened to the problem, instructed her to sit me down and remove my pets from the area. Was I going to turn into a pet-eating monster or something? I did as instructed. And then a major blow came. They were sending the paramedics.

Ohmigod.

This must be bad then, right?

I needed to call someone and tell them I was dying. No, not

a good idea, what good would that do? And not five minutes later the county fire department showed up. No sirens though. This is a good neighborhood and the sound would disturb the neighbors. Three fire-people came in. First-responder types.

"How old are you, ma'am?"

"What? My real age?"

"Do you feel pain?"

"Of course I do."

And then the paramedics showed up. Three of them. Three must be a magic number. Just like "Schoolhouse Rock."

I wanted to cry. I was loopy now. And crying. I told my nanny to take my kids to the mall or something. They would be traumatized if they witnessed my death. That wouldn't be good.

The fire-dude ran the situation down for the paramedic.

"We have a ??-year-old female, been bitten by a scorpion."

"Hey! Hey!" I felt like Archie Bunker.

He rephrased himself. "We have a 26-year-old female, been bitten by a scorpion."

He asked me about my symptoms, hooked me up to lots of machines. Oxygen. Blood O_2 levels. Pressure cuff.

"What's today's date?" They were flashing light in my eyes.

"Try another question. I never know the date."

"Do you still have the scorpion?"

I told him where it was and one of them went to investigate.

My hands were trembling. I was seeing spots. No, those were hornets outside my door. I made a mental note to call the exterminator.

"How much do you weigh ma'am?"

"Hey! Hey! I weigh what I'm supposed to weigh. I'm almost five-eight."

"A hundred and thirty-two pounds."

"Don't you see I'm a black woman, here? Put one-forty-five. Am I gonna die?"

At that point the scorpion finder entered. "This is a common bark scorpion. A baby. See the markings?" He was holding it between pliers. "I think I squoze the bugger to death."

"Oh, Lord."

"You should be fine. Unless of course you go into anaphalactic shock."

"Oh, Lord."

"But you would have done that already."

"Her pulse is coming down."

"Oh, Lord."

"No, no, that's good."

"Okay." I really do think I saw spots.

"We need you to sign releases if you aren't going to let us take you to the hospital."

"I'm not."

"All of our paperwork was written by lawyers, but don't be alarmed by that chance of death part."

"Jesus, Mohammed, and Buddha."

"You'll be fine. You'll need some Benadryl."

I thought a moment. Which box had the Benadryl?

"And you shouldn't go running or anything like that."

Dang. I really needed to exercise.

"Try to stay awake and drink water."

"Anything else?"

"Chocolate ice cream?"

Ben and Jerry's it is. Dang critters. Nature just seems to be lashing out at me this week.

Courtesy of the author

NINA FOXX, originally from New York, is the best selling author of five novels and the author of two industrial design patents. She has had a short story featured in *WanderLust: Erotic Travel Tales* and her fourth *novel, Marrying Up,* was successfully adapted into a musical stage play. She worked as an Industrial Psychologist specializing in human-computer interaction and is currently completing her third graduate degree, this time an MFA in creative writing, and working on an experimental film project based on one of her books.

Nina Foxx